SECRET KEEPERS AND SKINNY SHADOWS

Lee and Miranda

A novel by Mary A Russell

ISBN-13: 9781499262964
ISBN-10: 1499262965

Dedication

This book is dedicated to Jackie May. Your help digging out the research was invaluable. You kept inspiring me to get back to the computer. Jackie, you pushed me enough to get it finished. Thank you.

To Aaron Russell, for the encouragement to keep writing, and the valuable information to be able to complete the story.

Tracy Madigan Sheppard the best photographer in the world.

Last but not least, to my husband, Larry, who has always encouraged me to do whatever I wanted to do no matter how crazy it may be. He is always supportive and patient with me, and he is the love of my life.

Lillian's letters, which inspired Lee to investigate this case, are included in the back of the book.

Matthew 7:7b, Seek and you will find; knock and it will be opened to you.

Lee and Miranda

Lee and Miranda

PROLOGUE

Bridgetown, New York
Present day

"What the heck happened in here?" Their senses spiked, as they stood in Miranda's once immaculate kitchen. The cherry cabinet doors stood open and empty, all the contents were scattered on the granite counter tops and the floor. Her face turned ashen. She looked at the pots, pans, silverware and cooking utensils in front of their feet.

Lee's shoulders tightened. "Stay by my side. This room seemed to have more air a few seconds ago. He tugged at his shirt collar while gasping and expelling his breath." Don't panic, he told himself. But, he knew their eyes were following him everywhere, but who were they?

She peeled away from his side, picking her way through the debris, heading toward the light coming from the library. She halted by the door.

Walking forward he kicked a pot out of his path and stuck his head around the opened den door. "What a mess!"

"Miranda. I told you to stay with me."

"I can take care of myself. You're the one who's a bundle of nerves."

"That free will, will cause you real trouble someday, Miranda."

With a sweeping arm gesture, he planted his legs wide. "Fine, stay there. That free will is going to get you into real trouble someday." Shaking his head in frustration, he sucked in another deep breath.

"What was that?" Their heads jerked in the direction of the window as the wind sighed under the eaves, and rattled the panes. He shivered, then shoved his hands into his pants pockets, as he scanned the room. "Don't be afraid the sounds we hear are the moaning's of an old house trying to settle into its new body."

He pulled a mint from his pocket, tossed it into his dry mouth then sighed.

"I hear the noise all the time, it's startled me awake many nights."

He wrinkled his brow. "Miranda, are you sure you're okay?"

She cocked her head and smirked. "Yes, stop pestering me."

He clenched his jaw.

"Why did I open my mouth?"

"Miranda, do you hear that? Listen." The tendons on neck stiffened, a visible pulse pounding under his chin.

"No. I don't hear anything."

"I know, beyond a doubt, they're close." He continued. "They're always with me looking over my shoulder, examining what I'm learning. Leaving clues, they know will waste my time and fill my head with useless information."

"I agree. We could be chasing ghosts from the past."

"At this point in time, I don't know what to think of everything that has happened."

Was the constant whispering he heard real, or was his mind eavesdropping on his thoughts, he wasn't sure? He didn't know, and started to believe he was becoming paranoid or going crazy. Are the good guys becoming the prey, being stalked day after day, night after night? Had Miranda and Lee become the hunted?

"They can keep putting pressure on me but I'm unstoppable, Miranda. I'm sure they're trying to discourage me. Wishing I would give up, stop investigating, pack my clothes and run back to South Carolina."

"Will you?"

"Don't worry, I'll stay until this enigma is solved. I'm here till the end."

He glanced at the hair standing up on her arms. He watched the dread weave up her delicate cheeks and into her steady eyes, playing with his emotions.

He wanted to cross the room and sweep her into his arms.

His impulses tore at his soul and he asked himself if the price he would pay, be worth the effort.

Enduring more than enough caustic remarks from his wife's best friend and confidante, she'd never let him forget, Joan died before her time because of him.

He tried to remove the soft spot still beating in the corner of his heart for her. He considered her a kid sister and hoped she'd someday lose her snarky attitude.

Instead of moving toward her. "Miranda, you're safe, don't worry. I'll take care of you. We'll get to the bottom of whatever is going on here, we'll find out who they are."

She turned to face him. "I hope so. I'm counting on you to help me ferret the truth."

He thought it was easier to breathe now, he shrugged. Must be me. Nerves.

A smile moved across his lips. "Remember the phone conversations we had after I received your letter two months ago?" A chuckle bubbled from his throat. She pictured herself an amateur sleuth on the constant hunt for a mystery to solve.

"Yes, I remember."

"I resisted your pleas for help as long as I could, but you persuaded me to join your cause, convincing me, I should want to do this for Joan." He paused. "My memories of Joan, the way I treated her torments me day and night. Perhaps this will end the mental anguish."

***

Two days into the investigation:

"Miranda, I'm worried I may have made a mistake getting involved and putting our lives in grave danger. When I agreed to help you, it was a simple research project, but soon became something else. Three questions keep rolling around in my mind, keeping me up at night."

"What questions?"

"For one thing, what if we've reawakened the past by snooping around, digging up evidence?" He glanced in the next room.

"Lee, we're going to make enemies investigating this old murder, the police for one, and it's hard to tell who else will come forward before we finish this."

"Think about this. What if the heinous secrets buried for many years are starting to break their silence, crawling out of the cracks of time, crying out for the truth to be told?"

"Come on, Lee, aren't you getting a little too dramatic?"

"This is my last question. What monsters have we unshackled with our keys of curiosity and research?"

"I don't know, but it looks like a monster was turned loose in my house."

By now Miranda made her way over to Lee's side and whispered in his ear. "Are you going to stand there asking a bunch of questions or are we going to see if anyone is still in this house?"

He nodded. "Come on, whoever it is, might be in my room. Stay by my side." With one eye on Miranda, they tiptoed toward his bedroom at the back of the mansion.

They halted in the doorway, and stared into the dark room; a bright shaft of light lit up the floor and part of the bed in front of the slider.

Lee tapped her elbow with his, and nodded in the direction of the light. "It looks like they came in and left through the door."

They moved toward the opening. "Stay close. Don't be afraid. I'll protect you."

They peered around the curtain, with a perfect view of the patio and five acres of lawn leading back to the woods behind the mansion.

She shivered as the wind picked up, blowing its chill through the door. A dog barked in the distance, he saw a man dressed in black, running toward the woods.

"There! Look, do you see him?"

The man disappeared inside the cover of the black forest.

CHAPTER 1

Bridgetown, New York, February 1962

The bone-chilling cold wrapped its icy arms around Bridgetown, New York, an unassuming, bustling railroad town.

The inhabitants of this town didn't live, they endured life.

Bert Grayson spent his working career as a laborer for the Conn Railroad. The company owned the people and the town. Bert knew most of the people living in the houses in this hamlet, and would have been shocked by the repulsive secret they would, through the years, hide from the outside world while entrusting it to their children, and their children's children.

What a smug lot they were, conspiring with each other to take the secret to their graves, and many of them did. He would have trouble understanding how so many individuals could be involved in and with such an insidious cover-up, for more than half a century.

***

Like Bert, most of the townspeople worked for the railroad, building trains day after weary day.

But Bert stood out from the other men in stature and lifestyle. He stood a head taller than most of the men he worked with and he liked hard work. The monotony of it was what he didn't like.

The men who worked in the roundhouses produced train engines at a record pace, at the same time the smoke-stacks belched out heavy layers of toxic zinc, copper and lead. The poisonous metals penetrated their bodies, causing the workers to appear to glow. The line bosses kept the men building and repairing trains as fast as the Conn could force them to work.

While Bert was walking to the diner he looked up at the clouds of coal dust the train engines spewed out as they passed through town, leaving behind a fine, sticky grime. Particles of soot seeped into the houses through the unplugged cracks in the windows and doors. The thick, black blanket built up layer after layer on the roofs and sidings.

"Hi Bert, do you mind if I walk to the diner with you. I'm going to the meeting at the union hall tonight so I thought I'd catch a bite before I go," Henry said.

"Sure, I could use the company. I never liked to eat alone."

"What did you think of the little pep talk the bosses gave us today?" Henry paused, looking at Bert before continuing his thought. "They have a lot of nerve telling us their only concern was getting trains built, repaired and sold. We both know from the actions of the owners that greed drives the executives running the railroad to pollute the air, knowing they're protected by the corrupt officials running Bridgetown."

"I agree with you. From the mayor down to the cleaning help at City Hall, they're driven by two things, power and money. They'll turn their backs on all of us, the very people they're supposed to protect. Disgusting isn't it?" Bert said.

Henry nodded.

As they strolled the distance Bert thought about his father and how he recounted to him on a monthly basis the story of the Conn Railroad; the way it moved into the lush mountain valley surrounding Bridgetown in the mid-nineteenth century, building the railroad and town from scratch. Even the history books cited it as one of the best examples of a company-owned and run city. Bert's dad hounded him to go to work for the Conn so he could make good money from the largest employer in New York State.

In the 1960s, Bridgetown had become the railroad hub of the east. All trains going west from New York City passed through it, expanding its population generation after generation. Only a few lucky ones ever retired. Most of them died young as their bodies were poisoned by the black-death billowing from the smokestacks.

Bert fought alongside the other men to bring about change. They brought in the unions that grew in power, forcing the railroad to install pollution controls to clean the air and at the same time provide the workers with sick leave.

Bert was one of the more fortunate men who was assigned to work in the shops building boxcars, not in the roundhouses building engines. An injury on the job one day left him unable to work. After months of bargaining, the union forced the Conn to give Bert an early retirement with a disability pension check each month.

It wasn't a lot of money, but it was enough to support his drinking habit, along with some extra to help his sister Lizzie buy food and pay the utilities on the old place they shared.

***

"Bert, you're going to wear out the door on the mailbox. Your check will probably be in the carrier's hand when he comes today," Lizzie said.

"Well, I hope so. I have plans for tonight."

In the early evening Bert sat on the edge of the mattress on his old oak bed that once belonged to his mom and dad, who had passed away twenty years ago.

"Hey, Uncle Bert," Joan said, her ponytail of light brown hair bobbing in the air as she sauntered through his opened bedroom door, twirling her car keys on her finger.

"Hi, Pumpkin head. What's up with you? How's your old car running?"

While she answered his questions, Bert bent over to lace his boot, pausing for a second to pat his chest pocket.

"I've got my fingers crossed, hoping the old Chevy will keep running. It's going to be my only transportation when I start college in the fall."

From the corner of his eye he watched her walk over to his side. He glanced up, "Don't worry, Joanie. I'll make sure your car is kept in good running condition."

"You're the best uncle in the world. I don't know what I'd do without you. I've got to run now or I'll be late." She took a few steps toward the door.

Bert had time to finish tying one of his leather work boots and stood by the bed. "Hold on Joanie." She stopped, turning in his direction. "What are your plans for tonight?"

"Oh, I guess I should've told you, I'm going out with Miranda to the last basketball game and dance of the season."

He bent down as Joanie stood on her tiptoes and kissed him on the cheek. He reached up to rub off the lipstick she always left behind. "Have fun tonight." He put his big arm around her waist, squeezing her with a soft, affectionate hug. "My sweet Joanie, you always were my favorite niece. If my sister-in-law had lived long enough to see you grow up she would've been proud of her youngest girl." He grinned as Joanie broke into a smile.

"Uncle Bert, you're like a dad to me. I love you and Aunt Liz for taking care of us after our mom died. I don't remember her, but I'm sure she was beautiful and kind."

He watched her turn, leaving behind a soft scent of lavender and roses. She crossed the room to the door. He listened for her footfalls on the steps leading to the kitchen, and her soft voice. "Goodbye, Aunt Lizzie. I'm off to the game and dance."

"Don't be out late, young lady."

The door closed. His ear was tuned for the roar of her old Chevy as it pulled out of the driveway. He hurried to his bedroom window, brushing back the curtains to watch the car disappear down the winding dirt road. "Yes Joanie, your mom was beautiful and kind, just like you," he whispered.

CHAPTER 2

Present Day

Showing up at the office could have been the first mistake Lee made today.

For more years than he cared to remember, traversing from the houseboat that was his home to the space where he parked his car remained an enjoyable part of his morning routine. He never tired of the same sights while driving the winding coastal road to his job in the city, breathing in the fresh pine scent from the ancient spruce trees that kept the Appalachian Mountains green all year long.

Parking his Jag in the space marked, reserved for LP, he locked the car and hummed his favorite tune all the way to the elevator. Once inside he punched button twenty, enjoying the smooth ride to the top.

He said good morning to everyone as he passed by their desks. Pausing at the entrance to his office, he pulled a hanky out of his back pocket and polished the black lettering on the glass door. Lee Perkins, Associate Editor.

The men and women on the work room floor stopped what they were doing to watch him. A couple of men in the back were snickering, and winking at their co-workers.

Some pointed at him, mocking his movements. He was oblivious to everything going on around him.

Stepping through the door he dropped his papers on the empty corner of his desk, pulled off his coat, and went to his favorite spot in front of the floor to ceiling windows looking out over the city.

He stood tapping his fingers on the window sill, staring but not seeing the streets below. Lee enjoyed the sunlight streaming through the glass, warming his body and soul as it calmed his tormented mind. He'd spent a sLeepless night and was tired before the working day started.

With a heavy sigh he moved toward the desk and eased his tall frame into the chair. Through the wall of windows he watched the workers going about the business of book publishing on the workroom floor.

Sally Parker hurried through the door and handed him a cup of coffee. "Good morning, Lee. Another note is taped on your computer reminding you to learn to use it."

He glanced at the monitor, pulled the note off, and with a flick of his wrist tossed it into the trashcan without reading it.

"Thanks for the heads up. I would be lost without you. For twenty years the company has tried to force me to use a computer. I'm a dinosaur, Sally, what else can I say? I'm computer challenged and too old to learn now."

She nodded.

"Sally, you know better than anyone that I don't like change.

I have you and you're all I need."

Sally looked Lee in the eyes. "That's right, you always have me, and I do get the job done for you."

Lee knew he could depend on her to pick up the slack and do all the computer research for him without complaining, unlike some of the girls who worked in the office.

Of course, he always took credit for the work she did and he had no shame doing so. He was so caught up in his own importance that nothing else mattered. He thought the world revolved only around him.

"I have a lot of research to do today. I can't stay and chat any longer."

With that statement she scurried back to her desk.

Lee had a strange look on his face as he thought how odd her behavior was this morning. Sally always had time to chat. He shrugged. She must be behind with her work.

Later in the morning he was busy reading, sipping coffee and checking the calendar for jobs he had to finish. But he couldn't get the nagging thought out of his mind. Something must be in the air, but what? He tried not to think about it by going back to work.

He was engrossed in reading a new report when Ray, his boss and long-time friend, marched into his office, closing the door with a thud. "Lee, we need to talk."

Lee looked up, startled.

"I have bad news and good news for you. Which do you want first?" Ray planted himself in front of the desk and was silent for a few seconds.

Lee stared at him, waiting, thinking that it seemed like Ray was searching for the right words.

Ray folded his arms across his chest and cleared his throat while rocking back and forth on the heels of his shoes, clenching his jaw.

"Give me the bad news first."

"As you know, Wentworth Publishing has been making a lot of personnel changes in this office and company-wide."

Lee nodded.

"The competition is crushing us with the electronic readers. Then there's self-publishing. We're selling fewer printed books. I know you're also aware that we're going to downsize even more than originally expected." Ray uncrossed his arms and shoved his hands into his pockets.

Lee crossed his arms and leaned back in his chair. "Are you trying to say we're going to have to let Sally go?"

"No, that's not what I'm saying." Ray loosened his tie. "After much consideration, we'll be combining your job with two other positions. So, we'll be letting you go." Ray pulled his glasses out of his shirt pocket and rolled then around in his hand before he started to talk again. "Sally will fill your position, and we're going to replace the old printing equipment and hire some tech geeks to make our company more competitive while moving it into the twenty-first century of publishing."

Drops of sweat beaded on Lee's forehead. The aroma of coffee distracted him. Phones ringing out on the workroom floor sounded ten times louder than normal. All the while he was thinking, *Ray is firing me, why can't I think of anything except the smell of coffee, and ringing phones?* He was confused. Getting out of his chair, he crossed his arms and stared at Ray as he continued to talk.

Ray took a couple of steps back. "I can't tell you how sorry I am. This time, you're the most expendable employee. Look at it from our point of view. You're the only one in the office who still writes everything out in pen on paper. You've refused to learn to use the computers we've given you. You place all the burden of your job on Sally." Ray looked down and lowered his voice.

Lee glanced out in the work area looking for Sally, but didn't see her anywhere. He brought his attention back to Ray.

Twisting the wedding band on his finger, Ray continued, "I know we've been friends for years, but the business comes first. Today is your last day. You can leave now if you wish." Ray looked Lee in the eyes.

Lee's mouth was gaping open in disbelief at what he was hearing. He cupped his hands over his ears for a second before dropping them to his side. "Ray, what's the good news?"

"The good news is you'll get one year of severance pay. Even though you're too young for the full pension, our board of directors agreed to make an exception because you've been with the company for twenty-five years and you're a loyal employee. When the severance ends your pension will start."

Ray slid a small box from his jacket pocket, grabbed Lee's right hand in his and shook it, at the same time placing the small box in Lee's other hand. Then he turned and walked out the door.

Lee was too shocked and dazed to speak or move. His eyes followed Ray as he marched out, crossed the workstation floor and into his own office, closing the door.

Holding up the box he raised the lid, revealing an inexpensive gold Timex. Wentworth Publishing was written in black lettering on the white dial. He threw it, box and all, into the trashcan.

Panic was surging from his head to his toes. Leaning against the desk to steady his shaky legs he searched the office floor looking for Sally. She was nowhere to be found.

His arm wasn't long enough as he groped for the chair behind him. Flopping hard onto the seat all he could think of was, *What'll I do now?*

He sat at his desk for ten minutes or so trying to absorb what had taken place. The pension would be nice. Now he'd have time to do some things he'd wanted to do for years, like writing and traveling for pleasure. He was still too young to collect Social Security, but the generous pension would be plenty, for now.

Workers paused at his office window waving goodbye, others came in to shake his hand and to say they would miss him. It was evident everyone knew he was leaving except him.

His mind replayed how callous and insensitive Ray had been. He questioned how long he had known he was going to fire him, never letting on at the bar last night. They had talked for hours over drinks and Ray didn't say anything about work. Some friend he had turned out to be. Humiliation washed over him and he didn't know what to do. Lee knew it would be a challenge for him to continue a friendship with Ray after this—but Lee was smarter than that. He learned years ago not to burn his bridges behind him. After Lee collected his thoughts he decided the best thing to do was leave as soon as possible.

He'd have to find his way down to the storeroom, something he had never done because Sally always went there for him. He'd need a cardboard box to pack his stuff into. He kept thinking about Sally, and why she wasn't at her desk. He knew Sally, of all people, would be angry with Ray for firing him. She was made of better stuff than Ray, even though she would get a promotion from it.

Lee poked around in his bottom desk drawer, finding a flashlight. The bright beam of light was the only illumination as he picked his way down to the basement. Most of the bulbs in the hallways were burnt out. He could see large piles of rat droppings in the corners. In some places it was so dark he had to slide his shoe on the floor in front of him.

He was disgusted that the company didn't put decent lighting in the lower parts of the building. Oh, well, it didn't matter now what he thought.

He paused, feeling air under his foot. Flashing the light down he saw the steps, worn smooth from one hundred years of foot traffic, making them treacherous.

He would miss Sally, and he was sure she would miss him. She was his one true friend. He continued to mumble as he picked his way to the bottom of the steps and the lower corridor. He puttered along, flashing the torch at the top of each door looking for the storeroom. He opened a door, but it was a broom closet.

Then he was in front of it. To his surprise, the door stood ajar. He stepped inside, then paused, waiting for his eyes to adjust to the darkness.

On the other side of the stockroom a bare light bulb was hanging down from the ceiling on a long wire, casting dim light and shadows on the wall on the other side.

A quick glance around the cavernous space gave him the impression it was filled with thousands of books stacked on pallets, but he couldn't be sure because of the lack of light.

He was surprised to find a tall pile of cardboard boxes blocking his path.

As he picked one from the stack, he paused and turned his head, listening. He was sure he heard voices. By this time his eyes had become accustomed to the darkness. Silently he stared at the wall across the way. He was sure he could hear chatter and laughter from a man and woman in the far corner of the room. Clicking off the light it looked like there were two silhouetted images on the wall. Squinting, he strained to see who was there, then he realized who it was. In the shadows under that single dim light bulb stood Ray and Sally, locked in each other's arms in a passionate kiss. They were completely oblivious to his presence. In that split second the curtains were torn back and he saw the real truth. Ray had fired him, not because of his refusal to learn the computer, but to promote Sally to a new position. He raised the palm of his hand, tapping it against his forehead. He couldn't believe how stupid he had been. His face flushed with anger. He wanted to go over to them, deck Ray, then tell Sally what he thought of her, but he kept control of himself. It was as though a knife was being twisted in his heart. He was thunderstruck, betrayed beyond his wildest dreams by two people he thought he could trust with his life.

He couldn't believe he had missed all the signs of their affair, and how would this affect Ray's poor wife? The signs must have been everywhere, and he didn't see them, or didn't want to.

He turned his flashlight back on, grabbed the perfect empty box, and slipped out the storeroom door undetected.

Back at his desk, tossing the few belongings he had into the box, he sighed while thinking how pathetic he must look, that after twenty-five years he could pack all his stuff into a small cardboard crate. Picking up Joan's picture he placed it on top of the pile so it wouldn't get broken. Sally strolled into his office with a look of concern.

"Lee, I'm surprised and shocked to hear the news. It's hard to believe they would do this to you. Is there anything I can do to help? Do you need anything? Will you be all right?"

"No, thank you, Sally, you've already done more than enough. I'll be fine." He kept his eyes glued to the box.

"Well, if you're sure I can't help. I'll keep in touch and I'm going to miss you."

"Yeah. Thanks. Same here Sally, I think." He couldn't look at her.

When she turned around and walked back to her desk, Lee looked up in time to see her break into a smile as she sat in her chair and went back to work on her computer. He could hear her humming a tune to herself.

With a gentle pat on Joan's picture, he picked up the box, took one last look around the office then walked out of Wentworth Publishing for the last time.

On the drive home he replayed the morning in his mind like a movie, recounting every detail, hoping it might be a bad dream and he would wake up soon.

He couldn't believe what they had done to him in a matter of minutes. Twenty-five years of dedicated service, wiped out in a heartbeat. He lived and breathed editing and research for the company. Every six months he received offers from other publishing houses wanting him to come to work for them. Of course, when he stopped to think about it, there hadn't been any of those offers in the last couple of years. He had wasted so much of his life with Wentworth Publishing. He ignored Joan, his beautiful, compassionate wife, leaving her alone for weeks or months at a time. She was so understanding and loving. She told him many times, "Do what makes you happy, Lee." And like the selfish jerk he was, he did. He was glad Joan had Miranda as a friend. They grew up together and stayed friends through the years.

In looking back, Lee realized that because Joan had Miranda it made it easy for him to cut her out of his life. After all, his career was what was important. Joan would have to find her own happiness. He knew when he returned home after a long road trip that she would be waiting for him with open arms to welcome him back. What foolish regrets he now had, and he could never make it up to Joan, not now.

He ignored his family and friends, devoting his heart and soul to being the best in the business, and getting fired was his thanks.

CHAPTER 3

Bridgetown, New York, February 1962

When Joanie's car was out of sight Bert ambled across the room to the bed and sat on the edge of the mattress to finish lacing his other boot. He debated if he should put on his long underwear to keep him warm on the long walk to the bus, but he decided against it. It was too much work and he was anxious to get to town.

The house with all the furniture once belonged to his mother and father, and now it was his to share with his sister. He was born in the log cabin still standing across the dirt driveway. The family moved into the new house when Bert was twelve years old.

At the dresser he was combing his hair, making sure he looked respectable. As he turned away, he did a double take at the reflection looking back at him. He jumped, grabbing the dresser to steady his large frame. He gazed at the apparition perched on his shoulder staring back at him, rubbing his eyes in disbelief at the old goblin. He was scared because he only saw this ugly creature when he was drunk, and here it was looking back at him in the mirror.

Bert raised his voice. “Go away, Cadaverous, I haven’t started drinking yet.” He reached up with his big hand to brush him off. As he did it revealed an evil grin, showing its pointed teeth, then vanished into thin air as quickly as it appeared. Bert shivered. Wide-eyed, he watched in the mirror to be sure it was gone.

He knew seeing that thing wasn’t a good sign. He continued to stare long and hard into the mirror, thinking maybe he was going out of his mind, but he didn’t think he looked crazy.

He hurried for the door, turned into the hall and made his way toward the stairs. Passing the attic door he noticed it was standing open. He pushed it shut, locked it, and went down to the kitchen.

“You’re going to miss your bus to town if you don’t hurry.”

His taste buds perked up, smelling the fresh coffee coming from the cup Lizzie was holding.

Before she could offer him some he said, “Cadaverous, the old goblin, was sitting on my shoulder up there again.”

Lizzie set her cup on the table, turned, shaking her crooked finger at him. “It’s all our mother’s fault. If she hadn’t messed around with those evil spirits, doing all those weird things like stopping blood and blowing fire, you wouldn’t see the devil sitting on your shoulder all the time. Mark my words, Bert, that’s a bad omen.”

He got up from his chair, shaking his head. “Lizzie, shut up. Forget I ever mentioned it. You can’t blame our mother for everything. Janie and Joanie’s mother died seventeen years ago, but you’re the one who sees her standing at the foot of your bed in the middle of the night.”

By this time, he was half listening to her and thinking how tasty the coffee smelled. On his way to the door he stopped long enough to scoop up his wool hunting jacket hanging over the back of one of the wooden chairs. He slipped it on. He loved how warm and cozy it was as he buttoned it up.

The frosty February air sent a shiver through him when he opened the door, even though the sun was shining. Lizzie was mumbling something as he closed the door behind him. He breathed a sigh of relief to be out of earshot of her endless chattering. He thought about the poor man who might someday be her husband.

Bertrand and Elizabeth shared their ancestral home, built in 1899, in a little village south of Bridgetown. Of course, no one called him Bertrand. He was known as Big Bert Grayson.

Elizabeth was Liz to most people and Lizzie to Bert.

They were the only two of five children in the family who never saw marriage in their futures. One reason could've been Bert was too much of a drinking man while Lizzie was too prim and proper—all the men who came into her life never lived up to her expectations. Together, brother and sister continued to live in the old homestead that occupied a half-acre in the middle of one hundred acres of prime farmland in the lush mountains of New York.

Their mother and father passed away without leaving a will. This led to family battles over dividing up the estate, leaving five strong-willed children to settle it. Bert and Liz had permission from their siblings to live in the family homestead until one of them died, then the property was to be split up between the remaining heirs.

One of the heirs, Miser, the oldest sister, grew restless and unhappy with this arrangement. She wanted Bert and Lizzie kicked out and everything divided up right away. She didn't want to wait for her inheritance, but she had no choice. The majority ruled. That was the agreement between the five of them established many years ago.

Every Saturday Bert walked a mile and a half from his home to catch the afternoon bus to town. He knew he was running late so he picked up the pace, coming to the conclusion his work clothes weren't warm enough by the time he arrived at the bus stop. He stood waiting for the bus, thinking he should've put on his long johns, but at least he was smart enough to put on his jacket.

An icy wind started to blow, stinging his already windburned cheeks. He wished the bus would come soon. Shivering, he rocked back and forth from one foot to the other, rubbing his hands together and blowing on them for warmth, sending white puffs of smoke up into the air.

Today he was alone at the bus stop. Over his right shoulder, at the amusement park, he could hear music coming from a jukebox. The fans from the food courts filled the air with pizza and pepperoni, teasing his nose. It brought back memories of his teen years and Lillian when he worked at the park. The horses from the merry-go-round and all the other rides had been packed up and put away for the winter. The park owner made money through the cold months selling pizza, hoagies, and drinks to the locals, as well as an occasional traveler.

The long bus ride wasn't something Bert enjoyed but it was a necessity. A few months back he had demolished his truck coming home from a night of drinking, when he lost control and ran it over a cliff. The truck landed on the river-bank below and wedged between two trees, saving the truck and Bert from the chilling waters. The doctors said it was a good thing he was drunk. The booze kept him from freezing to death and relaxed enough to keep him from serious injuries. It was then that the police took away his driving privileges.

As the bus pulled up he hurried aboard, taking a seat in the front close to the heater. After a thirty-minute ride the bus deposited him one block from his favorite drinking establishment.

About ten o'clock that night the sky started spitting snow as he walked into the sixth bar on his list. The window sills, as well as the sides of the buildings, were soon blanketed white. The blinking neon lights of the bars and eateries on the south end reflected unrecognizable shapes on the new-fallen snow. The strong wind exposed shiny patches of ice, glazing the sidewalks.

When he stumbled into the next bar, he thought he noticed the same man in every bar he went into. He always came in after Bert, taking a seat in a booth with his back to him. He was a man who Bert knew from years ago, although he couldn't remember his name. What he did recall was that he didn't care for the guy. Determined not to let him spoil his night on the town, he soon pushed the thought of the man to the back of his mind and returned to his drinking.

Bert forgot about eating dinner, spending his last dollar on beer number twenty in bar number nine, the Squashed Frog, his favorite. He was drinking his Bud and doing his best to stay out of trouble, when the stranger started crowding back into his thoughts, intruding on his fun. He wished he had taken a seat in one of the booths away from the door, because every time a patron came in a chilling blast of wind followed.

His stomach growled from hunger in spite of all the beer. Gulping down the last of the brew in his glass he was ready to leave. As he wobbled up from the bar stool, a loud belch came from nowhere. He held his hand to his mouth, rolled his eyes from side to side, glad no one was paying attention. He moved his big hand in a slow swipe across his lips, as he staggered toward the exit. When he reached the door it swung wide open. A blast of icy wind took his breath away as he stared down into the face of a short, boyish looking man.

"Hi Bert, let me hold the door for you."

Bert blinked, staring at the man. His head was fuzzy from too much booze and lack of food and it took him a few seconds to come up with the man's name. "Thanks, Henry."

Bert liked Henry. He thought they connected on a personal level by being too shy to speak to people, but unlike Bert, Henry was a nice guy. Bert's friends and acquaintances were perceptive enough to know not to cross him, because those who did knew he had a way of taking care of them.

The giant of Bridgetown was the nickname they hung on Bert in his younger days when he went ten rounds at the old theater on Rainbow Street in a boxing match with John L. Lewis. Bert was one big, rough guy. His reputation was known around town, but in the south end Big Bert Grayson was respected by many, feared by a lot, and loved by all the women.

Bert stumbled out onto the street.

"Hey Bert, you better grab hold of one of those light poles so you don't slip and fall on the ice."

Bert saluted the guy and continued down the busy avenue.

He maneuvered his massive frame toward the light poles, swinging around some of them with one arm, waving and smiling at the passers-by with the other. A lot of them Bert knew by name.

The aroma of hot dogs and onions mingled together, drifting out into the street, teasing his nose, pulling him toward the little diner about two hundred feet ahead. He was confident he could make it without falling. After all, he didn't want to look like a common old drunk.

His hunger intensified with the aroma from the hot dog diner. Lizzie wanted to fix something for him, but he told her he would eat in town. Besides, Lizzie was busy primping while waiting for her new man friend to arrive. They were going out to dinner, then to see the new movie Dr. No. Lizzie was in love with James Bond.

He was now one hundred feet from the diner on the corner of Fifth and Tenth streets. The reputation of the diner had spread around the state. Hot dog lovers drove from all over to experience the best in the world at Jim's Diner. On weekends lines of men and women waited for hours to experience the taste.

As he muddled his way down the street, he paused every now and then to enjoy the sounds of the night. Loud voices of drunks cursing, the soft voices of women talking, loud jukebox tunes drifting out into the cold night air.

At last he was in front of the diner and still standing on his feet. He breathed a deep sigh of relief.

When he pulled the door open, heat wrapped around him like a warm blanket, causing him to wobble more. Once inside he hung onto the glass door for balance.

He didn't look around, wanting to get to the empty stainless steel red vinyl-covered stool to sit down before he fell over. He lurched toward the counter at the empty seat beside a man he knew.

With a thick tongue and slurred words, he managed to say, "Cain, it sure is cold outside tonight. I'm surprised to see you here so late. Your shift must have ended hours ago."

"Yeah, it did. I thought I'd get a dog and suds while I waited for my ride home. We worked overtime in the roundhouse.

The extra money always comes in handy this time of the year. Know what I mean? It pays for the heat in the drafty old house I live in. The old lady complains a lot about how cold the house always is."

He nodded in agreement, remembering the drafty old home he lived in. "I know what you mean."

Bert wobbled around on the stool, balancing himself. The diner was full. Some of the patrons were standing in the back, leaning on the walls drinking a glass of beer while talking to one another. He glanced around the room to see if he knew anyone. His eyes stopped at the back booth where he spotted the petite, dark-haired woman. She was facing a heavy-set man. Bert patted his wallet in his shirt pocket. Lillian's phone number was safely tucked inside. From the back, the man across from her looked like her piggish husband. Bert never understood why she put up with him.

He stared at her until she stopped talking, glanced up and made eye contact with him. The giant raised his hand

and saluted her, almost falling off the stool when he brought his arm down. She smiled and turned her attention back to piggish.

Bert paused at the third booth. What caught his eye was a woman sliding an envelope across the table to a man who took it, then quickly shoved it inside his jacket pocket. The woman's back was to Bert, but he thought she looked like Donna, one of his nieces who hounded him, trying to buy some land he didn't want to sell. He wobbled back around and continued his conversation with Cain.

"Would you lend me five dollars to buy a couple hot dogs and a beer? I didn't get to the bank so I couldn't cash my pension check. I brought it along thinking one of the bars might cash it for me, but they wouldn't."

Cain pulled a five-dollar bill out of his pocket and handed it to him. Bert noticed Cain's eyes stopped at the pension check sticking out of his shirt pocket.

"Sure, here you are."

"Thanks, you're a real friend." Bert pushed the five-dollar bill across the counter. "Jim, I'll have two dogs and a beer."

As Jim placed the hot dogs, beer, and change in front of him, Bert turned his head just in time to see Piggish turn around. He nodded at Bert before he turned his attention back to Lillian.

Bert took a big bite of his hot dog. "Hum," he mumbled. A mixture of ketchup, mustard and relish dribbled out of both sides of his mouth and slid down onto his chin, before lodging in his graying five o'clock shadow.

Cain handed him a napkin. "Better clean your face."

Bert rubbed the napkin around his face, smearing the mixture all over his chin and cheeks. As he put the napkin down the door opened and a blast of cold wind blew in. A tall man covered head to foot with soot hurried in, leaving black shoe prints behind him on the white tile floor. He headed toward the empty seat on the other side of Bert. Puffs of soot billowed into the air as he sat down, then settled on the floor beneath his stool. Bert looked over his way, and with slow, slurred words and a mouth half full of hot dog, said, "Looks like you had a long rough night, Clay."

"Yeah, I did. I'm tired and hungry." He nodded at the cook to take his order. Clay looked like a raccoon with the whites of his eyes shining through the black dust on his face. "Jim, give me three dogs and a six-pack to go."

He turned to Bert. "Yeah, shoveling coal for eight hours into the big boilers on a train engine is back-breaking work and I'm not getting any younger."

"Bert," Clay said, "do you want a ride home?" He craned his neck around Bert and nodded at Cain.

"Are you ready to go?" Raccoon eyes grabbed his bag of dogs stuffing the six-pack of Bud under his arm before turning to Bert.

"Cain and I are leaving now, Bert. I think you missed the last bus home. Why don't you let us drop you off? We'll be driving right past your place on the way."

"Okay, it's nice of you guys to make the offer. Sure, why not? I can stretch out on the back seat while you fellas drive."

On the way out the door with the two men, one on each side of him, he glanced over his shoulder at the woman in the back booth. She looked up and smiled. He watched her as the door closed.

They had a hard time getting Bert to the car. His huge feet would slip and slide, part from the ice and part from being stupefied by the alcohol flowing through him. They made it to the old blue four-door. Cain opened the car door, then helped Clay stuff Bert into the back seat, shutting the door. Cain got behind the wheel and raccoon eyes took shotgun.

The dark sedan slipped into the avenue, blending into the traffic flowing north. Bert's mind faded into blackness as he drifted off into a drunken slumber.

CHAPTER 4

Present Day

The day after Lee was fired from his job he made his second mistake by going to the mailbox.

It was on this day his suspicions collided with the evidence.

Lee now knew to follow the trail leading him through the door to the past and the clues to an old unsolved murder, presenting him with two choices. He could step across the threshold following the signs or seal the opening and walk away forever, but he wasn't a close the door kind of guy.

***

In the semi-darkness on the deck of his houseboat, Lee stood resting against the wooden railing with his legs crossed in front of him, sipping a cup of coffee and enjoying a perfect sunrise over the bay.

His eyes were glued on the horizon, watching the brilliant ball as it started to creep above the water line of the Atlantic. It splintered the sky with streaks of red and orange patches, reflecting a mirror image across the waters of the cove as it pushed the night away.

The sounds of silence were broken by the squawking of an occasional hungry seagull flying overhead looking for breakfast and the mesmerizing tide rolling in and out.

The clean fresh smell of a new day lifted Lee's spirits, if only for a little while. The serenity was satisfying, but right now his body and soul were still numb. Yesterday seemed surreal, as though it happened to someone else. He couldn't wrap his mind around the fact that they did fire him.

Lee, for some unexplainable reason, could sense something different in the air. He had never had a sensation like it, and couldn't put his finger on it, but it was there. As he turned to go back into his houseboat he stopped at the door and glanced up at the docks, scanning the area in all directions. He didn't know what he was looking for, as he rubbed the back of his neck and shook his head. What was going on?

He stood at the door searching the docks north past the expensive yachts and houseboats bobbing in their slips. Jim Goodson owned the yacht next to his boat and he was careful not to complain too much about the way Lee's houseboat looked. Jim only came to the docks a couple of times a year, the rest of the time his yacht sat idle in its moorings. It irritated Lee how the rich wasted their money.

His location on the docks gave him the opportunity to see everything that went on around the other boats that were close to his, when he was home. If he spotted something out of the ordinary around Jim's yacht, he would call him and relay the information. In appreciation, Jim would every now and again send Lee an expensive bottle of champagne or wine as a thank you.

For most of his adult life, Lee lived on the houseboat docked in slip number ten on the picturesque Taylor's Cove Bay. On the outside his home looked a little rough, but on the inside it was his version of a castle. Early March on the bay brought mild warm breezes, not that hot sticky muck that arrives on the first day of summer.

Around 9:00 A.M. Lee stepped off the usual fifty feet on the pristine wooden dock to check his mail. This was the first time he noticed the disgraceful shape his box was in. It was attached to an oversized, rope-wrapped piling on the well-maintained pier. It hung loose, dented, rusted, in bad need of a good paint job. It was almost as though Lee was seeing everything with new eyes since yesterday. Even the air had a different smell.

A yellow business-size envelope stood out in contrast to the dirty box. Lee pulled the mail out and noticed the return address. Seeing it was from Miranda he was Leery about opening it, thinking he didn't need this right now and at the same time speculating what she wanted from him, of all people.

She was like a manipulative little kid sister. In fact, he nicknamed her Kid. He never understood what Joan saw in her or how they remained best friends all their lives. Joan was soft, quiet, and gentle, the complete opposite of Miranda.

Miranda, as a child, was precocious. The year she was to go into third grade the school skipped her ahead two years. That's when she met Joan, in the fifth-grade. Joan took Miranda under her wing and they were inseparable from that day on. Miranda idolized Joan, and somehow they made it work through the years.

Ripping open the envelope while strolling back to the boat, he pulled a note out first, then noticed a handful of old letters along with copies of newspaper clippings tucked down inside. He theorized Miranda might be looking for some mystery to solve to occupy her time now that she was retired. She considered her twenty-five years as an investigator for the FBI her credentials that proved she was a brilliant detective.

He had to admit there were times when he called on Miranda to help research a project, and she always managed to come through with the information he needed.

From the first day he met Miranda he was jealous of her relationship with Joan. They were inseparable and dedicated to each other. Commitment was something he never gave to Joan. By her actions and inactions he could tell she never shared with him the things she shared with Miranda. What he didn't realize, or maybe deep down inside he did, was he didn't have a close relationship with Joan because he didn't want one, but he didn't want anyone else to have one with her either.

Lee's world revolved around him and his work. He stayed away from Joan for weeks at a time. He believed if he didn't have an emotional attachment to her his conscience wouldn't nag him for neglecting her. Now he lived with the haunting dreams that woke him almost nightly.

Miranda and Joan became soul mates. The closer they grew to each other the further the distance widened between Lee and his wife. He knew it, and didn't like the situation, but at the time Lee considered his job more important than Joan. It was convenient for him to keep the relationships the way they were. He didn't care about the emotional cost to Joan. What mattered was his mental state and the position he held with his company.

It never occurred to him that he might have been the problem in their marriage. He was sure Joan was the bone of contention. But now he was beginning to see the world and himself in a whole new way.

Maybe he had been misjudging Miranda all these years, and she wasn't so bad after all. As he remembered, she was drop-dead gorgeous, like Joan.

Miranda's technology skills were one of the reasons she secured a prized government job. She was the top in her class at M.I.T. Many of the major computer companies sent her offers to work for them, but her heart belonged to the FBI. She wanted to fight crime, serve her country and live a life of adventure.

He slid the paper out of the envelope.

Hi Lee,

I was cleaning out some of my old boxed up papers the other day when I came across a stack of letters.

They were written by a Lillian Grace who claims to know who murdered Joan's Uncle, Bert Grayson many years ago here in Bridgetown, but Lillian said she couldn't get anyone to believe what she was saying.

Jane had given her the letters.

Because you were gone so much, Joan decided to look into the murder to fill some of her lonely hours.

Joan kept running into brick walls, so she gave me the letters to read and asked me to look into the murder when I found the time.

I was busy with work as well as rebuilding this mansion, so I never took the opportunity to read them. As usual, they got shoved aside and ignored until now.

In fact, I forgot about them. It seems Joan did also because she never mentioned them again.

I did read them this time. Some are lengthy. I would like you to take a look at them as well. I was completely hooked after the first letter.

Joan and I were both older teens at the time of the murder. You know, best friends busy with school, homework, and boys. Nothing else mattered much back then. I don't remember much about the murder except it was never solved.

After you read the letters we could spend some time investigating this. Lillian weaves an interesting theory about Joan's uncle and his murder.

Out of curiosity, didn't Joan show them to you? If I remember right she told me she did. If she did, why didn't you take an interest in this for her? But I think I already know the answer to that question.

As usual, you dropped the ball, Lee. You pushed Joan and what interested her aside.

I no longer have access to the FBI websites, so I dig up the info on my own the best way I can, but it can be done with some good research skills.

I could be a big help to you if you decide to investigate this. If you don't, I will. In fact, I've already started looking up a few of the people this lady writes about. We can work our way through this just as we have many other projects. I can't believe the book company you work for would let you get by without using a computer. Oh well, in any event you always have me and my geeky brain and expert computer skills.

Take a vacation and come here. We can investigate this together. You can stay with me. I think we could get along for a couple of weeks, anyway. After that, who knows? I have a room in the house where you can live with all the comforts of home and you won't be under my feet. If you had ever traveled with Joan when she came to visit you'd know that she always stayed with me.

Anyway, you still remain my favorite guy, because you were Joan's one true love even though your one true love was the book business.

You need to lose yourself in something since Joan's death. It's been almost three years now. That's a long time to grieve her loss. It's time for you to start a new chapter in your life. You should get away. This is the perfect opportunity to do so. Call me. You have my number. It hasn't changed.

Miranda

The newspaper clippings about the murder along with the letters written by Lillian Grace, who said she knew who committed the murder, was all it took to lure Lee to New York State with the goal of clearing his conscience, and maybe getting a good night's sLeep. He would look into the murder for Joan and then the tormenting thoughts, sLeepless nights and dreams might go away.

CHAPTER 5

Bridgetown, New York, February 1962

The mud-rutted alley was dark except for an occasional backyard lamp, and the brilliant full moon shining down on the naked ancient oaks that stood on the properties behind Thirty Chestnut Avenue. The moonlight wove a twisted path down through the tree branches, casting skinny shadows that looked like tall dark men leaning against the wooden fence enjoying the night.

The opaque dark patches were hiding a hideous sight in the back lane behind the hovels where the locals lived.

Small piles of snow lay against the wooden fence that had boards kicked out in different spots, but there were two gone beside the grisly scene.

The inhabitants of the run-down houses on the avenue couldn't imagine the giant man filling the space on the ground within a few steps from their homes. It wasn't the best part of town, but they thought it was pretty safe until now. The people who lived there knew the bars outnumbered the homes, but never had anything like this taken place before.

The wailing of sirens and rhythmic pulse of the blue flashing lights on the police cars pulled curious neighbors out of their warm beds. They drifted out into the night to investigate the noise, but not all of them were surprised; some were frightened. Some had already been out and about.

Wide-eyed adults were wiping sLeep from their eyes. Women were holding their bathrobes closed with their hand.

"What the heck is that? Am I seeing what I think I see?" the woman said. They all seemed confused by the sight in front of them. They walked back and forth, gathered in groups and pointing in disbelief.

"Look, he's almost covered with snow," John Williams said, pointing at the big man's body. He was sitting in the snow slumped over, with his feet straight out in front of him. His arms dangled at his sides, hiding his hands in the snow.

"Oh, how hideous," one man said.

"I can't look at it again. It's too horrible. Such a repugnant sight," the short woman said as she turned away after a glance, quickly covering her daughter's eyes.

"Watch your step John, don't slip on the bloody ice," his wife said.

"Look at the blood. It's gathered in pools in the ruts and starting to turn to ice. The snow around the body looks like someone used an airbrush to spray everything red," the tall man said.

"Look, his head is lying on his shoulder," one man said as he moved closer to the giant's body. "Look at that slice in his neck. It goes from his ear to his Adam's apple. No wonder his head is flopped over."

"Get back, move away from him," a policeman said. "Get away from that body. You shouldn't be there."

The residents were pressing nearer, some standing next to the body in the bloody snow. The man who was told to get away kicked the giant's lifeless shoe as he walked away, blending back into the hushed crowd. The two policemen trying to keep the people away from the scene glanced at each other, shaking their heads in disgust at the man's gesture.

"Okay, folks," one of the policemen said, "it's time to move away. This is a crime scene. Go back to your homes, please. Take the children inside. They shouldn't see this. Make room for detective Jones, he's coming down the alley."

"Officer, what do we have here?" The officer rushed behind the detective, grabbing the arm of the man following him.

"Hey buddy, you can't come in here."

Jones looked back to see what was going on. "Oh, he's okay. He's from the newspaper. He can come over here with me."

The reporter smirked at the officer, making his way over to stand beside Jones, with his pencil ready to write.

"As you can see, it looks like murder." He looked from Jones, back to the smirking reporter.

Jones stopped in front of the body and turned, watching the residents drift back into their houses. Some of them were peeking out their windows, continuing to watch what was going on. "It looks like the whole neighborhood was out here," he said, looking at the officer who was setting up the wooden saw horses around the scene.

"We got them away from the body as soon as we arrived on the scene. We got here a few minutes before you did," the officer said. He moved over in front of the barricades, turning his back to Jones and the reporter. "Go on now, head back to your homes," he said to the remaining stragglers.

The reporter was staring at the body while writing fast, probably describing what he was seeing.

As he glanced from the reporter to the body, Chief of Detectives Jones said, "I'll say this—from the number of footprints around the body I think it took a lot of men to bring down this giant of a man."

The reporter stared at him, waiting for more information.

Sliding a pipe from his coat pocket, he put it in his mouth, clenched the stem between his teeth and reached into the other pocket, pulling out a pack of matches, noticing that it was his last one. Ripping it from the book he struck it on the striker patch and listened for the hiss as he watched it break into a blaze. He sucked on the stem of the pipe, each breath pulling the flame down into the bowl, as white smoke swirled from the sides of his lips and disappeared into the air.

Breathing in the sweet smell, Jones looked at the reporter and said, "Cherry tobacco is my favorite."

The reporter nodded.

After a couple of puffs, he held the pipe between his fingers. "This is a gruesome sight."

The reporter nodded in agreement as he stared at the body.

Jones moved his eyes in a slow circle around the mangled body that lay sprawled in front of him, almost covered by snow. Pushing his hat back on his forehead, Jones looked down at the body, hoping that it wouldn't take long to solve this murder.

"This would have to happen to me," Jones said, looking over at the reporter. "I'll be stuck on this case until it's solved. And that might delay my retirement. Things like that always seem to happen to me."

The reporter stared at the body. "Well, I'm sure of one thing."

"What's that?"

"I'm sure this poor man didn't want to be murdered."

Jones stared back at him and paused before speaking. "I know what I said sounds cruel and hard-hearted, but I've been waiting a long time for this retirement. Oh, well, forget I said anything so stupid. We need to get back to the business of this murder."

"I'm all for that," the reporter said.

Taking his hands off his hips he stuffed the now cold pipe into his pocket. He pulled a pair of white gloves from his coat, putting them on. He didn't like the cotton gloves. In cases like these the blood always leaked through onto his hands. He didn't like touching dead bodies.

Leaning over the body he brushed away the snow, pulling the victim's head back onto his neck to get a better look at his face. Jones stepped back a couple of feet, moving so fast he almost fell in the slippery snow.

"What the—?" he said, pausing for a minute as he sucked the air. "What is that all over his face? It looks and smells like dried mustard, ketchup, and relish. The welt between his eyes looks like someone belted him with a blackjack." He looked up at the reporter, shaking his head.

He repositioned the man's head back on the right shoulder shuddering a bit as he let go of it. Wrapping his hand around the arm of the blood-soaked jacket, he pulled it out of the snow to examine the palm of the right hand.

"Look at that. It's covered with black powder burns and dozens of pinhead-sized holes." He looked up at the reporter. "It looks like someone used a bird shot pistol or rifle. They must have pulled a gun on him and in a defensive reaction he grabbed the end of the barrel with the palm of his hand as they pulled the trigger."

Dropping the blood soaked sLeeve back into to its original spot, he grabbed the other one to examine the hand. It was clean except for some black and blue marks on the knuckles. "It looks like he put up a good fight," he said as he let it drop. He pushed the bloody snow around looking for clues, hoping to find a weapon. He wanted to find something that would make this case a quick easy solve. Pulling open the red and white checked jacket his eyes landed on what looked like a check sticking out of the victim's shirt pocket. With careful precision he slid the paper out, and for a few seconds he stood examining it.

"It looks like we know this man's name," Jones said to the reporter. "This is a Conn railroad pension check made out to Bertrand Wyatt Grayson, Appleton, New York. I guess robbery wasn't a motive." He dropped the check into the plastic bag the officer was holding open for him. "Label that evidence bag number one," he said.

"Yes, sir," the officer said, pulling out his marker.

Jones shifted his eyes, trying not to look at the oozing neck as he pulled a worn, brown wallet from the other shirt pocket. He could hear the faint sounds of a crying baby coming from one of the houses behind him. He turned his head, looking in the direction of the sound. Lights were on in all the homes. He could see white puffs coming from the tops of the chimney stacks, dissolving and filling the air with fireplace smoke. He turned back to the wallet.

"His expired driver's license," Jones said, "confirms he's indeed Bertrand Wyatt Grayson. Let me see." He paused as he fingered through the bill compartment. "Two dollars in the bill compartment." He was about to drop the wallet into the second bag when he noticed a small piece of paper pushed down in the corner of the bill compartment. He plucked it out and unfolded it. Without thinking, he read the phone number loud enough for the reporter to hear, "944-823-1415." Jones glanced at the reporter, shrugged, then dropped the wallet and paper into the waiting baggie.

Jones took a couple of steps back from the body. "It's a shame, isn't it?" he said as he stood with his chin cradled in his right hand. With a wide-eyed steady gaze, he studied the body.

"What could Grayson have been involved in to die like this?" He paused. "From my years of experience as a detective, I know people often hide the seedy side of their lives from their loved ones. My question is, what was Grayson hiding? Maybe the phone number will give me some answers."

The detective looked up in time to see a man coming down the alley, pulling a gurney.

"Oh, better move back." He took the reporter's arm, guiding him away from the body. "I see the coroner coming."

"Good evening, Joe. Where's Leslie?" Jones asked as the coroner came to a stop in front of the body.

"What's so good about it? Leslie called off tonight," he said, shaking his head. "Of all nights for this to happen. They said he had to go out of town or something. I don't remember."

After completing his examination, Joe and the officer wrapped the body in a sheet and placed it on the gurney.

Jones looked up to see a Bridgetown fire truck pull up and stop at the end of the alley behind the waiting ambulance. He could hear the men talking.

"I'll get the hose," the tall fireman said as the two of them jumped out of the truck. The short one turned on the water and ran to catch up with the tall one, dragging the hose toward the scene of the crime.

"I'll help you," he said, grabbing the hose. Just then the two firemen halted in their steps, staring at the gurney as the coroner pushed it past them to the waiting ambulance.

The tall one had his eyes riveted to the blood spots leaking through the white sheet. Jones could see him shiver. They started down the alley again, coming to a quick stop when they reached the spot where the body had been.

The short fireman sucked in his breath. "Look at all that blood. It's everywhere."

Jones approached the firemen just then. "I want you men to wash away the snow from that spot," he said, pointing. The firemen turned the hose in that direction, pulling the handle. The water rushed out, melting the snow down to the bare ground.

He watched, hoping to find a knife, gun, or something useful.

"Look at that, not one single clue."

"Thanks for coming out, fellas," Jones said. "I'm disappointed we didn't find anything." The firemen walked back to the truck, dragging the hose behind them.

"All that remains now," he said to the reporter, "is finding someone who knows something. And what are the odds of that?"

The reporter shrugged.

With the reporter by his side he questioned the neighbors and people in the local bars.

When they were finished, Jones looked the reporter in the eyes and said, "I'm heading back to the office now to file my report."

"Okay. I need to get back to the paper and write up my story so it'll make the morning edition." The reporter paused.

"Jones, thanks for letting me get close to the scene. I know you didn't have to."

Jones nodded as he walked away.

CHAPTER 6

Bridgetown, New York, February 1962

Later that night on the outskirts of a town a few miles south of Bridgetown, a man pulled his truck to the side of the road, stopping in the middle of the hill. He put the gearshift into park but left the motor running. He glanced down the road, then checked his mirrors for headlights coming from behind. When the coast was clear, the driver slid out. Walking around the back of his Chevy he stopped at the guardrail, looked around in the dark, and then threw the gun over the hill. It landed with a clang in the rocks, weeds and brush on the creek bank below. He walked back around the truck through the exhaust fumes rolling from the tail-pipe filling the night air, got in and drove off.

The headlines in the morning edition of the *Bridgetown Mirror* screamed in bold black print:

> ***Retired Conn Railroad engineer murdered***
> *The body of an Appleton man was found against the wooden fence in the alley at the rear of 30 Chestnut Avenue. Big Bert Grayson's lifeless*

body was discovered by a group of teens on their way home from ice skating late last night.

Fifty-eight-year-old Grayson often frequented the local bars in Bridgetown at the south end. This area is known for its rough bars, loose women, and knock-down, drag-out, fights.

The investigators traced Mr. Grayson's steps from a string of local bars to his last known location, Jim's Diner, where he borrowed five dollars from someone. He met two men there and was last seen walking toward a dark sedan in the parking lot of the diner with these two unknown men.

Bertrand lived with his sister Elizabeth and was retired on disability from the railroad.

The family members at first thought robbery could be a motive until they learned he didn't cash the disability check he had received that week. The police discovered it was still in his shirt pocket when they found his body. His brother Benson told the Mirror it wouldn't have been easy to kill Bert, and that he was a popular guy around the bars because of his size and strength. Police are speculating that more than two men might be involved. If robbery wasn't the motive, was it revenge or jealousy? Or a love spurned?

> *The police are leaving all angles open. Grayson was a patient at the State Mental Hospital. He was released three weeks ago.*

The *Mirror* included a composite picture of one of the companions Bert Grayson was last seen with.

CHAPTER 7

Present Day

Lee carried Miranda's letter into the kitchen, dropping it on the counter top. He took a seat on the bar stool, trying to decide if going to Miranda's was the smart thing to do. He could also tell from reading the letter that she hadn't changed much through the years.

He often thought Miranda never got married because there wasn't a man alive who could live with her.

At Joan's funeral, he didn't spend much time with Miranda.

He was anxious to lose himself in his work, trying to take his mind off his wife.

With his elbows resting on the black granite countertop and his legs straddling the stainless steel stool, he was soaking in the sun filtering down through the skylight, warming his shoulders while at the same time soothing his beat up ego.

He dumped the remaining contents of the envelope onto the counter top, spending a couple of hours reading the letters and newspaper clippings. He meditated on where the key might be and if Miranda was looking for it.

Three months after the murder, the police stopped investigating, claiming they had no new clues to go on. There was a composite picture of one of the men they said Bert left the diner with the night he was murdered.

Lee studied the picture, and was thinking about the letters while twisting his hair with his finger, a habit he'd tried to break, but couldn't.

His mind was all over the place. He recounted every detail of being fired and betrayed by his best friends, Sally and Ray, the murder and what he had learned so far. The letters were intriguing to him, spiking his curiosity about the murder and Lillian. Then there was Joan.

Miranda was right. Three years was long enough to mourn. He could never forget Joan but it was time to move on with his life and begin to live again. He was growing lonely and needing female companionship, even if it had to be Miranda.

He made a promise to himself, right there and then, that today he would begin the next chapter of his life. As he was daydreaming it dawned on him. These must have been the letters Joan gave him to read many years ago. Being the self-centered man he was, he handed them back, telling her he was too busy for such nonsense. Cringing at his own words he sat shaking his head in disgust as those thoughts stung his conscience, and how his words must have hurt Joan.

He made a vow that day. If it took the rest of his life, he would investigate and solve the murder of Joan's uncle. He also vowed to be there for others who might reach out to him, to help solve the unsolvable, and in some way in his guilt ridden mind he would also be making it up to Joan.

Maybe then the haunting and sLeepless nights would leave him. He never thought of himself as a particularly brave man, but he would do what he had to do. Somewhere deep inside he would find the courage to face the threat of death, if that was what it took.

The scent of pine drifting in from the mountains traveled through the screen door, the roaring of boats moving in and out of the bay, mournful sounds of an occasional tugboat horn moaning in the distance, all reminding him why he loved this place so much. Joan had a fondness for this spot on the docks. She said it centered her.

Lee now wished he could go back into the past, redoing that one thing if nothing else. And as it happened, destiny had put the letters in his hands for a second time. Now he'd have the opportunity to wash his conscience clean.

He reached for his cell to call Miranda. "Hi, Kid, how are you?"

"Scrappy as ever, Lee. When are you going to get off the Kid thing? I'm a little too old for that now. So, are you coming soon?"

"I read the newspaper clippings and the letters. It all sounds interesting. Are you sure there's enough room?"

"I'll make room for you. This place is big enough for both of us."

"Thanks . . . Kid. I have loose ends to tie up here before I can leave, so it'll be a couple of weeks."

"Okay, Lee. I'll look for you then. Bye."

He made a trip to the bank to transfer money out of his savings and into his checking account to use as traveling money.

He couldn't shake the uneasy feeling that something wasn't right.

After reading the newspaper accounts and the letters again he was hooked on investigating this murder. He decided he would let Miranda tell him about Lillian.

One of his goals was to change his opinion about Miranda and forget the past. He'd work to see only the best side of her.

He never enjoyed the legwork that came with research. He only enjoyed putting the pieces together. Sally did most of the work, and without her computer skills he would have been fired long before this. Sure, he traveled to dig out the hard to find information, but the bulk of the work was done by Sally on the computer.

He couldn't figure out why he had the feeling someone was watching him.

CHAPTER 8

Present Day

Robert had them turn the new laser satellites in Lee and Miranda's direction. He gave orders to the techs. "I want to know everything they say and what they're up to. I want eyes and ears on them all the time."

The lead tech looked up at Robert. "Don't worry, boss. We won't miss a thing. We have everything where it should be."

Robert loved new technology, and now because of it, he was sure what he had waited for all these years was finally within his grasp.

CHAPTER 9

Bridgetown, New York, March 1962

The moaning wind whistled in the eaves, slamming rusted pieces of loose aluminum siding onto the house, sending them screeching all the way to the ground.

Lillian was halfway down the third page when George's big hand slammed down on the desktop, ripping the papers from under her fingers. The violent force sent her pen sailing across the room where it bounced off the dirty white wall, leaving big blue ink splatters before hitting the floor and rolling to a stop against the paint chipped baseboard. She screamed and on instinct wrapped her arms around the back of her head, waiting for him to smack her.

When she realized he wasn't going to hit her, she looked up at him. It was at that moment she realized what he was about to do. Her mouth gaped open in disbelief, and she begged, "Please don't do this George. Please don't."

His big meaty hands crumpled the pages into a ball as he rushed across the room to the fireplace, tossing the wad of paper into the flames.

"There," he said, planting his hands on his hips and whirling his upper body around, his bloodshot eyes looking directly into hers. "That'll take care of that. I don't want to see you doing any more writing, Lillian. Do you understand me?" he hissed between clenched, rotted teeth.

She jumped as a strong gust of wind smashed a tree branch against the living room window, and watched a new crack start to grow in one of the panes.

Her eyes narrowed to slits as she fixed them on George.

Water leaked from the corners, running like rivers down her cheeks. She wiped them on her dress sLeeve, but soon they were gushing and she was unable to control them as she watched the flames lick and devour her papers until there was nothing left but ashes.

George glanced in her direction, then tilted his head back, as he laughed and snorted at her. "You're a dumb one, you are.

I don't want you writing about that murder and making me look bad," he said. "What's done is done. Forget about it.

That old drunk got what he deserved."

He stomped into the dark kitchen, jerked open the refrigerator door, and grabbed another cold Bud from the shelf.

She could see him from where she was sitting. The bulb from the opened refrigerator door was like a spotlight, illuminating his fat, pig-faced head. She hated him. She hated him even more than when he was slapping and kicking her around.

Lillian watched George shove his stubby fingers into his baggy pants pocket, she could see his hand moving around inside. When he pulled it out his fingers were gripping the church key he always carried.

All the while he ignored her as she sat at her desk holding her head between her hands, sobbing in soft, hushed, uncontrollable whimpers, watching him out of the corner of her eye as he locked the flat hook on the waffled edge of the metal bottle cap and flipped it.

"Ah," he said, "I love that sucking sound the lid makes as it releases the smell of fresh beer."

He stuck his nose up into the air, breathing in the droplets of beer still hanging there.

His eyes shifted down, watching as the bottle cap slid, bounced, and rolled across the kitchen floor. It wobbled and came to rest against the other five in a round shallow spot worn into the old linoleum.

She watched him with hatred in her eyes, as his pig lips locked around the opened bottle. Sucking and snorting, he swigged the beer as fast as he could swallow it. Some of the froth ran out the sides of his mouth, creating white rivulets that streamed through his whiskers. When the foam reached the front of his dirty T-shirt it expanded the wet circle that was already there.

He pulled the bottle from his lips, breathing hard. "Don't bother me anymore, Lillian. I'm going to finish watching The Red Skelton Hour."

He belched, wiping his mouth with the back of his hand while waddling back into the living room, where he plopped his wide body down into the big faded blue velvet chair.

Outside the wind had died down as fast as it puffed up.

She watched as George fell into a drunken slumber in front of the TV.

It was as though her body would only move in slow motion. She forced herself to get up from the desk chair and into her bedroom. Locking the door, she fell across the bed, crying herself to sLeep.

The next morning, through tear-swollen eyes and with determination in her heart she started to write again. This time, she waited until George had gone to work. Sitting at her writing desk she wondered who she could contact—then the answer came to her.

She was sure Bert's sister would believe what she had to say. She would write what she knew in the letters and mail them, one by one, year after year, to Elizabeth. Then someone else would know the truth about the murder.

CHAPTER 10

Present Day

Lee spent the next few weeks tying up loose ends in preparation for his stay with Miranda, packing everything he thought he would need or couldn't live without.

The sun was bright that day as he walked out to the dock keeper's hut and found John.

John was hired by the corporation that managed the harbor to do repair work and keep the marina looking perfect for the wealthy clients who chose to moor their vessels in this expensive coastal bay area.

"How are you, John?"

"Fine, Mr. Perkins. Thanks for asking."

"I'll be leaving tomorrow for a visit with a friend in New York. I don't know when I'll be coming home. I plan to keep in touch with you from time to time. Here's the phone number where I can be reached if you need me." Lee shook John's hand, giving him a folded paper with the number on it.

"Thank you, Mr. Perkins. Don't worry yourself. I'll look after your houseboat. Stay as long as you want."

"Thanks again, John."

He made his way back to the houseboat, pausing every once in a while to enjoy the seascape unfolding in front of his eyes, colorful boats and yachts bobbing in their slips on the blue-green waters of the bay. He would miss this panorama that had become part of his life. He ambled down the steps on his boat to the main deck and stood resting his back on the railing. He crossed his legs and folded his arms over his chest to watch the sunset.

He opened his cell. "Hi, Kid. I'll be on the road early in the morning, arriving at your house sometime tomorrow. I appreciate your hospitality. Oh, and Miranda, I may stay with you longer than a couple of weeks."

"Okay, you can stay as long as you want to. I'll look forward to seeing you again. Sometimes it gets lonely rambling around in this big house. I'll see you when you get here."

"Miranda, one more thing. I'm working on changing my attitude. Maybe you could help me deal with that issue."

"I'll be glad to help you."

"Thanks, Kid. Bye for now."

He stood on the deck watching the sunset and rolling around in his mind his attitude toward Miranda. The red ball dipped into the ocean and bright stars dotted the dark sky.

He was hoping that time had changed Miranda. He shook his head. Well, maybe it had changed him, too. In a lot of ways he wasn't the same man he had been a couple of weeks ago. He was seeing a side of his personality that he didn't like.

He couldn't shake a nagging feeling of uneasiness.

Before he got into bed, he set the alarm for five o'clock. That would give him a full day of driving in daylight. He didn't like driving at night.

That night he tossed and turned, dreaming and waking every hour. All the past weeks' happenings wouldn't leave, and his guilty conscience haunted him.

Unable to sLeep, he got up, loaded the car, and before daybreak he was driving north on I-95. This would be his first visit to Miranda's new home.

CHAPTER 11

Present Day
Bridgetown, New York

Hours later, Lee turned into an imposing entrance that stood open, with the words "Wind Swept Acres" on an ornate arch across the top. Stopping the car just outside the wrought-iron gates, he could see the mansion was almost hidden by the winding tree-lined driveway. This is classic Miranda, he thought.

She had restored the two-hundred-year-old all-brick mansion from the ground up. The original owner was the man who financed and built the Conn Railroad.

The mountains behind the house were breathtaking. The locals called this the high peaks area. In front of the house the plush acres of manicured lawns, expensive trees, shrubs, small ponds and gardens added to the beauty of the old place.

The brick house emerged intermittently through the old oak trees guarding the cobblestone driveway with its many curves, looming large and spectacular.

He stopped his Jag at the inviting house and got out. The front door opened and Miranda strolled across the wide porch, followed by a tall, husky, good-looking middle-aged man. They descended the steps together.

"Hum," Lee said under his breath. He wasn't aware that Miranda had a male friend. He studied the man as he walked toward him. He looked six-foot-four, with muscles bulging on his arms, in stark contrast to Miranda's tall, slim figure. Lee thought he looked more like a bodyguard than a lover. There, he was making assumptions about people in his own egotistical way, when in most cases they turned out to be wrong.

Miranda marched right up to Lee, invading his space, stopping she stood on her tiptoes. Her lips were almost touching his, and her perfume was intoxicating. Lee smiled.

"Hi, Lee. I see you haven't lost your killer smile. It's good to see you. It looks like you're thinner and taller than I remember. What, maybe six-foot-six?"

Her breath smelled of sweet mint. She stepped back about a foot and stuck out her hand, with a curt grin. Lee continued to smile as they shook hands.

"Six-foot-seven. I'm not sLeeping too well at night—insomnia,

I guess. I can see you're as soft spoken and beautiful as ever." Lee continued to hang onto her hand as he stared at her. She pulled her hand away. "I imagine you can't sLeep at night from a guilty conscience."

"I knew I could count on you for words of encouragement."

He paused for a couple seconds, looking her up and down.

"It doesn't hurt that after all these years you're still drop-dead gorgeous."

She turned in the direction of her friend. "Lee, this is Adrian, my house-carl."

"Your house what? What is a house-carl?"

"Well, I guess it's a fancy word for a butler."

Adrian reached out his hand, flashing a big smile that revealed perfect white teeth. "Hello, Lee. If there's anything I can do for you while you're here just let me know. I'm always around. I do the cooking, cleaning and whatever Miranda wants. So don't hesitate to ask."

Lee pulled his hand from Adrian's and shook it in the air.

"Thank you, Adrian. I'm glad my fingers aren't broken."

"Sorry about that. I forget myself at times."

Lee smiled at Adrian, thinking, *He does whatever Miranda wants*, imagining what that would be. He looked at Miranda, shrugged and mouthed the words, house-carl?

As though Miranda could read his thoughts—or because it showed all over his face— she said, "Adrian takes care of the house and cooking so I'm free to do whatever I want. Don't think you can flash that handsome face at me expecting me to melt the way Joan always did." Miranda's eyes flashed, then narrowed as she stared at him.

"Right on, Kid. Whatever you say."

"How was the drive up?" Miranda asked.

"It was smooth sailing all the way. Stopped a couple of times for a break, but that was about as exciting as it got."

Lee opened the trunk and started to pull out his suitcases.

"Here, let me help you with that," Adrian said. He pulled the bags out.

"Your place is so big. A two-story brick beauty. Are those the original pillars?"

"Yes, they were the biggest expense to restore."

"I can see the money and work that went into the house. It looks like it was a labor of love."

"Yes, it was. There were times when I thought it was a money pit, but now that it's finished it was worth all the time and money I invested."

"How many acres do you have here?"

"It's just a bit over one hundred and thirty-five."

Lee walked beside Miranda as they approached the house and ascended the steps, crossing the porch and into the vestibule.

"This room is spectacular. You have great taste. The wide crown molding was always my favorite. The dark hardwood floors—are they in every room?"

"Yes, and they're all original and took a ton of money to restore."

Scanning the spacious room, he remembered Joan's comments: Miranda fell in love with and bought the old place at auction for a great price when it was in shambles and only days away from being razed. Lee remembered commenting to Joan that Miranda must be trying to reach the future while living in the past.

"Have you learned anything new about the woman and her letters?" Lee turned and made eye contact with Miranda.

"Yes, but first I need to tell you this. Let's take a seat at the counter. Adrian brewed a pot of coffee."

Lee sat on the stool beside her.

"About two hours ago I had an interesting visitor. The doorbell rang and I thought it was you."

"Who was it?"

"It was a nervous, geeky looking man about forty years old.

He wanted to buy the letters. I told him I wasn't interested in selling them at this time. If I changed my mind I would call him if he would leave his name and phone number. He said he would give me a thousand dollars for them and I asked him why he wanted them. He said he was a local historian and collected old letters written by people from the area."

"Wow. Did he leave his name and phone number?" Lee took a sip of coffee and listened intently to what Miranda said.

"No, he said he would contact me again in a couple of days."

"How did he know you had the letters?"

"That's the exact question I asked him." Miranda put her arm on the counter and looked Lee in the eyes.

"What did he say?"

"He said that I told a friend of mine who told a friend of his and his friend told him that I had some historical letters he might be interested in buying."

"Well, did you mention to your friends that you had the letters?"

"I guess I mentioned the letters to a few people I met around town in my excitement after reading them."

"But you didn't tell them what they said, did you?"

"Yes, but I told them not to tell anyone. I guess they told."

"Listen, Kid, I would think you of all people, especially with your background, would know to keep your mouth shut."

"Oh, Lee, what harm has it done? He was just a guy wanting to buy the letters."

"I can see a local historian being interested in those old letters, but paying a thousand dollars for them makes no sense," Lee said.

Miranda pulled a folded piece of paper from the back pocket of her designer jeans and handed it to him. He couldn't help but notice that her nail polish matched her lipstick, a soft shade of pink.

"Here's a note from the man who tried to buy the letters. He handed it to me just before he went to his car. He said he had to leave, they were watching his every move, and he had to get the letters before they did. I asked who was watching him and were they watching him now? He said my life was in danger too. I laughed out loud. It sounded too preposterous, like something straight out of a mystery novel. He hurried away to his green Ford, got in and drove off."

Lee unfolded the paper and read it out loud.

> *Right now is all of time that exists. All past time ends where the future begins. You should take heed of the experiences of the past as they will shape your future. The letters will lead you if you know how to follow the clues in them. You should push forward redeeming the time and your life.*

He stared at the note for a few minutes, clenching and unclenching his jaw. *What have I gotten myself into?* He glanced up at Miranda, who was staring back at him.

"What does that mean?" he asked. "Is he trying to tell us to back off or to keep going? You should take heed of the experiences of the past as they shape your future while redeeming the time and your life. What's he telling us? That the answers are in our research and will lead to who killed Joan's uncle? And why would he tell us that when he was trying to buy the letters for himself, or was it for someone else?"

"You got me, Lee. Those are all good questions, and I'll bet that some if not all of what Lilly says in her letters is true."

Lee stuffed the note into his pants pocket.

"What do you mean 'Lilly'?" he said. "You sound like you're old friends with her."

"After reading her letters I feel like I've known her for years. You read them, don't you feel that way?"

He put his cup down on the counter. "Well, I feel I know and understand her, but I'm not sure I'd say I feel I've known her for years. We've got a lot to think about."

"For right now I should get you settled. Follow me to where you'll be staying." Lee followed Miranda down a long hall leading to the back of the house. "You can have access to the rest of the house, except for Adrian's quarters on the other side, and stay out of the upstairs—that's my domain. You shouldn't need to go up there at all."

"What if I need to go there for something?"

Miranda narrowed her eyes. "You stay out of my bedroom areas unless you're invited. And I don't see that happening."

"Okay, but I'm not that easily discouraged, even with big old hunky Adrian around." He flashed a playful smile.

"Oh!" She stopped and stared into Lee's sea blue eyes.

"Adrian has been with me for a long time. I don't know what I would do without him."

"I'll bet."

She opened her mouth to say something, then stopped short, turned, and opened the door in front of them.

"This is where you'll be staying. It has a full bath and a walk-in closet. I see Adrian has already brought in your bags.

As I said, Adrian does the cooking. We're not formal diners, he usually eats with me, and you're welcome to join us."

"Wow. This is nice."

The large room had a small seating area with glass doors leading out onto an expansive wooden deck with a couple of chairs and a chaise. Lee strolled over to the patio doors to take in the view. Stretching out behind the house was a field of grass with shrubs, trees, a small pond surrounded by chairs and cement benches for seating. The lawn stopped at the edge of a stand of tall trees that led into the forest at the foot of one of the high peaks mountains.

"Does your property go back to the woods?" Lee asked as Miranda joined him in front of the doors. She held up her hand and pointed to the distance.

"No, it goes back to that mountain."

"It must be nice," he said.

"The privacy is wonderful."

Lee had to admit that Miranda provided him with all the comforts of home. He turned and glanced around the room. On the dresser on the far side of the room was an eight-by-ten framed photo of Lee and Joan. It had been taken when they were on their honeymoon. Out of the corner of his eye he could see Miranda watching him.

"I didn't know you still had that picture. Joan was so excited to give it to you."

"I know, and I was excited that she wanted me to have it. This is the room Joan always stayed in when she came to visit. She felt at peace staying here, and we had a lot of good times together."

"If only I had taken the time to come with her. I made a vow to solve this murder for Joan no matter how long it takes. I intend to see it through to the end. I hope you will be with me." He turned and looked Miranda in the eyes.

"Better late than never I guess. I, too, wish you had taken the time to come and visit with Joan. She had become so lonely toward the end. Yes, Lee, I will be with you to the end of this, no matter what that turns out to be. Joan would have liked to see this finished," she said, pulling away from the moment. "Let's move on to other things." She pointed to the closet. "You have plenty of space to put your clothes. I'll leave you so you can unpack, or I can have Adrian do it for you, if you like."

"That's okay, I can handle it on my own." *Yeah, right. I don't want Adrian handling my underwear*, he thought. "I'm sure Adrian is busy getting dinner ready." He placed his suitcase on the bed, then opened it and started to unpack.

"When you're finished, come out to the computer room, it's down the hall on the left. We'll have a few minutes to look at some things before dinner." Miranda moved to the door and began closing it behind her.

"Okay, thanks, Miranda."

She stopped and poked her head back in the door. "That's better. I like my name."

He looked up from his suitcase, nodded, smiled, and went back to unpacking. After putting his things away, he stretched out on the king-size bed. It was just right. He was staring at the ceiling mulling things over in his mind.

He got up and shook his head to clear his brain, then made his way down the hall where he found Miranda. She was hard at work on a computer in a spacious office and library combination room. She looked up at him. He stopped in his tracks and stared at her. He was thinking she had become more beautiful with age. Miranda broke the silence.

"Adrian will have dinner ready in about thirty minutes. It's getting late. We waited so we could eat with you."

"Thanks. That was considerate."

"It was Adrian's idea, not mine. You can sit in this chair." She shoved a computer chair in his direction.

He pushed it over beside her and sat down. "Well, my curiosity is way beyond ready to learn what you've found out," he said. "When are you going to let me hear all about it?"

"I know you want to hear all about the research, but it's getting late. I'm tired. All I want to do is eat and go to bed. I have exercise classes in the morning, and I need to get my rest. I think you should wait until tomorrow. You look pretty tired to me."

"I might have trouble sLeeping, thinking about everything."

"Tomorrow, after you've finished going over what I've learned, we should look into everything Lilly has to say to see if the people she talked about really did exist. Or, for that matter, who she was. All we know about her is what's in the letters. We don't even know where she's from."

"After I review the information you've dug up I think we should visit Joan's sister Jane to see what she can tell us about all of this."

"That's a good idea. It's been a couple of months since I've seen Jane. We've both been too busy to get together."

Lee stood, "Oh, I didn't know you spent time with Jane."

Miranda stopped typing long enough to shoot an irritated look in his direction. "There are many things you don't know, Lee. Jane and I go way back. She's single now, so we go out for dinner every now and then."

At that moment, Adrian called for them to come to dinner.

After eating, Miranda turned to Lee and said, "Good night.

See you in the morning."

He smiled and said, "SLeep tight, Miranda. If you get lonesome, you know where I am."

She glanced at him, shook her head in frustration, and stomped upstairs. Lee chuckled to himself on his way back to his room mentally and physically tired. He was about to flop on the bed, but his attention was drawn to the photo on the dresser. He picked it up, studied it, and then placed it back in its spot. He ran his finger around the edge of the frame. *I'll make it right, I'll solve this murder for you, Joan.*

CHAPTER 12

Present Day

For the last twenty years Lee, like F. Scott Fitzgerald, put into practice training his mind to operate while holding two opposing ideas at the same time and still retain the ability to function.

When Lee was faced with a situation that appeared to be hopeless, he never gave up. He became more determined to turn it around. His big weakness was being a sucker for the underdog and a beautiful woman.

At sunrise the next day, perched on a stool in Miranda's kitchen and resting his elbows on the counter, Lee scanned the local morning newspaper. Out of the corner of his eye he noticed Miranda standing behind the counter next to Adrian, reading the other side.

Miranda grabbed the paper. "Give me that," jerking it from his hands with her eyes fixed on the front page.

"What the heck, Kid? Please, here, have the paper."

She ignored him and flopped it onto the counter. Her eyes darted back and forth on the page then she stopped and looked up at Lee while tapping her finger on a picture on the page.

"Lee, this is the man who was here yesterday trying to buy the letters." She turned the paper toward him. "That man, right there."

He gave the article the once-over, making comments while reading it. "It looks like James Robinson was killed on impact, hit by a train when his car stalled on the tracks at Blake's Crossing. Sure enough, it says he was the local historian in Bridgetown, and had a wealth of knowledge about the area and the people."

Lee glanced up.

"I guess it wasn't my life that was in danger after all, it was his," Miranda said.

"At least now we know the man's name," Lee said, twisting a few strands of his hair while pondering this development.

Miranda interrupted Lee's thoughts. "Okay Lee, the guy was killed after coming here. Could his death be tied to his interest in the letters? And what about the people he said were watching him? Who are they and why would anyone want those letters? This gets more intriguing by the hour." Miranda crossed her arms and leaned back against the counter gazing at Lee.

"Listen, Kid, it could be a coincidence, just a car-train accident, as the paper said. It happened at night so maybe this Mr. Robinson drove onto the tracks. His car stalled and he couldn't get it started."

Miranda glanced at Lee with a confused look. "Okay, so why didn't he jump out before the train hit him?"

Lee got up from the stool and shook the kinks out of his legs. "I don't know the answer to that one, but there must be a good reason. It looks like this is going to be dangerous to be involved in, maybe I should do this on my own. I can stay in a local hotel so you won't be connected."

Miranda glared in Lee's direction and scowled. "Oh come on Lee, this hasn't scared me. I could protect both of us. Right now we should finish up here and get started with everything we have to do. We have a busy day ahead of us."

Adrian handed Miranda a glass with a red creamy smooth drink in it. She took a sip. "Hum, thank you, Adrian. It's just the way I like it."

Lee watched her lips as she sipped the smoothie. "Don't tell me that smoothie is all you're having for breakfast?"

"At my age I need to be on a diet and working out all the time. And from the looks of you, you should as well. What are you, two hundred and fifty pounds? That graying hair around your temples shows your age and working out might be good for you. Speaking of, I have to be at the gym pretty soon."

"Hey now, wait a minute. I'm in great shape," Lee said as he fingered his slightly bulging belly. "I'm all lean muscle, getting a little pooch here, that's all."

Miranda strolled over to the garage door. "Okay, Lee."

Miranda had once told Lee that her family often accused her of being flighty or hyper, with the attention span of an ant, which he knew wasn't true. He figured her family saw her this way since she took on new projects constantly and handled multi-tasking with ease. That was one of her greatest assets. She was a Pisces. She often looked and acted like she couldn't make up her mind when in reality she was focused and choosy.

"I was hoping," Lee said, "to hear what your thoughts were on Lillian and the letters."

"You need to read what I have so far. I did a lot of research, but not a lot of investigation. I thought I'd wait to do that with you." Miranda shifted from one foot to the other and turned around to face Lee. The tone of her voice changed.

"Here's what I think so far. The letters to Elizabeth are a journal of Lillian's struggles seeking the truth about Bert Grayson's murder. She was trapped in a marriage with a man who ruled with an iron fist. He hit her and shoved her around when he was drunk. To me, the letters revealed this woman's journey through a not so forgiving world, trying to change hearts and minds in a desperate attempt to seek happiness."

"Oh come on, I read the letters too. It sounds like you're agreeing with her even before we find out if she's telling the truth or making up all that stuff we read."

"Not at all. As a woman, I can empathize with the situation she found herself in."

"Now what do you mean by that? Are you saying as a man I can't empathize with her?" Lee squared his shoulders.

"Yes and no. As I read each letter she sucked me into her world by exposing her raw feelings, explaining how each person, place and event changed her life, driving her to the actions and reactions of the narcissistic, disturbed person she in the end became."

His eyes widened in surprise to hear her talk about feelings in such a natural tone. "So... are you saying you think she was nuts?"

A frown formed at the corners of her mouth. "That's not nice. Make no mistake about it, I wouldn't say she was as disturbed and confused as she appeared to be. I think she was a victim of events, manipulated by a corrupt police department, mafia figures, and the other people involved. I think cold calculating men worked to cover up the truth that Lilly knew and they tried to silence her by making it look like she was a crazy woman."

He shook his head. "If what you're saying is true why didn't these people just kill Lilly?"

She gave him a half smile. "I thought about that as well. The conclusion I came to was, there were already too many bodies piling up. Any more would attract the attention of the federal government. Nothing brings in the FBI faster than an extraordinary amount of murders in a given time period in any town. They track that kind of information."

He nodded in agreement, "You would know that better than I would."

"At the time Joan gave me the letters, she said the people in her family didn't think Lilly actually knew her Uncle Bert. The family unjustifiably accused her of being one of those nut cases who read about a murder, then would try to get involved with it somehow. Joan said her family knew the woman was a mental case."

Lee took a couple of steps in Miranda's direction. "I don't think you should just assume that what this woman says is true. She could very well be crazy."

She took a couple of steps back while holding his eye contact. "In my opinion as an FBI profiler, I think all of the incidences she mentions worked together to drive Lilly to live on the edges of her own psychosis. I think it's evident as you read each letter."

He smiled and touched her elbow. "So you're saying that she drifts in and out of reality?"

"I know after all these years it'll be difficult to prove what she says, but what kind of detectives are we if we can't dig up the evidence?"

He nodded.

"I have to run or I'll be late for my appointment at the gym. You should have enough time to look at that material while I'm gone. It'll be interesting to hear what you think."

"One thing before you go. After I read the newspaper clippings and letters, I placed a called to the Bridgetown police to make an appointment with someone to go over the case with me. That was weeks ago, and I haven't heard back from them."

She shot a wide-eyed glance at Lee and pushed his hand away. "That isn't unusual, murder cases are considered open until they're solved. I can understand their reluctance to talk with you, but they should give you something."

"I gave my number to the secretary where they could contact me, it would be nice if they would call while I'm here, saving me a trip back to this town."

The look in Miranda's eyes softened for a second. "You can stay with me as long as you want to, and as long as you remember your place. I now have all the time in the world since I retired," she said.

Lee returned the smile and ran his fingers through his hair. "Thank you," he said as he cleared his throat. "Now I have all the time in the world as well."

"Why? What do you mean?"

"The day before I received your envelope in the mail, the publishing house fired me." Lee looked down at the floor as he spoke. He couldn't bring himself to make eye contact.

"What? Why?"

He looked up in time to see her put her hand on her hip, cocking one leg out slightly.

"My good friend Ray is the one who axed me. He said I was the only editor who still wrote everything out on paper. They invested in expensive computers for me and I never even tried to use them."

Miranda threw her hands into the air. The keys in her hand jingled on the way down to her side. "What did I tell you? Years ago I told you, you should learn to use a computer but, oh no, not you. You could get by without learning to use one."

Lee looked back down at the floor. Miranda stepped forward, and with her finger gave a gentle tug under his chin lifting his head up. Lee moved back a couple of inches.

"As I was saying, before I was rudely interrupted, Ray told me they were combining my job with two others and Sally Parker would replace me." He watched Miranda's eyes grow to the size of quarters.

"Your assistant? How humiliating. They really stuck it to you.

It almost makes me feel sorry for you." The corners of her mouth turned down. She reached out and took his hand in hers patting it trying to comfort him. "Lee I'd like to say I'm sorry, but I did try to warn you. Someday you'll learn to listen to me.

But that did have to hurt."

"Is that a bit of sympathy I detect? Thank you, but I'm past it all now, and what's important is this murder case."

She pulled her hand back from his, moving back to the door. "Maybe a bit, but being computer savvy in this day and age is almost a necessity in any business. I'll be back in an hour or maybe sooner. I have to go. Try to finish reading that stuff before I get back so we can discuss our plans and lay out a course of action going forward."

CHAPTER 13

Present Day

Lee made his way across the expansive Tudor-style living room, stopping in front of the floor to ceiling windows that looked out onto the driveway. He followed Miranda's expensive car as it disappeared into the heavy mist rolling in off the mountains. He stared up into the sky. He could feel someone watching him—but who and why?

The silence in the big house was deafening. He didn't like it. The quiet allowed him too much time to think about the past, present, and future. The past he couldn't change. The present he could manipulate, but the future filled him with renewed hope. Remembering the vow he made to solve this murder for Joan, he felt he could control and change the direction he was going.

He couldn't shake the feeling that his and Miranda's lives were in danger, especially since the death of the local historian and the warning he gave Miranda. He sensed that everything that happened so far was somehow tied into the murder and the letters. What else could it be?

Miranda was always a private person and lived alone for reasons she never shared with him, but he was sure she shared them with Joan.

To live alone for such a long time she must enjoy the solitude. Of course, he didn't know the real role Adrian played in Miranda's life either. He was still trying to piece that together. Maybe he was a bodyguard pretending to be a housekeeper. After all, who ever heard of a house-carl? Maybe he was her lover to be available at her beck and call. He thought how silly that sounded and he shook his head, trying to clear his thoughts.

As he did so the silence was broken. "Lee, is there anything I can get for you before I leave?"

"Nothing I can think of, but thanks anyway, Adrian." Lee watched him walk out the same door Miranda used.

Miranda, living the life of a single lady with a heart that's locked up and refuses to empty itself of its secrets and loneliness. He thought maybe he was the only one she didn't open up to. Keeping him at arm's length with a rough persona made him wonder if she was hiding some deep, dark secret. For someone he had known for so many years there were many things he didn't know about her.

Lee knew from experience that living alone wasn't a formula for success. Every time he looked in the mirror he could see the gray hair spreading from his temples and weaving paths to the front of his head, the deep crow's feet around his eyes and mouth, all signs of aging beyond his years.

After three years his heart had started to wither because it didn't answer to the beat of another. Looking back on everything that had happened he was beginning to wonder if his heart ever answered to the beat of another person. Perhaps his heart was answering to the beat of his successful career at the publishing house. It was hard for him to admit he didn't take the time to get to know the real Joan.

Miranda seemed to be warming up a little from the way he remembered her. She was still a dazzling beauty. No wonder Adrian stayed with her. She was his eye candy.

He turned around to move back into the kitchen when his eyes stopped on a large framed picture hanging on the wall above the sofa. It was of Joan and Miranda, taken shortly before Joan passed away. Lee stared at it for a couple of minutes. He was reminded of Joan's soft, kind and gentle nature. It was in her eyes. He held his head between his hands while thinking what a jerk he had been.

He retrieved his glass of juice from the kitchen, then went back into the living room, found a comfortable spot on the sofa, picked up the notes and started to read.

CHAPTER 14

Present Day

Lee finished the notes when he heard the door opening. Miranda walked in, and he watched her stroll to the kitchen and drop her keys and purse on the countertop.

"Have you finished reading?"

Lee stood and stretched, rocked back and forth on his heels. "Reading always makes me sLeepy. I'm not a speed reader. I did finish your notes and you're right—I'm hooked. I know a lot of time has passed since this took place but we might get lucky and find someone who remembers this lady as well as the murder."

By this time Miranda was in the living room, standing in front of him. He found it hard to concentrate on what she was saying. She was so beautiful.

"I've done some of my own digging around on the computer," Miranda said. "Lilly did spend a lot of time in the mental institution, but I don't know if it was for protection from George or sickness. Several months after the murder Lilly was in and out of the hospital."

Lee stared into her brown green eyes, listening to her soft voice. "Come on Miranda, let's take a ride and get a drink."

While Lee drove he peppered Miranda with questions.

"What did you find out about George?"

Miranda shifted in her seat to face him. "Well, he was hard to track down. He was twenty years older than Lilly. Short and stocky, from the description on his draft card. He left the army because he was too old to serve any longer and took a job on the Conn railroad here in Bridgetown, working as a laborer."

"So you think Bert and George worked together at the railroad."

"Yes, that must be where he met and knew Bert. I couldn't find any of George's family. Maybe they will pop up somewhere as we continue to look into this. It's like they dropped off the edge of the world." She took a breath.

Lee broke in with a question. "Didn't Lilly say in one of her letters that she divorced George, married Hap Mills and later divorced Hap before she remarried George?"

"Yes, she did say that, but I could only find a marriage to George. Why do you ask?"

"Would this have been something she made up or the truth? It's a good place to start to see if Lilly is lying," Lee said.

"I don't know about that, it could be poor record keeping back then, but we might come up with something," she said. "Why are you pulling over to the side of the road?"

He brought the car to a stop pointing in the direction of the mountains. "What a great view," he said. "People pay a lot of money for a view like that." He glanced in her direction.

"I did pay a lot of money for it, when I bought that old house." She shrugged and grinned.

His attention was taken by the blue lights flashing in his rear-view mirror. He swore under his breath as he watched the policeman get out of the car and walk to his side of the car.

Lee lowered the window. "Did I do something wrong, officer?"

"Are you Lee Perkins?"

"Uh, yes, I am. Did I do something wrong?"

"No, I was on my way to Miranda's to talk with you." The officer leaned over and looked into the car.

"Hi there, Miranda."

"Winslow, what do you think you're doing? Why did you pull up behind us? We weren't doing anything wrong. And how did you know I would be in this vehicle?"

"Wow, Miranda, so many questions," the officer said. "Don't get your panties all twisted. We knew Mr. Perkins was staying with you. Come on Miranda, it's a small town, word gets around."

"What do you want, Winslow?" she asked.

Winslow directed his attention back to Lee. "I have a message for you from the police chief. It seems they were able to squeeze in some time for an appointment between you and Captain Woods for tomorrow at one P.M. That's the only opening they have available. I told the chief I would drive down and give you the message and I spotted your car pulled over to the side of the road."

Winslow grinned at Miranda. "I'm still waiting for our date you promised me, Miranda."

"That'll be the day Winslow. I never promised you anything, now leave us alone."

Lee smiled at Winslow as he glanced in Miranda's direction.

He could see the cold stare she was giving him.

Winslow backed up and tipped his hat. "Be seeing you around."

Lee grinned at him, and watched in his mirror as he got back into his car. "I think that is a good example for us to witness, how brazen the police are in this town," he said. "You're going with me tomorrow Miranda, whether they like it or not."

Winslow pulled out and drove south.

"Our own personal invitation. They send a cop down to tell us. How connected are you in this town?"

"Oh, Winslow. He stops me every chance he gets, trying to get me to go out with him. I think he's disgusting. I don't like him, don't trust him, and I would certainly never go out with him."

"I can't say I blame him for trying."

She nodded, turning her head away.

"Let's get back to what we were talking about," she said. "Lilly did mention a lot of different men in the letters. She must have known these guys from the hotel where she said she cleaned and tended bar. Do you know where you are going?"

"No, but I was sure you would tell me how to get to a coffee house," Lee said.

"The Dr. Denny she talked about," Miranda said, "has since passed away and the hospital wouldn't release any information about her or Bert."

He noticed how animated Miranda was as she talked like a marionette puppet without the strings.

"Turn right here."

Lee followed her order. "What would you think of placing an ad in the local newspaper asking for information about the murder of Bert and any information about Lilly that someone would like to share?"

"Great idea," Miranda said. "I'll place the ad right now from my iPhone. It should make tomorrow's newspaper."

"At this meeting with the police tomorrow we can question the police chief about the young historian who was killed in the accident last night."

"They could have called instead of sending Winslow,"

Miranda said, typing the ad text into her phone. "I'll cancel my exercise class for the rest of the week. I need some time off anyway."

Miranda pointed to the parking lot of the coffee shop and he found a vacant spot to pull the car into.

CHAPTER 15

Present Day

The fogged over storefront windows with streaks of dirty white residue caught Lee's eye. "Hum, looks like a greasy spoon," he said.

"You can't always go by looks."

"You would go in there and have coffee?"

"It's not as bad as it looks, don't be so fussy, Lee."

The wooden sign with faded white letters on a red background was swinging back and forth. A single rusty nail kept it from falling on the head of the next person who walked under it. The rusted knob wiggled in Lee's hand as he turned it pushing the door open. To his great surprise it was like walking into a different world. The aroma of freshly brewed coffee was incredible. The place was packed with people chatting while soft rock music played in the background. Clean, neat tables were spread around the expansive room.

He found a table in the back and ordered coffee.

"You drink way too much coffee," Miranda said. "It's not good for you. No wonder you can't sLeep at night."

He smirked. "I was thinking about Lillian's remark in one of the letters when she said the aluminum siding wouldn't burn. It's hard to believe that anyone would think like that. Pretty funny, isn't it? She must have believed the house wouldn't burn because of the siding. What a nut case."

"Nevertheless," she said, "I'm willing to wait and see what we come up with before I pass judgment on her." She raised an eyebrow and pursed her lips as she gave him the evil eye.

"Don't look now," Lee said, his voice dropping lower so only she could hear him, "but I think that man sitting by himself two tables back is trying to hear what we're saying."

"What makes you think that?"

"The way he is sitting in the chair with his head cocked in our direction while pretending to study his coffee cup."

"Oh, come on Lee, he could have a lot on his mind or he could be thinking about something important."

"Okay, let's get back to the letters," Lee said. "In her letters, Lillian was sure Cain and Clay Bliss were the people who murdered Bert. Did you look up anything on them? Did you check the mental hospital? Was the book ever published? Isn't it interesting that she said not many people knew about her or of her?"

"She was probably a shadow person. You know, she listened to peoples' conversations and then went home wrote down what they said to create her book, and she mixed fact with fiction," Miranda said.

"I think there could have been a love triangle. According to Lilly there was—or was she making that up? She mentions in the second letter this Mr. Merritt. How does he figure in this whole mess? She never explained that."

Lee paused, as he now understood why Miranda was so interested in this murder.

Miranda stared at Lee. "I think there was a love triangle, but not the kind you're thinking of."

"You're right. It was a love triangle of a different kind," Lee said. "According to Lillian, there was the gay thing with the detectives. I can't remember the detective's name who made a pass at Bert, and Bert nearly killed the guy. It all got pretty messy after that."

The man two tables over picked up his coffee cup and moved to the table beside Lee and Miranda. Lee tapped Miranda's wrist. She shifted in her chair to look, then nodded at Lee.

"I think money, revenge, and love are always motiving factors in any murder," Miranda said.

"And I think all three played into this murder."

The man at the table next to them stood up and approached them. He cleared his throat. "Excuse me," he said, "I hear you are looking into the Grayson murder. I think there are some things you should know."

Lee looked at Miranda and back to the man. "How do you know that?"

"Talk around town," he said. "I'm Derrick. You don't need to know my last name."

"I'm Lee and this is Miranda," Lee said. "You don't need to know our last names either." Lee hesitated, sizing the man up, trying to decide whether he was a threat.

Miranda was the one who said, "Have a seat."

The man nodded, taking a seat at the table.

"So, what do you know?" Lee asked.

Derrick looked over both shoulders. "You can never be too careful," he said. "I must be quick, and leave before they catch me talking to you. But they probably already know I'm here.

"You see, Clay and Cain Bliss were my cousins. Cain is dead now, but Clay is alive. He still runs part of this town and remains tied to the mafia. Something else, he's as nasty and mean as he ever was. At the time of the Grayson murder they had their tentacles wrapped around the policemen, detectives and every official in this city."

Lee interrupted. "I don't understand how Cain and Clay could gain that much influence and power. Was it their connection to the mob?"

"You would understand if you knew the power of the mob and the corrupt police at that time," Derrick said.

"I think I'm beginning to get it. We were visited by a policeman today," Lee said.

"You might not be aware that Cain was killed in a work accident in Maryland in the fall of the year of the murder, and Mr. Merritt was someone involved with the Mafia as a money runner. His death was called an accident by the Bridgetown police, if they're to be believed. If you follow the trail of Mr. Merritt, you will find the information you're looking for."

Derrick looked around nervously. "Now I have to leave." He got up and hurried out the door.

As they watched him exit the building, Lee said, "Do you believe that? People are popping up everywhere we go with information about this murder."

"Wow. What did we get into?" Miranda said.

"We should head back to the mansion," Lee said. We have a lot of research ahead of us. It's pretty interesting that Clay Bliss is still alive."

They paid the bill and got back into the car.

Lee looked at the sky as he was driving. "Look at those clouds rolling in from the mountains. They look like snow clouds. I hope it doesn't snow. I hate the snow. And it is a lot colder up here than I thought it would be. I didn't bring a heavy jacket."

"You can borrow one of Adrian's jackets," Miranda said.

"He'll be gone for three weeks on vacation. We do get some of our heaviest snows in March, so we could be in for one."

Lee glanced at Miranda and held her gaze. "Thanks for the offer, but if I need a jacket I can go buy one."

He smirked at her and turned back to driving. The storm worried him, snow was one of the big reasons he lived in the south.

Miranda start to work on the case. "The guy Lilly talks about at the cleaners was a black man who was in and out of prison for petty robberies. The cleaners and the house where Lilly lived with George have both been torn down. An expressway runs through the property now."

Lee nodded to show he was listening. "Well, one thing we know for sure after reading the letters is that Lilly didn't trust the police then, and we shouldn't trust them now," he said.

"After our visit from Winslow, I agree with you."

"I think it's a crying shame that you no longer have access to the FBI website. It might make it faster to find some of this stuff."

With a heavy sigh, Miranda said, "Lee, are you complaining already? You're a bottom feeder living on other people's information. Think of all we've learned that wasn't in the letters or the newspapers."

"Well, that might be true, but when the book I'm going to write revealing everything we have and will learn about this murder is published, you won't think I'm such a bottom feeder then."

As Lee pulled the car into the driveway, he could see a woman standing on the front porch waving at them.

"Who's that?"

"From here, it looks like my cousin Nancy from Bridgetown. I wonder what she wants. She never comes around unless it's to gossip," Miranda said.

"Well, we could use some gossip right now. It might be good information."

"Hi, Nancy," Miranda called as she closed the car door.

"Miranda! Who's your handsome friend? I haven't met him." She smiled at Lee, and he smiled back.

"Hello, Nancy, I'm Lee."

"What an unexpected visit," Miranda said. "Come in. It's cold out here."

"Yeah, it looks like it's going to snow," Lee said.

"What brings you out my way, Nancy?"

"It's all over town that you and this handsome fella are looking into the Grayson murder."

"Oh, great. Just what we wanted to hear," Miranda said.

"I wanted to add my two cents. Miranda, you were probably too busy with school and the boys to remember Ron Grayson who died of a heart attack at age forty-five. He had been nosing around the Bridgetown Police Department trying to dig up information, but he kept running into brick walls. And then, suddenly he died from a heart attack." Nancy took her glasses off, rubbed her eyes, and put the glasses back on, resting them on a nose too tiny to hold them up, her close set blue eyes twinkling as she talked.

"That's it?" Lee said. "Didn't the family check on the information they were given?"

"Not as far as any of us could find out," Nancy said. "The few brave souls who did speak up were soon squashed by the rest of them."

"It makes me wonder about some of the family, and if they were involved in the murder," Lee said.

"Nancy, did you ever hear of a Lillian Grace, who was in love with Bert?" Miranda said.

"No. Oh my goodness, that sounds too delicious. I don't remember ever hearing anything about her. I don't have time right now to hear the story, but I'll come back, and I want you to tell me all about it, Miranda. Right now I have to be going. It was nice to see you." She looked over at Lee, "And your handsome friend. I hope my information helped."

"Oh, it did Nancy every bit helps," Miranda said as she walked Nancy to the door and said her goodbyes.

"With each new person we talk with, we get a better idea of what Bert was like. Now we just need someone to tell us about Lillian," Lee said.

CHAPTER 16

Present Day

Lee picked up his papers to move his reading into the computer room to be close to Miranda. After ten minutes he realized what a mistake that was. The smell of her perfume was intoxicating. He was having trouble concentrating on the notes. All he wanted to do was grab her and take her to bed.

"Okay, let's get back to Lilly. Is she paranoid or is she frightened of Clay and the police?" he said.

"It would be interesting to find out if the police department still has links with the crime syndicate," she said.

"Lilly has sucked me into her world, I'm right there with her in 1962, experiencing her emotions. What a terrible life she lived," he said.

Miranda stopped what she was doing and turned around, crossed both her arms and legs, then with a gentle lifting she bounced her foot up and down. She always looked Lee straight in the eyes when she talked to him. Her eyes were men killers. "Yes," Miranda said, "she pulls on the heart strings."

Lee tried to shake Miranda's eyes out of his head by getting back into the conversation. "Do you know where they buried Bert?"

"Yes, it was on his military record," she said. "The cemetery is a short drive from here. Why?"

"I'd like to check out this one bit of information. Lilly writes that Hap is buried too close to Bert's grave. We could go to the cemetery and find out if she knows what she's talking about."

Miranda stood, grabbing her purse and keys in one swift motion. "Good idea. Let's go."

They put on their coats, got into Miranda's car, and drove south. Lee continued to pick Miranda's brain about the information in the letters. "The key, Miranda. We need to find the key to her deposit box."

"I know, me too, but right now we're checking this information. We'll work on the key when we get back to the house."

"Okay, fair enough. Lilly mentioned in one of the letters a couple watching TV were shot by a kid. Was there anything about that in the papers?"

"That's a good question, Lee. There were different accounts of the murders in the newspapers. Some of the people interviewed said the couple ran a drug and prostitution house that the police protected. They said some of the policemen split the money it brought in. Of course, the police denied those comments saying the people making those statements were drug users making up lies to get back at the police department."

"Well, you know what, Lilly could be right," Lee said. "The corruption in the police department could run into high places.

But the bigger question in my mind is why do you think Lilly blamed herself for Bert's murder?"

"I don't know. I thought about that as well, she makes the statement more than once in the letters. Here we are."

A long neglected cemetery came into view on the right. She turned the car onto the grass and gravel rutted road. Numerous headstones had fallen over, and some were almost hidden by the tall grass. Some of the grave markers were starting to slide down into the river that ran behind the forgotten place.

She stopped the car and they got out, not knowing where to look for Bert's headstone.

"Kid, you go in that direction, I'll go this way."

Miranda nodded, wading through the tall grass and weeds.

In a few minutes she called out. "It's over here."

As he approached the spot, he could see her eyes scanning the Grayson tombstone.

"Look over there."

His eyes followed her raised arm in the direction of the road. There it was—Hap Mill's headstone.

They walked over to where Hap was buried, which was about ten feet from Bert's grave.

"His real name was Hap and he was a lot older than Lilly," Miranda said.

Kneeling, he spread open the tall grass to read what was carved on the stone. "This guy was born in 1890 and died a few years after Bert. So he didn't serve in the army with Bert. Maybe Lilly only lived with Hap but didn't marry him after she divorced George the first time. Think about it, back then who would know the difference?"

"Lilly must have had someone bring her here since she didn't drive," Miranda said.

He stood and made his way over to where Miranda was standing.

"I'm not sure about that theory. She could have sent someone to this cemetery to check out Bert's grave while at the same time putting flowers on it for her. They could have told her that Hap was buried behind Bert."

"True. But I still believe she was here. I can sense it."

He stared at her. "Oh, come on, what kind of a detective are you? Agatha Christie would be ashamed of you."

She looked at him. "Oh, really, Mr. Smarty Pants. I don't think so. A lot of times her detectives went on a gut feeling in their investigations, and they usually turned out to be right."

He cringed as Miranda's eyes turned to cold slits again. Shivering, he thought that he wouldn't want to get into a real fight with her.

They tromped back to the car, and as Lee opened the door he stopped and scanned the area. *Who's watching us, and where are they?* Miranda paused as well. He could hear the water rushing over the river rocks and squawking birds flying over their heads. In the distance, on the far side of the wheat field at the edge of the woods, two deer stood with their heads pointed straight at Lee.

He turned his head back to the river as a man dressed in hunting clothes with a shotgun cocked over his arm pushed his way through the tall weeds and up the riverbank. He was moving in their direction.

"I been watching you two. What are you doing here?"

"Well, who are you and why do you want to know?" Lee said with a steady gaze, while moving between the man and Miranda.

"My name is Ron Alley. I was told there was a stranger in town nosing around about the Grayson murder. I don't know either of you," Ron said as he stared at Miranda.

She closed her car door and walked toward Ron. At that moment Lee stepped in front of her saying, "Well, that makes two of us. I don't know you either. So, Ron, who told you there was a stranger in town asking about the Grayson murder?"

"The people of this town don't want the Grayson murder stirred up. I'm warning you. You're getting into something dangerous."

By this time Lee was in Ron's face. Ron took a few steps back.

"We aren't looking for trouble, Ron... just answers," Lee said.

Ron shifted his weight while moving his gun to his other arm. "Whatever you're looking for, I encourage you to stop. Leave the murder alone. It happened a long time ago. Leave it alone. You might find out something you don't want to know."

"Do you mean like maybe the name of the person or persons who bumped off Grayson?" Lee said, holding Ron's gaze.

Ron started to open his mouth to say something, then stopped. He turned his back on Lee as he started walking toward the river, forging through the water then up the bank on the other side. They watched as he disappeared into the tall grass.

The dark clouds forming overhead smelled like snow.

"What do you make of that?"

"I don't know, but someone has spread the word that we're looking into the murder," Lee said.

"As far as I know the only people who knew were the police."

Lee rubbed his eyebrows. "How about all those people you talked to after you read the letters, Kid?"

"Well, them too, I guess. But I didn't tell them we were going to investigate the murder. I only told them I had the letters and what they said."

Lee looked at Miranda.

They got into the car heading in the direction of the mansion.

On the drive back, Lee couldn't get Adrian out of his mind.

He left this morning, Miranda said.... he would be gone for three weeks on a long deserved vacation. Adrian told Lee he would never leave Miranda alone in the mansion, or; wondered why.

CHAPTER 17

Present Day

Back at Miranda's mansion, an intruder jimmied the sliding door leading into Lee's room and slipped inside. He spent twenty minutes in the mansion, and as he finished his mission he exited the same way he came in.

CHAPTER 18

Present Day

Back at the mansion, Lee stood in the doorway of the computer room clearing his throat. "I don't know about Lilly," he said, stepping across the threshold. "I wonder if she had anything to do with Bert's murder. She says several times in her letters that it was her fault, that she could have prevented the murder. I don't know if I trust her. She writes that she only likes tall men, but her husband George was only five feet six inches tall. She said she wouldn't marry a man who drinks and beats women. George did both." Lee gave Miranda a quizzical stare.

"There are a lot of inconsistencies in the letters. She repeats herself often, but that may be because of her state of mind. She did tell Elizabeth that she forgot what she said from one letter to the next, and she was still under a doctor's care. These are the kind of things that make me think she was a nut case, but I'm willing to wait and see until we've researched all this information," Lee said. "If only we could find one person who she said she gave a copy of the first five chapters of the book to. There must be other letters out there somewhere."

"Finding the other copies may fill in some the holes in this investigation," Miranda said. "Why does she keep bringing up Mr. Merritt, as Derrick did?"

"How can we follow the trail of Mr. Merritt when we can't find out anything about him?" Lee said.

"Derrick must think we can or why would he have said that?" Miranda asked.

"How could Lilly have known all these people? I get the feeling when reading her letters that she lived in fear for her life."

Miranda stared at Lee as he talked, while tapping her fingers on the desk.

"I agree. And why do you think she flitted around from subject to subject? She did it in all her letters," Miranda said.

"Okay, I'm pretty sure this is the way it went. Lilly started to write a letter, stopped to do something else, after a couple hours or maybe even days she came back to write again. Then she'd put in the letter what she's been doing between writing sessions," Lee said.

"Okay," Miranda said.

"Did you do any checking on this niece who was fighting with Bert, trying to buy the land from him?"

"I couldn't find out anything," she said. "We'll have to wait and ask Jane about the niece."

There was a loud knock at the door. Miranda ran to answer it, and Lee heard her sigh as she opened the door.

"Winslow, what do you want?"

"Now, Miranda, is that any way to talk to me. Where's your manners?"

Hearing the conversation Lee moved toward the door. "Hello, Winslow, what brings you here?"

"May I come in, or are you going to make me stand out here all day?"

"Well, I guess if you have to, come in and have a seat."

Miranda stepped back to let him by.

"Now, that's more like it, Miranda."

"Since you're here, Winslow, I have some questions for you," Lee said.

"Okay. Hope I have the right answers."

"It seems that everyone in town knows we are looking into the Grayson murder," Lee said.

"Yes, it's all anyone can talk about."

"Do you know anything about the police department at the time of the murder?" Lee asked.

"Would you be honest enough to tell us the truth?" Miranda added.

"I know a lot about it," Winslow said. "I do the history research for the department."

"Great. Could you tell us what you know about a Detective Elway?"

"What do you want to know?"

"Was he gay, for instance?" Lee asked.

"Well, I don't want to comment on someone's personal life, but it was always suspected that Elway and three other detectives were. Everyone throughout the department and the town suspected, but in those days no one talked about it or admitted to it. Things like that were hushed up. It was rumored that Elway made a pass at Bert and he beat Elway up, almost killing him. Then for revenge Elway set Bert up to be murdered. That theory makes perfect sense to me, but proving it is another thing."

"Winslow, I'm shocked that you would share this with us. I had you pegged as one of them in every way," Miranda said.

"I could sense that you didn't trust me, but I have a personal interest in this murder being solved. I could get into a lot of trouble if the department finds out I was here."

"What is your personal interest?" Lee asked.

"The department isn't aware that my dad was friends with Bert Grayson, so I would like to see his killer, if he is still around, brought to justice. I don't think my dad knew, but I was friends with Bert's son."

"What? Wait, he had a son?" Lee said.

"Oh, yeah. He was a nice guy. All the girls liked him. He was killed a couple of years ago in a hunting accident."

"What was his name?" Miranda said.

"John Wiggins. He took his mother's last name since Bert wouldn't marry her, Bert told her he was in love with someone else and it wouldn't be right to take a wife you weren't in love with. Bert supported John and his mother until he died."

"Who else knows about Bert's son?" Lee said.

"No one as far as I know, except maybe some of the family, but I'm not sure about that."

Lee looked at Miranda and back to Winslow. "So are you telling us that you are willing to help with the investigation?" he asked.

Winslow smiled. "I would love to help, but I have to be careful. I could lose my job—or my life. These people don't mess around."

"How do we know the police didn't send you as a spy to find out what we are learning?" Lee said.

"Well, I guess you don't. So you will either trust me or not use me." Winslow smiled and winked at Miranda. Her face turned pink.

"One more question, Winslow," Lee said. "Did you happen to know a Sara Dowell?"

"You mean old Piano Legs Dowell? Yeah, she was our speech teacher in school. Why do you ask about her?"

"Her name came up a couple of times and I wondered who she was. Why do you call her Piano Legs?"

"She had wide legs filled with varicose veins, we thought they resembled a piano keyboard. I know—not a nice thing to say, but we were kids." Winslow stood. "I have to go, they keep track of us all the time. I took a chance coming here."

Lee and Miranda walked Winslow to the door, watching him as he got into his police car and drove away.

Lee looked at Miranda. "Did you believe any of that?"

"I don't know, he sounded sincere, but it was too unbelievable."

"Well, I guess we'll have to wait and see if he does help us," Lee said. "By the way, Miranda, I found out some information on Clay," he said with a Cheshire cat grin.

"You did? How did you do that?"

"While you were at the gym I googled him."

"Wow, I'm impressed. So, you do know how to use a computer?"

"Well, maybe a bit more than I let on. I picked up a few things watching Sally."

"Oh, I see, you're a piker."

Lee put his hand on his chest. "How could you talk to me like that?"

She laughed out loud. "You're impossible. Let's get back to work. So what did you find out about Clay?" Miranda sat at the table, crossed her feet, and stared at Lee as he shared what he had found out.

"Since Clay is still alive and living in this area, we will need to be careful. He was a dangerous character then, working as an enforcer and local bookie for the mafia."

Miranda interrupted Lee. "Now wait a minute, you mean he made people pay up on bets by beating them up?"

"Yes, my dear. Or, worse yet, if they didn't pay, he killed them.

I found an old newspaper article that told of a man here in town—who, by the way, is still alive— who placed a bet on a football game with Clay and lost."

"Did you say he is still alive?" Miranda asked.

"Yes, and living in Bridgetown. The guy's name is John Fink.

I think he is related to Derrick. After losing the bet Fink refused to pay up. Clay followed this guy to the unemployment office the following Monday morning. He waited outside, and when Fink stepped out onto the street, Clay grabbed him and demanded his money."

"Wow, this is one nervy guy."

"It gets worse," Lee continued. "When Fink refused to hand the money over to him, Clay pulled out a gun and shot him, in the middle of a busy sidewalk in broad daylight. By the time the police arrived Clay had shot him twice then kicked him into the street." Lee paused.

Miranda sat back in her chair. "He was one mean guy," Miranda said.

"They arrested Clay and the ambulance took Fink to the hospital." Lee sat down in his chair.

"That poor man," Miranda said.

"Clay only spent a couple of days in jail," Lee said. "Now isn't that suspicious?"

"Sounds to me like corruption ruled then," Miranda said.

Lee walked into the living room. Stopping in front of the windows, he stood watching dark clouds rolling in over the mountains.

"Well, Kid, I think that incident backs up Lilly's claim that the police protected Clay along with his mob ties. They arrested him once before on numbers running and enforcing for the mob. He only spent a couple of days in jail on those charges."

By this time Miranda was standing at Lee's side looking at the mountains as the sky grew dark. "They look like snow clouds to me," Miranda said.

"I think Lilly is sounding more convincing all the time. By the way, Kid, did you learn anything about Robert Mason?"

"Yes, he was a local historian and writer. That's all I've learned about him so far. He's living in Florida somewhere around Miami."

"I wonder if he's still in Florida or if he's visiting here in Bridgetown," Lee said, as he turned toward Miranda.

"Why would you say that?"

"Because this guy could still be looking for Lilly's book, the one he tried to get from her back then."

"Lee, that's the silliest thing you've said yet. Why would he still want the book?"

"I don't know, Miranda, but my gut feeling is that he is here looking for the book."

"Lee, it seems whoever they are would go to any length to get what they wanted."

"That's right, Kid. From where I'm standing, it looks like the bodies are beginning to pile up in this investigation."

"This hasn't turned out to be as easy as we thought it would be," Miranda said.

"Lilly makes the statement that she wasn't afraid of George anymore in her eighth letter. Then I remembered reading on George's military record," Lee said, "that he died in November of the year before. She knew he couldn't reach out from the grave to slap her around ever again."

"It's interesting she has a sister still alive in a nursing home in upstate New York with late stages of Alzheimer's,"

Miranda said.

"I should go see her sister. Would you look up the address for me?"

"When were you going to go? I have some things to take care of here and can't go with you," Miranda said.

"That's okay, Kid, I have a GPS. I can find the place. You stay here and take care of what you need to do. Are you sure you don't mind staying by yourself? I mean, with Adrian gone. He doesn't leave you alone."

"I'll be fine, Lee. It should only take you a couple of hours to drive up and back. You should be back here before dark. I can get a lot of research done while you're gone."

She handed Lee his coat, along with the phone number and address of the nursing home, while walking him to the door.

Lee paused, turned back to Miranda. "I wonder if the family knew George beat and kicked Lilly around."

"I think they did, Lee. If it was my relative living with a guy like George, I would probably suspect that she admitted herself to the mental hospital from time to time for protection from an abusive husband."

"So it is possible that any information about the book may be lost unless Lilly's sister can remember something," Lee said. "I hope this trip won't be a waste of time." He raised his eyebrows at Miranda.

"We seem to be running into a lot of dead ends," Miranda said.

"Yes, but dead ends aren't all that bad. We're finding that a lot of what Lilly said was true. Tomorrow should be interesting with the interview with the police, and the ad comes out in the paper."

CHAPTER 19

Present Day

Lee pulled into the parking lot of the Safe Haven Rest Home forty-five minutes later. At the front desk, he told the receptionist he was there to visit Kathy Wilson.

"Hum, you're not on the list of visitors for Kathy." She looked Lee directly in the eyes.

"Yes, I know that, but I was a friend of her sister Lilly. She asked me to stop in and see Kathy if I was ever in the area."

"Well, okay. I'll take you back to her room."

When the nurse opened the door, his eyes stopped at a small, frail looking women sitting in a chair by the window. Lee walked in and took a seat in the chair beside her. She stared at him with a blank expression.

"Do I know you, young man?"

"Kathy, my name is Lee Perkins. I would like to ask you some questions about your sister, Lillian."

Kathy broke into a faint smile. "Do you know Lilly?" she said as she leaned closer to Lee.

"Well, I'm an acquaintance of hers." Lee took Kathy's hand in his, patting it gently. "Kathy, I need you to think hard, if you can."

She nodded.

"Lilly wrote a book. I think she hid it in a safe deposit box in a bank somewhere."

Kathy's face lit up. "Yes, but I'm not allowed to tell anyone where Lilly hid it."

Lee raised his eyebrows. "You mean you know where it is?" he whispered.

"Oh, yes, I know, but I promised Lilly I wouldn't tell anyone where she hid it. Because she exposed the police for the corrupt men they were. Why, that no good Mr. McCune, he was nothing but a numbers runner and enforcer for the mafia back then."

She stopped and put her finger to her lips. "You can't tell anyone I told you that. I promised Lilly I wouldn't say anything."

"Don't worry, Kathy, your secret is safe with me. Now, to get back to where the book is. You can tell me. Lilly wouldn't mind. She wanted me to get it to clear some things up for her."

"Well, I guess it would be alright to tell you. Lilly was more afraid of Robert Mason getting it than anyone. I miss Lilly. Did she say when she was coming to see me again? She didn't like Robert. He was trying to get her money." Kathy paused. "Then there was that Indiana druggist she married. She said he was the only guy who ever treated her right, and what did he do? He up and died from a throat infection, three weeks after she married him. Poor Lilly. She had the worst luck with men and love."

"You don't have to worry. I'll make sure Robert doesn't get it," Lee said. "Do you know where Lilly hid the key?"

Her eyes glazed over as she smiled. "Oh, yes. I have it around my neck. Lilly said I was to keep it safe for her." She put her hand up to her neck, pulling on a gold chain inside her nightgown. When she slid it out, Lee could see a large ornate key on the end.

His eyes widened.

Kathy smiled. "Here it is, but don't tell anyone I have it. It's a secret."

"That's the key?"

"Yes. It's the key to my heart. Lilly has one just like it. Isn't it beautiful?"

Lee's face dropped as he patted her hand. "Yes, Kathy, it's beautiful."

Kathy stiffened and looked at Lee with wide eyes. "Who are you and why are you holding my hand? What are you doing in my room? I don't know you." She grabbed the buzzer next to her chair. Lee tried to stop her but was too late. She pushed it.

The door to her room flew open. "Nurse, I don't know who this man is. I want him to leave." Kathy turned her head away from Lee.

"Sir, you will have to leave now, or I'll call the guard." The nurse pointed to the door.

"Yes, okay, I'm going. Goodbye, Kathy." Lee stood, shaking his head as he made his way to the door. In his car driving back to Bridgetown he called Miranda and told her what had taken place.

CHAPTER 20

Present Day

Lee opened the door of the mansion and walked in, dropping his keys on the counter as Miranda stuck her head around the corner.

"Hey, Lee, sorry you didn't find out anything."

"Do you remember in Lilly's last letter, she said she put some jewelry and coins in a safe deposit box?" Lee said.

He made his way into the computer room and took a chair next to her. She stopped working, looking up at him with a smirk.

"Yes, I remember that she also said she hid the key to the box in a safe place," Miranda said.

"One thing I know for sure, it won't match the one Kathy has around her neck. We need to find the real key. What did that last paragraph in the letter say?"

Lee stood and began pacing back and forth in front of her, trying to contain his anger. He was still angry with Kathy for not telling him what he wanted to know.

"Kid, do you think Kathy knew what she was talking about, or was she delusional when she said she knew where the book was?"

"You're the one who talked with her. What do you think?"

"We need to head on down to Florida, get that manuscript, and maybe the extra bonus of jewelry and coins."

"Stop pacing, Lee, and calm down. I've been dying to find that key."

He stopped and looked at her.

Miranda got up from her chair and walked out to the living room, stopping in front of the window to stare at the mountains.

Lee moved over and stood beside her. "I was disappointed after reading the last letter," he said. "Lilly seemed to change her attitude, or maybe she resigned herself to the fact that she couldn't change city hall. Maybe she gave up the fight, being too old to care anymore. In any event, it was a different Lilly from the other letters. If it wasn't for the key and what might be in that safe deposit box, her last letter would have been a bomb."

"I was disappointed, too, except for the key thing," Miranda said. "Or was it that Lilly had so successfully sucked me into her world that I had become emotionally invested in her life after only a couple of hours of reading? Then at the last minute, she slammed the door on me in her last letter. Lilly seemed removed from her love for Bert, the murder, and who committed it. It made me believe she wrote off that part of her life."

"Lilly may have written off that part, but we haven't, or at least I haven't. We need to think about that key. I think banks only hold a safe deposit box as long the rent is paid on it. Then what do they do if no one claims what's in it? Do they have to hold it for a certain period of time, or do they empty it and throw away the contents? And how do we know which bank? Was it in Bridgetown or in Florida? But first, we need the key."

Miranda walked over to the sofa, taking a seat on the end. "Yes, we have a lot to look into. Maybe the ad in the newspaper will help. That is, if anyone even remembers the murder or Lilly." Miranda raised an eyebrow and pointed her finger at Lee. "Maybe we need to read the last part of Lilly's letter again. Maybe she was giving us clues and we didn't recognize them."

Lee picked up the letter again. This time, he studied the last two paragraphs.

CHAPTER 21

Present Day

P.S. My book was never published, but I put the manuscript in a safe deposit box at my bank. Everything should be okay there. I put the key to the box in an envelope and put it in a safe place.

Love never dies; it just mellows with age. Friends and lovers help hide what we hold dear. Bert always held the secrets to my heart. As he protected them in life, he will protect them in death. Oh well, at least the manuscript is in a safe place now, in a place where I know that old coot Robert Mason won't be able to get his fingers on it.

As Lee finished reading the last two paragraphs the doorbell rang.

"I'll get it." Miranda sprinted to the door.

From Lee's position in the room he could see the surprised look on her face when she swung the door open.

"If isn't a ghost from the past, Ridgeway Tarkington, get in here and give me a hug. You're still a big old good looking guy."

She wrapped her arms around the neck of a tall well-built man. He stepped into the vestibule and scooped her up in his arms. A white toothy grin broke through his five o'clock shadow as he planted a kiss on her cheek. Lee was instantly jealous. Miranda looked like a little kid in this big guy's arms.

"You're still as beautiful as the first day I met you." He placed her back down on the floor.

"You always could charm the boots off a cowgirl."

"Yes, but I could never charm yours off of you, and not for lack of trying."

Her face flushed, and she turned toward Lee while touching his elbow. "Come in. I would like you to meet Lee Perkins, a fellow research investigator."

He stuck out his big hand and shook Lee's with a tight grip. "Lee, I'm glad to see Miranda has a friend to share this big house with."

"Ridge." Lee shook his hand.

He grinned at Lee.

"Wait a minute. Lee and I don't share anything. Lee is staying with me as a guest while we work together on an investigation. That's all there is to it." A wide grin broke across Ridge's face as he looked at her.

"Miranda, whatever you want to call it." Ridge glanced in Lee's direction.

She wrapped her arm around his, guiding him into the living room. "Come in and sit down. Can I get you something to drink or eat? And what are you doing in this part of the world?"

"You know me. I'm still hung up on diet cola."

"I know what you mean. That has been my vice since you introduced me to it way back when."

"As to what I'm doing here, I'm sure you heard that Chuck Darrell passed away a couple of months ago. I couldn't make it for the funeral, so on my way to Maine to investigate a dig site, I decided I'd stop and spend a few hours visiting with his family."

"I did read in the paper that he'd passed away. He was six years ahead of me in school. I didn't know him; I just knew of him. He was a big shot in the local government, wasn't he? I thought you were friends with him, but I wasn't sure."

"Yes, we were friends in school, but after graduation we went our separate ways and lost contact with each other. He was one of the comptrollers for the city before he died."

"I wasn't aware of that. But I'm glad you're here."

"While leaving the Darrell's today I thought I'd just pop in and say hello to you. Sorry I didn't ring you first, but I didn't think you'd mind."

"My door is always open to you. Don't feel you ever need to phone ahead. I know—I've been in those situations myself. I'll get your diet for you," she hurried into the kitchen.

"Ridgeway," Lee said. "That's an unusual name, was it passed down to you from a member of your family?"

"It's my father's name, he pinned it on me, saying it would make a man out of me. I don't know what he meant by that statement, but it is what it is." He shrugged as he looked eye to eye with Lee.

She entered the room carrying the soda. "Here you are, Ridge, just the way you like it—no ice."

"Thanks, you're the best."

"Ridge, I heard you retired from the FBI a few years ago?"

"Retirement for me is wonderful, now I can immerse myself deep into my passion, archaeology."

Lee was half listening as he watched the two of them interact. Ridge's eyes gleamed with an inner light of confidence and lit up his rugged, tanned faced. Lee was questioning the jealousy he was feeling about this guy. He watched her melt at his every word. He wondered if Ridge was the reason she made it clear that she wasn't interested in him in a romantic way, but he wasn't ready to give up on her yet.

She must be madly in love with this guy and he isn't aware of her feelings for him. She's secretive about certain aspects of her life, but isn't everybody? Do we ever completely reveal ourselves to people? Lee shook his head to bring his attention back around to what Ridge was saying.

"The FBI job would provide money and security for the future, which by the way, Lee, is how I met Miranda."

He nodded in acknowledgment.

"Miranda was a great partner, I trusted her with my life for the couple of years we were together in the field until she took a promotion, breaking up our team." He smiled at Miranda.

Lee thought it was amazing watching her dissolve into her chair. Lee knew his suspicions were right—she did have a strong desire for this guy.

Ridge finished his diet and stood to leave.

"Wait," Miranda said. "Before you go, we'd like you to take a look at this and tell us what you think it means."

Miranda handed him Lilly's letter. She couldn't take her eyes off of him as he studied it.

"If this Bert's grave is around here, I'd say dig around the headstone. It sounds to me like she buried the key there. If it was me that's where I would look first."

Together with raised eyebrows they glanced at each other.

"My thoughts were leaning in that direction," Lee said. "Thanks for confirming what I was thinking." Lee smirked at her.

She glared back while nodding. "Sure, you were." Then she turned back to Ridge. "Thank you. It seems you arrived at the right time. It doesn't matter what Lee said. We weren't sure how to go forward with this information."

"Glad I could help you. Anytime I can assist you, call me. Would you let me know if you find anything around the grave? I would like to know if my thoughts panned out."

"Sure. I'd be glad to. I'll call as soon as we find out anything."

Ridge smiled at her and looked over at Lee. "I've got to get going now if I expect to be in Maine by tonight. Thank you for your hospitality. Lee, it was nice to meet you. I hope our paths cross again in the future now that we have a mutual friend. Miranda, it's always good to see you. I'll keep in touch."

"I would like that." I'll call you."

Ridge shifted his stance and winked at Miranda. It looked like he was flirting with her. "Call me. You have my number." He bent down, and kissed her on the cheek. "Bye for now. Keep in touch," he said softly. He turned and walked out the door, crossed the porch, down the stone steps, and got into his waiting Hummer.

They stood in the open doorway watching the car weave down the driveway, passing the tall trees and turning north onto the main road.

"So, you worked with him at the FBI?"

She opened her mouth to say something, then stopped short, raised her eyebrows and gave him a glassy stare. "Don't be so clingy. Ridge and I worked together. Of course, we were close. Ridge watched my back and I had his."

"I'll bet he was watching more than your back."

"Oh Lee, you're hopeless, you sound like a jealous lover. As long as you remember we're working together on this research project and that's as far is it is going to go. If or when it goes beyond that, I'll let you know."

"Why are you so defensive? What is it with you? You tease me and pull me close, then when I move toward you, you push me away."

She turned toward him with her hands on her hips, her face muscles tightened. "You may have perceived that I was drawing close to you when in reality I was just being a kind person, so get over yourself, you're not all that much and more."

"Okay, okay, Kid, just forget about it. Let's go back to finding the key." he took a seat on the sofa.

"Good, that's what you're here for, nothing else. Just a researcher. Get it?"

He rolled his eyes, shrugged, and offered her a smile. "You know, it's scary that you can find out so much information about people from the Internet and they have no idea that you're doing it. I can see now why you think you're a real detective. A real-life detective wouldn't have the money to own all this expensive equipment. Or live in this big house or travel at will," he threw his arm in a sweeping motion around the room. "This roomy office with its expensive furnishings and up-to-date computer and other equipment."

"You sound jealous. What good is money if you can't spend it and enjoy what it can buy? My parents left me well off when they passed. My dad made a lot of good investments in the stock market. I made some wise investments with my dad's money while I was working, so now I intend to enjoy the rest of my life doing what I want, when I want, and the way I want."

"Okay, okay, don't get your panties all twisted. I was kidding you."

Miranda plopped in her seat in front of the computer. He watched her as she briefly closed her eyes taking a deep breath, then exhaling. Her fingers were working the computer keys. She looked up then shoved the other chair at Lee. He grabbed the back of it.

"Pull up a chair."

He pulled the chair over beside her. "What are you looking for?" he asked.

"I was hoping to find out what banks did with abandoned deposit boxes. It says here that they are required to keep the safe deposit boxes for years, even after the person stops paying for it. After repeated efforts to contact the owner of the box without success, they can then empty the contents and, by law, they have to send the items in it to the state. The state holds them until they are claimed, but the length of time the banks can hold the box isn't listed, so I guess they could hold the box for any length of time." She paused.

"That looks like a link to check for abandoned boxes," he said, pointing to the screen.

Miranda clicked on it and a site box came on the screen to put in the state and the name of the person who might have had a box at a bank. Miranda typed in Lillian Grace, Florida. Luck was with them when an abandoned box in her name appeared in Osprey, Florida at the East Tampa Bank. It even gave the account number, 574109.

She turned to Lee. "Can you believe that?"

"No, I can't. It might be another Lillian Grace. We have to consider that point, but the bigger challenge would be finding the key, and if we do find the key, you have to be the owner or a relative, it says here."

"Well, Lee, if we find the key and go to Florida, I could be a relative. Who would know? I could say I was her niece."

CHAPTER 22

Present Day

Lee's busy morning faded into afternoon. Miranda was riding shotgun singing along to "Big Girls Don't Cry" on the radio. They were on their way to Benson, five miles down the road. He was going over the murder in his head, along with the investigation and how much he had learned about Bert's life. He intended to stop at the cemetery on the way and dig around Bert's tombstone or maybe Hap's, looking for the key that Lilly may or may not have buried there.

He pulled onto the grassy, gravel rutted road, stopping the car next to Bert's grave. He popped the trunk lid before getting out. Miranda took the shovel out of the trunk and went right to the headstone.

Closing the door he paused, leaning on the side of the car.

The air was cool and crisp, and the sky was growing darker by the minute. In the far distance he could hear mighty peals of snow thunder echoing off the mountains. Lee was hoping it wasn't going to snow. He pointed his face up to the sky, enjoying the few rays of sunlight breaking through the dark clouds.

He turned in the direction of the water rippling in the shallow river that ran behind the cemetery. The water was low. In some spots it was dried up, exposing a dry path to the other side across rocks held into place with a black muck.

On the other side of the river was a wide field. Squinting, he focused in on a lone deer feeding on winter grass at the edge. A flock of wild turkeys were scratching and eating what they could find. White mist formed small clouds rolling up the mountainside and disappearing into the sky. The mountain range encircled the wide valley, standing like sentinels guarding the land and the secrets it held. This was truly a place that stood still in time. The land hadn't changed since the first day he set foot on Joan's doorstep over thirty years ago, but the people living in the valley were now a second generation of secret keepers.

Big black crows were squawking and landing in the distance then flying off again. Lee looked around shaking his head, while thinking, *In a few more years this place will be so overgrown no one will be able to see it from the road.*

He glanced in Miranda's direction. She was standing with her legs crossed, leaning on the shovel handle. She followed him with her eyes as he ambled over, stopping at her side.

Without speaking, Lee studied Bert's tombstone, while ignoring Miranda.

"Oh, are you ready to do some work, now that you're done daydreaming?" she said with a smirk.

Lee continued to ignore her, thinking she could be sharp-tongued at times. "Well, Kid, should we dig here?"

Lee knelt in the thick grass and started to pull it from the ground on his side of the stone. Large clumps of dirt clinging to each handful, he piled it up to his right.

"If anyone drove by the cemetery and happened to look in our direction, they would probably think we were cleaning up an overgrown tombstone of a loved one."

"Good thought, Lee. I agree."

"I can feel someone watching us."

"Oh, not that again. Come on, Lee, enough is enough."

"No, Miranda, the hair on the back of my neck is standing up."

He stood and did a three-sixty. "Nothing. That's so strange. Why do I keep having that feeling?" Then Lee spotted someone in the parking lot behind the chain link fence of the factory across the street.

"Look quick." Miranda stood. "HIT THE GROUND, KID!" The sound of gunfire echoed through the mountain valley. Miranda's body crumbled under the weight of Lee's as he fell on her, shielding her from a bullet. He looked up in time to see someone jump into a waiting car, speeding north on the highway.

"Lee, get off me, I can't breathe." She was pushing and shoving him. He didn't realize just how tiny Miranda was until now.

"I'm enjoying this. It might be the only time I get to be on top of you."

She was still pushing him away. Lee jumped up. He was breathing hard, trying to catch his breath he walked around Bert's stone, brushing off his pants and jacket. He grabbed Miranda's hand, pulling her to her feet. His breathing was beginning to slow down and his heart wasn't beating as fast.

Lee could see Miranda was still shaking when she put her arm through his, all the while darting her head from side to side. He didn't know what she was looking for.

"That was too close, Lee. This little research project has taken a dangerous turn. I think I'll start carrying my gun."

"Do you think so, Miranda?" Lee could breathe normally enough to talk now. "I have a gun in the trunk of my car. I'm getting it out and strapping it on."

"What are you doing carrying a gun in the trunk of your car?" she said, still holding onto his arm as they walked back to the car.

"Some of the places I would visit for research weren't always the safest, so I bought a gun and was licensed to carry. At times like this, I'm glad I took the time to do it."

"Thanks, Lee, for trying to protect me. That was close. Your instincts and quick actions saved one of us from a bullet."

"I guess you believe me now."

Lee opened the trunk, leaned in, unlatched a compartment on the side and pulled out a holster with straps. He unwrapped it to reveal a .45 magnum.

"That's a lot of gun. Do you know how to shoot it?" she asked, wide-eyed. A strong, gust of cold wind nearly blew her off her feet, pelting her with snowflakes. He steadied her with one hand.

"You bet I do."

Lee took off his jacket and strapped on the gun, then put his coat back on. He patted the part of his jacket hiding the gun.

"Now let's get into a real gun battle. I'll be ready the next time."

"Wait a minute, Lee. We should only use a gun if there's no other way to solve the problem." She closed the trunk lid.

He was glad his heart had stopped racing and he could breathe normally again. "I got a quick glance at the shooter," he said. "I couldn't make out who it was. All I could tell was it looked like a man. One thing is for sure, Kid, someone wants us dead, or they are trying to scare us off."

He looked at Miranda. "Are you okay? Do you want me to take you home?"

He was still a little shook up. Miranda's breathing was almost back to normal. He supposed it was because she had experienced being shot at, that she recovered so quickly.

"I'll be fine. It's been awhile since I was last shot at by someone. I had almost forgotten how scary it was."

"Do you still think I'm paranoid?" Lee said as he started to pull the weeds and grass again.

"No, at least not this time. They could have killed one of us. I think it was a warning to back off our investigation. We must be getting close to whatever or whoever they don't want us to find. But I still think you're a paranoid narcissist." She smirked.

"Kid, you're hopeless, do you know that? You can't admit when you're wrong. It isn't in you, is it?"

"Let's get back to digging around the stone," she said.

They worked together clearing grass and weeds again.

"Can you still see the deer standing at the edge of the field or did the shot scare it off?" Miranda asked after a while.

They stood gazing toward the distant field.

"I don't see anything there now. Maybe they were shooting at the deer," Miranda said.

Lee looked at her, 'I can't believe you said that."

Miranda was pulling weeds and piling them up as fast as Lee, ignoring his remark.

"I wish I had thought to bring gloves," he said.

She stopped working, he looked at her as she put her hand in her jacket pocket. "Here, I forgot I brought you some." She pulled out a pair of gloves and handed them to him.

"Hum, nice, blue sticky on the palms. Thanks."

"You're welcome. Have you spotted anything yet?"

"Nope, not on this side. How about you? I'm about ready to move over to Hap's tombstone and start looking there."

"Well, not so fast Mr. Impatient. I'm not sure, but it looks like there's something here right up against the stone, but I can't seem to get it loose."

He grabbed the shovel and made his way around to her side of the stone.

"Let me try to wedge it loose with the shovel." He poked and prodded at what looked like a small rusted metal box inside a dirty plastic bag.

"It won't budge. I guess we'll have to dig a hole around it."

He shoveled, being careful not to hit it, then the box dropped into the hole. They exchanged glances, and Lee brushed the dirt off the top of the box.

"It appears to be a couple of inches wide and deep. But it still looks almost as good as the day it was put in the ground. Even the worms didn't bother it. There doesn't seem to be any writing on the plastic bag," Lee said.

She pulled off her gloves and picked up the box between her index finger and thumb. She shook it. "Nothing, I was hoping to hear a key rattle in it."

"If there's a key in there, it may be glued to the inside with rust," he said.

He couldn't believe their luck, now to get it open and see the contents.

Both of them were on their knees in a praying position looking down at the box Miranda now held in the palm of her hand, unwrapping the plastic layer by layer. When at last the box was exposed, there appeared to be a thin layer of rust coating the metal.

"Well, for heaven's sake, open it."

"Be patient, I don't want the thing to fall apart. Look how rusted and fragile it seems to be. It's been in the ground for who knows how many years."

He couldn't take his eyes off the box. It was as though it would vanish if he did. Watching as Miranda turned it he saw a small latch.

She sucked in her breath. "Cross your fingers." With a gentle touch she tugged on it.

He stiffened, holding his breath, then the lid popped, dropping rust and dirt on the palm of her hand and revealing a piece of clear plastic wrapped around a strip of paper that was about two inches long. He reached in, taking out the contents.

"Be careful."

"Kid, why are you whispering?"

"I don't know unwrap the darn thing."

Lee was unfolding the wrapping with slow measured movements.

"STOP, RIGHT NOW!"

Lee jumped and his heart started racing. He slid is empty hand inside his coat and put it on his gun. Before she looked up, Miranda put her hand holding the box behind her back.

Lee slid the plastic into his front coat pocket.

"What are you two doing down there? You vandals come in all ages and sizes, don't you?"

Lee turned to see who was behind him as Miranda looked up. Their eyes met the angry gaze of a big whisker-faced guy, as they stood at the same time.

"Oh, sorry, Miranda, I didn't know it was you," he said. "I didn't know you had anyone buried in this cemetery."

"Oh, for heaven's sake, Gus, you scared me to death. We were trying to clean up around this overgrown tombstone of my family friend."

Lee pulled his hand from inside his coat, leaving the gun in the holster.

"As I said, I'm sorry. Some of us from the neighborhood have been taking turns watching this place because there have been so many vandals around here this last year. They don't respect cemeteries like they used to."

"Gus," Lee said, "someone was standing in the parking lot over there across the street earlier and fired a rifle at us. Did you happen to see who it was or know anything about it?"

"No, sir. I don't know anything about that. I was driving by when I spotted you two. You mean someone was standing in the parking lot over there watching you guys and shot a gun at you?"

"Yes," Lee said, "then the person jumped in a car and sped away."

Gus turned to the field across the river and pointed. "Maybe they were shooting at some of the deer that come out at the edge of the woods over there."

"Well, why would anyone shoot right over our heads? We could have been killed," Lee said.

"I don't know, sir. It's interesting that you would say that because there have been a lot of strange goings on around here lately."

"What do you mean?"

"There have been a lot of strangers in town lately. They've been snooping around, asking questions. There's this one old guy who must be in his eighties or nineties asking about some Lillian person."

Lee exchanged glances with Miranda. He was sure they were both thinking the same thing.

Gus continued. "This old guy approached me at the park the other night asking me if I knew a Lillian somebody. I told him I never heard of her. I asked him what his interest was in her but he just mumbled, "never mind," gave me the evil eye and walked to his car."

"Why did he think you would know anything about a Lillian?" Lee asked as he shot a glance at Miranda.

"I don't know. I was sitting at one of the park tables with my friend eating pizza when Milton brought up the murder of that Grayson guy from years ago. We were discussing it and what we thought happened, when the old coot sitting at the table next to ours came over and wanted to know if we knew this Lillian something. I can't remember her last name."

"What did he look like?"

"He was well dressed and walked with a cane. He had on a go fast hat with a scarf wrapped around his neck. As I said before, he looked to be about eighty-five years old or older, and he smelled like mint."

"Was he alone?" Lee asked.

"When he walked toward the car, there was a man holding the door open for him. The old guy got into the back seat, the other man went around, got in the driver's seat and the car drove north."

"Are you sure that was all he said?" Lee asked.

"Well, that's all I can remember right now. If I think of anything else, I'll give Miranda a call."

"Okay, thanks anyway." Lee patted him on the shoulder, "You did a good job, Gus, thanks." Lee smiled at him.

"Anyway," Gus said, "sorry again for scaring you and your friend. Miranda, if I were you I would be careful out here. It's hard to tell who might sneak up on you," Gus said as he turned away and rushed back to his car parked by the side of the road.

They watched him as he checked for coming traffic before he opened the door to his gray Buick and slid into the front seat.

Rust fell to the ground when he slammed the door closed and drove off.

"Gus is the guy in the neighborhood who watches out for everyone. He's an old teddy bear, well maybe more like a big gentle panda bear. He acts and sounds gruff, but he's as gentle as a lamb, with the heart of a lion, who would do anything for anyone, even you."

CHAPTER 23

Present Day

"Come on, Lee, we can take this back to the house and look at it away from prying eyes."

"That's a good idea, but we need to go into town even though I'm still shaking a little from being shot at and startled by Gus. If we get this part of the research finished, we'll have accomplished a lot today. As much as I want to see what's in that paper it can wait until we get back from town."

Miranda rolled her eyes and stared at Lee. "Are you kidding me? How can you wait? We've found lost treasure."

"Grow up. It'll keep until we get back. I feel the information we'll find at the library will be just as important as whatever is in that plastic wrap, which we hope is the key."

"I could take it out of your pocket." Before she finished the sentence she pulled it out of Lee's pocket and unwrapped it. Lee watched as the key dropped into Miranda's hand.

"Wow, who would have thought that it would be there?" Lee looked around, checking for prying eyes, then back to Miranda who was staring at the key.

"The key has been here all this time, but is it the key to her safe deposit box in Florida?"

"I think you're jumping to conclusions. It could be to a bank here in town. How would we know?" Lee said.

"There is one way to find out. We are going to that bank in Florida. Besides all that I checked with the banks here in town and none of them listed a box to her," Miranda said.

"It might be a wild goose chase," Lee said.

"I'm booking us on a flight to Florida for early tomorrow morning right now," she said, pulling out her phone. Miranda rushed toward the car, but before they got in, she opened the trunk, put the shovel in and closed the lid.

Lee put the key back into his coat pocket then gave it a pat before getting into the car.

After getting into the car, she turned toward Lee, looking him square in the eyes. "I think you're right. Our every move is being watched, but by whom and for what I don't have a clue. It may be about the letters, I don't know. Or it may be about the money and jewelry or all three. We'll have to be patient. Maybe by stalling we can flush out whoever it is, but this I know; we should guard the letters, and now the key. This thought keeps rolling around in my head. How did they, whoever they are, know that we were coming to the cemetery? Has my house been bugged? Maybe there's a bug in this car. What do you think?"

Lee shrugged. "Well, if there's a bug in this car we shouldn't be talking about it now. Oh, sure so now you're admitting I have been right all along. And maybe Robert Mason is here and having us watched to get the letters or the manuscript. Lilly said he hounded her for the information.

But why? What's in the letters that would be of value to him?"

"I'm not admitting anything Lee. It's my intuition kicking in, that's all. But I think from this point on we need to be extra careful where we go and what we say. And yes, I'm beginning to think it's been Robert Mason all along and we were thinking it was the police or someone in the local government."

"Listen, Kid, I think there are two things going on here. One,

I think the police are involved and don't want us to uncover the real murderer because it will expose one of their own, and two, I think Mason is after the letters but the question is why?"

Lee put his foot to the gas pedal and eased the car up to the road, while Miranda turned up her sixties music, humming as Lee drove south toward town.

He reached over and turned down the music. "It's a shame this town has seen its better days. Look at it, it's been neglected like the cemetery."

Benson had a charming, old-fashioned, yet forgotten look. It was a dying run-down place. The streets still had the original red brick from the 1800s. The brick mills closed down in the mid-1900s causing major layoffs and the town never recovered from the loss of its second largest employer in the county. The abandoned railway station that was now home to animals, homeless people, and drug dealers, was once an important stop on the rail line from Bridgetown to Harrisburg. The library was small but easy to locate on the corner of the only busy intersection. It was housed in one of the few new buildings in town.

Lee parked in the small lot and they entered the building. They were the only people there except for the young librarian. After Lee explained what he was looking for, she pointed him in the direction of the yearbooks as a place to start searching.

From the 1930 yearbook, Lee found Lilly's senior picture. She was a nice looking petite girl with short dark hair. At least it looked dark in the black-and-white picture.

"Listen to this," Lee said. "Lilly Sanders: Happy-go-lucky all day long. If she isn't chattering something is wrong."

"Now that sounds like the Lilly in the letters," Miranda said.

"Oh, listen to this, she was a contestant in an oratorical contest. You'll never guess who the coach was. The junior oratorical contest of the class of 1930 was held in the auditorium of the Methodist Church on May 3, 1929. The contestants were ably coached by Miss Sara Dowell.'"

"At last we've found Sara."

"She has to be who Lilly spoke of in the letters and Winslow talked about," Lee said. "So it would seem Lilly kept in contact with her through the years. Finding her might answer a lot of our questions."

"Yes, if she's still alive. Flip back to the faculty section so we can see what Sara looked like," Miranda said.

Lee flipped the pages. Sara taught English 2 and 3. She graduated from college, Upper New York, A.B. She taught at the high school five years.

"Yuck. She sure didn't get any awards for good looks."

"Lee, what a mean thing to say. She couldn't help the way she looked."

Miranda walked a few steps behind Lee as he carried the book to the librarian. She made copies for them and Lee paid her.

They were adding information hourly about the Grayson murder and the people involved with it and in it.

After getting into the car, Lee programmed the GPS. "I put in the address of the house Lilly grew up in. I want to see what it looks like."

They followed the directions to the address at 705 West Fifteenth Street, not far from the library.

"There it is," Lee said. "Wow, it's beautiful, what a great old Victorian house. It is a gracious looking place, isn't it?"

"Yes, it is, Lee. Turn the car around and let's drive back out of town toward Jane's real estate office."

"Okay." As Lee did a U-turn and pulled away, he took another look at the house. "Yes, I could picture Lilly living there," he said, watching the house grow smaller in the rear-view mirror until it was out of sight.

They drove through the underpass of the railroad bridge. The nursing home on the left had a few old people, bundled up in blankets, sitting in wheelchairs on the pillared front porch. The town smelled like old people everywhere Lee went, and he couldn't get the smell out of his nose. He turned into the real estate office parking lot on the left. There was only one car there, a new Buick.

He pulled into a space, as a whistle turned into a siren and fire trucks roared by. Lee watched them speeding up the street.

"There's Jane's car. We're in luck to find her here," Miranda said.

He held the door open for Miranda. Jane was in the office to the left side of the reception room. Lee peeked around the door as she looked up.

"Lee, what a surprise. How nice to see you, it's been awhile." She got up and walked around her desk, putting her arms around his neck, giving him a warm embrace. Jane looked at Miranda, walked over to her, and gave her a hug.

"It's always nice to see you, Miranda."

"Yes, it's nice to see you as well. We should get together more often."

"Yes, we had some good times. Lee, how are you doing? It's been what—three years since Joan passed?"

"It gets better with each new day. I don't think that's something you ever get over. I could never forget Joan, but life goes on. I still have trouble sLeeping at night."

"Yes, Lee, I know what you mean, I miss my sister terribly, but it's time for you to move on with your life just as I've had to do since Reggie passed away. Life is full of pauses that break our hearts and leave us floundering around grasping for something to comfort us, but what we do with the fragments of time that are left reveals a lot about who we are and who we've become."

"Wow, Jane, you said that so well it was as if you were reading my mind."

"Lee, if you don't mind me asking, what brings you to our little town?"

"Well, Jane, of course . . ." He shifted position nervously in his chair. "I wanted to stop to visit with you for a while, and I have some questions as well."

"Lee, that's not the way I remember it, but never mind me, go on."

He paused for a second, knowing all too well what Jane meant. She understood what haunted him day and night.

Miranda spoke up, "Jane, about ten years ago Joan gave me some letters that were written when we were teenagers. They were from a woman who said she knew who murdered your Uncle Bert. She wanted me to take a look at them and if I had time snoop into what the woman said. I took the letters and told her I would, but I was too busy to read them. I moved the letters from one spot to another always meaning to read them, but didn't. In all the shuffling around they landed at the bottom of a box of my papers."

Jane nodded, shifting in her chair.

"A while ago," Miranda continued, "I was working on some long overdue cleaning when I came across the letters again. This time, I decided to read them." Miranda paused, and made a sweeping gesture with her hands. "I couldn't put them down. They were compelling reading. The lady who wrote them seemed a bit confused, contradicting herself at times, but nevertheless, they were compelling. They were written by Lillian Grace and addressed to your Aunt Elizabeth. When I finished the last letter, I was so intrigued by what she said I contacted Lee."

Without turning her head, Jane's blue eyes moved to Lee. "What did you think after you read them, Lee?"

"I was hooked. Miranda and I discussed them, and together we decided to investigate the murder on our own."

"Oh, I wouldn't get too wrapped up in the letters," Jane said with a laugh. "That woman was crazy. She couldn't have known Uncle Bert to say the things she said." Jane paused. "What did she say that makes you think she knows what she's talking about?

Aunt Elizabeth gave the police copies of her letters. They said they checked out everything and none of it was true.

They also said she was crazy, had delusions, and saw connections with all the murders that took place in Bridgetown to Uncle Bert's murder. Did you know she was in a mental hospital for quite some time?"

Lee stood, pacing back and forth. "Jane, I can see why you would laugh, she does sound crazy, but we have worked on hours of research already and a lot of what Lilly said we're finding out was true."

"Jane, did you read the letters?" Lee asked.

"Yes, I did read them. Well, maybe I only skimmed the first letter and didn't read it. I guess I didn't look at any of the other letters either, but more than fifty years have passed since then.

I don't remember a lot of what I did read, except there were a few lines she wrote that gave me the impression she couldn't have known Uncle Bert to write such silly things."

"I have a question for you. Why did you give the letters to Joan?" Lee stopped pacing, looking directly at Jane.

"I guess, like Miranda, I was doing some cleaning in the office one day and came across the letters in my desk drawer.

Joan was in town that week for a visit. In fact, she was sitting in the same chair you are, Lee. I showed her the letters and told her the story. She said she'd like to read them, so I told her to keep them, they were of no value to me any longer." Jane paused, smiling at Lee. "It would be nice to have closure on the murder, finding out who did it and why. At this point in time I think the why is probably more important than who did it, because after all these years the person or persons who committed the murder are probably dead by now, but you never know what could turn up."

Miranda folded her arms in front of her and looked at Jane.

"No, you don't," Miranda said. "We may uncover all the secrets surrounding this murder, you never know. We're sure of one thing, someone thinks we are getting too close."

"Why would you say that?"

"We stopped at the cemetery where your uncle is buried and someone took a shot at us."

"What!" Jane said with a nervous laugh. "That's crazy, who would do such a thing?"

"That's the same question we had."

"Wow," Jane said, shaking her head.

"Then Gus showed up and about scared us to death. He said a lot of strangers were in town nosing around."

"Oh, big old lovable Gus," Jane said.

"Miranda and I were so intrigued by the things we read in the letters that I had her place an ad in the *Bridgetown Mirror*. It'll run in tomorrow's paper."

Jane turned in Lee's direction and crossed her arms on top of the desk. "What does the ad say?"

"We asked that anyone with information they would like to share about the murder or Lilly to contact us, for a possible book," Lee said.

"Jane, Lilly lived here in Benson and graduated from high school in 1930," Miranda added. "Her maiden name was Sanders. She was also married in the church down the street."

"I didn't know that," Jane said. "How did you find all that information?"

"I found her wedding announcement in the 1934 *Benson Herald*, after spending hours searching the Internet," Miranda said, "digging a bit here and a bit there. After a trip to the library this morning we now have a lot more information about her and her family. Lilly was a popular girl, busy in high school."

Lee studied Jane as Miranda was talking. She was petite like Joan except she was eleven years older. She was in her seventies and still good looking, with eyes that sparkled when she smiled.

Jane turned in Lee's direction. "Lee, fifty years is a long time. Most of the people involved in and with the killing are no doubt dead, and not a lot of people are going to remember the murder." Jane paused for a moment. "My uncle was a gentle giant. He lived a rough life that had transformed his blue eyes to a dull gray and his rugged handsome complexion into a scarred, twisted, sagging face. His heavy drinking, bar fights, and that terrible accident all did their work in transforming him into someone who none of us knew any longer. But he was a nice man, at least to his family."

Lee interrupted Jane. "Was he your dad's brother?"

"Yes, Uncle Bert and my dad had the same personality. Physically they were exact opposites, there were no strangers to either of them. Everyone they ever met would walk away thinking they were my uncle's or my dad's best friend." Jane moved her hands from the desktop to her lap.

"It's obvious someone didn't like Bert," Lee said, "and Lillian Grace seems to think she knows who."

"So, you think Lillian was telling the truth and wasn't some nut trying to get attention?" Jane asked.

"Miranda and I are going to try to either prove or disprove the statements Lillian made in the letters. Would you happen to know this address?" Lee handed a piece of paper to Jane with the address written on it.

"Why, yes, this is a good address, that's the high-end real estate section of town. Who did you say lives at this address?"

"We don't know who lives there now," Lee said, "but that's where Lillian Sanders Grace grew up."

Jane's mouth dropped open. "Are you kidding me?"

"No, we're not kidding," Lee said. "We pulled that address from Lilly and George's wedding announcement."

"What was her maiden name again?" Jane asked.

"Sanders," Lee said.

"When I was in high school there was a drug store in town, it was Sanders Family Drugs. I wonder if her father operated that business."

"Is the drug store still there?" Lee asked.

"There's a drug store there, but it's no longer Sanders. A chain bought it out about ten years ago. They've added onto the building and completely remodeled it." Jane stood and walked to the window. "Her family had to have money to live at that address," she said as she turned, looking at Lee. "You and Miranda have found so much information in such a short period of time. Too bad the police didn't do their job investigating back then. They could've learned the same information if they'd wanted to. Well, good luck with the rest of your research and the ad. I hope it's profitable for you. If I can help, you know where to find me, both of you have my phone number."

"I do have one more question," Lee said. "In Lilly's letters, the said Bert told her about a sister or a cousin or someone who was trying to buy some land from him and he refused to sell it because he didn't like the person. Do you know anything about that?"

"Huh, I would say Uncle Bert had to tell her that bit of information. There is no other way she could have known. So, maybe she did know him after all." Jane walked over and sat in her chair, crossing her legs.

"The person who tried to buy the land was my cousin Donna. She would get into knockdown, drag-out fights with my uncle about the land. About once a week Donna would drive up to my Uncle Bert and Aunt Elizabeth's and start fighting with my uncle. Aunt Elizabeth would phone daddy to come up and break up the fight. Mind you, my little dad between these two. It would be funny if it weren't so serious. I don't mean to mislead you. They didn't hit each other, but there was a lot of serious name calling." Jane chuckled and shook her head. "Donna hounded my uncle about it, in fact, she was relentless. I think her mom, Aunt Miser, was encouraging Donna to try to buy the land, but Uncle Bert refused to sell it to her."

"What reason would Miser have to goad Donna to be so relentless?" Lee asked. "Why did she want Donna to have it?"

"I don't know. That's a question I often ask myself. Maybe Aunt Miser wanted to acquire all the estate, and Uncle Bert's land would make it that much bigger."

"Miser," Lee said. "What kind of a name is that to give a kid?"

"Back in those days," Jane said, "they named people after relatives, friends and places, who knows where they dug up the name Miser."

"Greed is a great motivator," Lee said, "compelling a person to commit an act that under normal circumstances would be foreign to them." Lee moved across the room and sat in his chair. "Where was the twenty acres of land, and how did Bert get control of it?" he asked.

"When the twenty acres in question came up for sale next to the home place, Uncle Bert bought it for five thousand dollars, but he had it deeded just in his name, so there was no attachment to the home place. Donna said she wanted to live on the property, but Uncle Bert didn't want her there. Donna never married, and after she came home from the Air Force she worked as a prison nurse in southern New York."

"Donna sounds like she might have been a bit on the rough side, and would have been in the know with the police with access to low-life criminal elements," Lee said. "Maybe she hired someone to commit murder then paid off the local police to cover it up."

Jane nodded. "I guess it would seem to point in that direction."

Miranda chimed in. "Sounds to me like a motive for murder."

"Yes," Jane said, "I guess it does, but Donna was such a quiet person. Other than fighting with Uncle Bert, it would be hard to believe that she could do something so evil."

"Jane," Miranda said, "do you know if the police investigated any of the family members for the murder?"

"They never investigated any of us. Reggie and I used to talk between ourselves wondering why they didn't, especially since Donna was trying to gain ownership of the property."

"Do you know if anyone ever told the police about Donna and her efforts to buy the property from your uncle?" Lee asked.

"I didn't, but I don't know what the other family members may have told them."

"What was your reason for not telling the police about Donna?"

"At the time, the thought crossed my mind, but I couldn't bring myself to betray a family member."

"Even though this family member may have committed murder?"

"I couldn't do it at the time, Lee. I do regret it now, but it's too late. Donna died about ten years ago."

"Did Donna ever get the land?" Lee asked.

"Yes. After Uncle Bert died, Aunt Elizabeth received the property from Uncle Bert's estate. Then about five years later, she sold it to Donna. She had a log house erected on the land and lived there along with her widowed mother, who died shortly after moving in. Donna continued to live there alone until she died. Again, I did think it strange that the police didn't investigate the family."

"Do you know if Donna was in Bridgetown the night your uncle was murdered?" Lee asked.

"Yes, I do know she was in Bridgetown. I was with Aunt Elizabeth when she cornered Donna to find out where she was that night and if she was at the hot dog stand. She told us she was, but it must have been before Uncle Bert got there because she said she left around ten o'clock that night."

Lee looked at Miranda, smiling. "All right, Jane," Lee said, "let's get down to brass tacks here. Lillian wrote in her letters that your uncle had a pet name for her, she said he always called her Lilly. Why would she mention that one thing?"

"Well, it's an interesting statement. Uncle Bert liked to use pet names for women he cared about. As an example he never called me Jane, he always called me Janie. In the same way, he always called Joan, Joanie." Jane paused and nodded. "From that one statement alone, I would say she must have known him."

"One more thing," Lee said. "Would it be okay to drive up to the property and look around? I'm sure Miranda knows how to get there. It would be helpful to see where all the things we've talked about took place."

"I'll call my son Johnny and let him know you'll be looking around the old place. I'm sure he won't mind."

"We've taken up enough of your time, it's getting late," Lee said as he stood and smiled at Jane. "Thanks again for all the information, Jane."

"Oh, no, thank you."

Lee glanced around the well-appointed office. "Jane, it looks like you do well in your real estate business."

"It makes a decent living for my son and me. Johnny runs the office most of the time now because I'm semi-retired, but I still have deep connections around town, so if I can help with anything let me know. I'd like to be kept informed of what you learn from your research."

"Of course, Jane. I'll keep in touch with you," Lee said.

"Oh, and Miranda, we need to get together some night for dinner. It's been awhile. I miss our times together."

"I'd like that, Jane, call me."

"Oh, I almost forgot to tell you this," Jane said. "A neighbor who lives across the river from the home place or the farm we've been talking about, called and asked me to meet her there. She said she had something for me. When she showed up she pulled a rusted coffee tin from the trunk of her car, and as she handed it to me the smell of kerosene filled my nose. I gazed down into the can, swimming in the liquid was a small handgun." Jane paused and looked at Lee. "Then she told me this story," Jane continued.

"Two months after my uncle's murder her husband had gone fishing in the river that ran behind their house. As he was slogging through the brush at the edge of the riverbank his boot caught on something. He bent over, parted the weeds and saw the rusted gun. He brought it home, put it in this can, and covered it in kerosene so it wouldn't rust anymore. He told her not to tell anyone he found it, that it might be involved in the Grayson murder. It was a small bird shot handgun."

Lee glanced in Miranda's direction, and back at Jane.

"So, she promised her husband that she wouldn't tell anyone, but since he's passed away she didn't think it would make any difference now."

"What made her husband think by finding the gun that it would connect him to the murder?"

"I didn't think to ask her that."

"Wow," Lee said. "Do you still have the gun?"

"Yes, I put it in the shed. When you go to the home place, tell Johnny you'd like to look at it."

"Do you think the police would check the pellets they pulled out of Bert's hand against the gun in the coffee can?" Miranda asked.

"If you'd like to take it to them, I don't care," Jane said. "It's up to you, but I don't know if I'd trust the Bridgetown Police."

"You're right, I'll send it off to the FBI. I still have a few connections in the department, and they can confirm the results for us. The FBI can obtain some of the pellets from the Bridgetown Police evidence department."

"If they still have the evidence and haven't gotten rid of it," Jane said.

Lee glanced at Jane, thinking that was a strange statement. Smiling at Jane, they said their goodbyes and made their way to the door. Lee held the door open for Miranda as they left the office.

Standing outside the door, Lee could see Miranda scanning the buildings lining both sides of the street. "When did this part of town get so dumpy?" she said.

"It sure is. Jane may want to think about the possibility of moving her office to a safer area." Lee opened the car door stopping short of getting in, as his eyes followed the line of buildings and trees surrounding them.

"What are you looking for? It's almost dark."

"I don't know," Lee said. "I can sense someone watching us, but who and why? Can't you feel the eyes following you, Miranda? I can feel the hair on the back of my neck and arms standing up again."

Lee turned toward the office. He could see Jane's face as she stood at the window, watching them. He saw her walk away from the window, then he heard the deadbolt latch on the door. He thought that maybe she sensed the watchers as well, and he'd bet she knew who they were. He guessed she probably knew as he did—they were the second generation who knew the sins of their fathers and mothers.

Lee slid behind the wheel. For a few seconds they sat in the car looking for something; anything, it didn't matter. Lights were flipping on in the buildings and houses, radiating a warm soft glow from the windows. The smell of exhaust fumes hung in the air from the passing vehicles. The light polls started to flicker on one after the other down the avenue.

The full moon filtered light down through the treetops, casting long skinny shadows onto the sidewalks and streets.

Lee shivered at the eerie scene.

He tapped Miranda's leg and pointed. "There. Did you see that?" He was pointing toward the big house on the hill in front of them.

"What? I didn't see anything."

"You didn't see the curtain move? Someone was at the window. When I looked up, whoever it was stepped back and the curtain closed."

"We're running out of time tonight, Lee. We won't be able to fit a visit to Jane's home place until tomorrow sometime."

CHAPTER 24

Present Day

Hidden by the dark shadows of the tall trees in the moonlight, Randy picked his way to the patio doors. He slid the knife into the space between the doorjamb and the lock. In a flash, he had the door open and was in the room. With the small flashlight between his teeth, he moved like an apparition, his steps were undetectable. With the skill of a magician he opened the black briefcase on the closet floor, but they weren't in there. In one smooth fluid movement he found the computer room. The drawers and books didn't give up what he was looking for. Fifteen minutes later he'd searched everywhere, but couldn't find them.

The sound from the opening garage door told him it was time to leave, and in a swift and silent rush he exited.

***

As the overhead door closed, Lee watched Miranda put the key into the door lock, push the heavy door open and hit the light switch. The first thing she saw were pots and pans scattered around on the floor.

“Oh no, what the heck happened here? Look at this mess.” Miranda lowered her voice to a whisper. “It seems we had a visitor.”

***

Randy bounded down the wooden patio steps, running across the well-kept lawn. With the skill of an acrobat, he zigzagged his slim body around the cement seats and the pond behind the house, with his eyes on the dark forest in front of him.

***

“Or still have one,” Lee said in soft tones. “Now do you still think I’m imagining things?” He put his index finger to his lips, tapped Miranda on the shoulder, and whispered, “Wait here, Miranda. Let me check the rest of the house to make sure there’s no one here. You go back into the garage, lock the door and call the police on your cell.”

“There’s no way I’m waiting in the garage. I’ll be right behind you.”

“This isn’t the time to argue with me. Just get into the garage and call the police.”

“Okay, okay.”

Lee watched Miranda grab the garage doorknob before he turned and pulled his gun out of the holster. He was about to start walking, following the papers littering the hall, when he thought he heard a noise and paused, “Oh,” Lee said, as Miranda ran into him almost knocking him down.

"Miranda, what are you doing?" he whispered. "I told you to wait in the garage."

"I was never good at taking orders. It caused me a lot of problems when I worked. Anyway, two weapons are better than one." Miranda crossed the kitchen and pulled open a bottom cabinet drawer, felt underneath, loosened some tape and turned to face Lee. He gave her a wide-eyed stare.

"Now this is a weapon," she said, holding a .40 caliber semi-automatic pistol in her hand.

"What the devil? You keep that in your kitchen?"

"Yep, and I haven't had to take it out until now."

"Do you know how to use it?"

"I hope we don't have to find out. Now, we better get going because whoever is in here is probably falling asLeep waiting for us to come after them."

"Okay, okay," Lee whispered. He put his hand down to his side, nudging Miranda to stay close to him. "We're making so much noise I'm sure that whoever was here is certain to be gone by now."

They moved as one body, stepping over the books and papers scattered in the hall, glancing in every room on the way. They all looked the same—drawers emptied and the contents thrown onto the floor. In the library, the shelves were bare and the books filled the center of the room.

"It's a good thing the bookshelves were attached to the walls," Miranda said, "or they would probably have pulled them over as well."

"What in the world could they have been looking for?" Lee asked.

"One guess, and I say the letters."

In Lee's room the patio door stood open about a foot.

"It looks like they came in and probably went out through this door." Lee inched over to it peered around the curtains and could see outside. "Look quick, Miranda, someone is running into the woods."

Miranda jumped to the open door.

"Did you see him?"

Miranda shook her head, "He was too fast. I didn't see him."

Lee and Miranda stood at the door staring into the night. In the distance they heard the roar of an engine, listening as it faded into the night.

CHAPTER 25

Present Day

Miranda walked from room to room, shaking her head.

"Oh Lee, it'll take hours to clean this up. Of all the times for Adrian to be gone."

Detective Mann took notes as he walked around the house surveying the mess.

"Lee, show the detective where we think the intruder broke in."

"Come with me. We think the interloper went out through these doors, into the woods and followed the path through the trees." Lee pointed in the direction of the woods.

"Patrolman Jones." Jones was soon standing at the detective's side. "I want you to take your flashlight and go into those woods out there." He pointed to the back of the property. "Follow the path through the trees and see where it goes."

"Yes, sir, right away." The patrolman pulled a flashlight from his belt and hurried out the door.

Lee watched Jones make his way to the woods, then disappear as he walked into the black forest. Every couple seconds Lee could see the light flickering between the trees, then even that was gone. The detective turned toward Lee.

"We've had a rash of burglaries in this area in the past few weeks," Detective Mann said. "We think its kids hunting for drugs or money, or both. Whoever it was probably won't be back. Can you tell if there's anything missing?"

Miranda cast a glance at Lee and back to the detective.

"I can't tell right now, but I'll call you if I find that anything has been stolen," Miranda said.

Ten minutes later the patrolman was back.

"Did you find anything?"

"The path led to a power line clearing on the other side of that stand of trees. There were four wheeler tracks on the blacktop road going south toward town."

"Okay, thank you, Patrolman," the detective said. "Since there's nothing more we can do here tonight we'll be going now." The detective moved toward the door.

"Lee and I appreciate you coming out and investigating," Miranda said.

Detective Mann held her gaze. He looked like he was going to say something, but didn't. Lee followed Miranda as she showed the detective to the door.

"Have a good evening, Miss Witherspoon, Mr. Perkins."

Lee thanked the detective again as he closed the door.

Miranda turned, shaking her finger at Lee. "Do you think that detective was like one of the crooked police Lilly talked about in her letters? Why do you think they were after the letters? If the letters were what they wanted, or it could be an enemy I made while working for the FBI. Would they just now be coming after me? No," Miranda said, second-guessing herself. "I still think it's the letters they were after." She crossed her arms and stood in front of Lee, tapping her foot. He could tell she was thinking, as he interrupted her thoughts.

"That's my guess, but why?" Lee moved over to the windows staring at the night. Then he turned to Miranda.

"Where did you put the letters after I gave them back to you?" Miranda moved back to the computer room, stopping at the wall beside her desk. In one quick move, she kicked the baseboard just below the snow scene painting. Two sections of the hardwood floor moved sideways, and a metal safe started to rise from below the floor. She stooped, opened it, and pulled out the letters, waving them in the air. After putting the letters back in the safe and tapping the baseboard it disappeared into the floor in a smooth, silent motion, keeping its contents safe.

"You sure are full of surprises, aren't you?"

Miranda turned and walked toward Lee, stopping two inches from his face. "You don't know the half of it."

Lee nodded. "Ooh, sounds intriguing. Come on Kid, I'll help you put this place back together."

He started to pick up books, placing them back onto the shelves, nodding and listening to Miranda.

"Lee, I appreciate your help. With the two of us working on putting this house back together it shouldn't take long." Miranda started to put the room back in shape.

"This is, for the most part, my fault," Lee said, "nosing around in this town asking questions about the murder. I'm afraid your life is in danger because of me, so until we find out who we can and cannot trust, we need to watch each other's back."

"I agree, but I'm the one who found the letters, then told a lot of people about them, not thinking that anything like this would happen. So in many ways, a lot of this is my doing, not yours."

Lee was stacking books as fast as he could. "This is just the beginning," he said. "Our ad is coming out in tomorrow's paper. What kind of interest will surface then? Or what kind of visitors will we get? I don't understand why this fifty-year-old murder would stir up such a hornet's nest or that anyone would even remember it."

Miranda finished with the computer desk and helped Lee with the books. "I don't either, Lee, but it'll be interesting to see who comes out of the woodwork and why."

"Maybe it's not so much about Bert Grayson as the letters. Or maybe both. Lilly may be right about the murder. Maybe the killer is still out there," Lee said as he finished filling the first bookshelf. "Miranda, what are you doing with all these books? Have you read all of them?"

"I love the smell of an actual book, not an e-reader. There's something about touching the paper in my fingers, turning the pages and the satisfying feeling of finishing a story. Yes, I have read every one of them." She nodded at him. He wasn't paying attention to what she said.

"Jane is still alive," he said, "so there's no doubt in my mind that there could be a lot of people from that time period hibernating in Bridgetown with the information they thought was safe. I believe the children are protecting the secrets of their mothers and fathers. It's only a matter of ferreting out who they are, and exposing them so they open up with the information they have or think they have about the murder or Lilly."

Thirty minutes later Lee placed the last book on the shelf.

"What about the guy who tried to buy the letters and was killed that night in the car-train accident?" she said.

"I doubt if we'll ever find out why he wanted the letters,"

Lee said. "Why does someone take a chance breaking into a house looking for we think but aren't sure is the letters? The information in them must be of value to someone, but who could that someone be? We must be missing something important in the letters."

"This is all so crazy and dangerous, but don't worry. I can protect you, Lee."

He stood and held his arms out in front of him. "Thanks, Miranda, I don't know what I would do without you. All kidding aside, whoever these people are, they're not going to give up. I believe we're getting close and they're getting desperate."

Lee followed Miranda upstairs.

In the middle of the staircase, Miranda stopped and turned. "Don't get any ideas, Lee, we're cleaning and putting things away. That's all. Then right back downstairs."

Lee shrugged and kept walking.

"You don't have to worry about me. I can take care of myself," Miranda said. "I've been doing it for years, but the important thing is I can run real fast."

"I'm not blind, you're in great physical shape, but no one can outrun a bullet."

Lee helped finish with the upstairs, then down to the kitchen where he stood looking across the room at her. She was so self-confident. Her radiant eyes were staring, but not seeing, looking all around, especially behind her. She jerked her head in the direction of the creaks and groans of an old house getting used to its new body. The unknown was always hard to defend against.

He saw the fear behind her eyes. As hard as she tried to hide it, he could tell deep inside she was scared.

CHAPTER 26

Present Day

At 8:00 A.M. the next morning they arrived in Crooksville, Florida, and rented a car. The bank was opening as they parked in front. It seemed empty except for a few tellers who appeared to be rushing to open their windows.

A pinched face young girl about twenty years old walked over to them. “Can I help you?”

“Yes, thank you,” Lee said. “I would like to get into my deposit box, number fifty-two.”

“Okay, just one moment, please.” She scurried off and soon came back with a key.

“Follow me, please.” She stopped turning toward Lee. “May I have your key, please?” He handed it to her and they continued into the vault.

She slid her key, then his into the slots, turning them together. The door swung open and she pulled out a long wide metal box and set it on the table behind them.

“There you are.” She walked out and closed the door.

Lee turned to Miranda with a look of surprise.

“Wow, Lee, that was easy.”

"Yeah. Do you think it was a little too easy? Better hurry before they realize their mistake," he said as he grabbed the lid.

To their great surprise, when he opened it the manuscript was on top. Miranda grabbed it as the door to the vault opened. Like a magician, she shoved it into her purse. A tall pox-faced man slipped in and closed the door. Lee looked up in surprise.

"Don't take anything out of that box, the girl who let you in here is new. She isn't familiar with the way we do things around here. There are rules and everybody goes by the rules. Besides all that, there's a lot of money that's owed to the bank for holding your box," he said as he took it from the table and closed the lid. Lee stepped away from him; his breath filled the room.

"You'll have to pay the fees to have access to this box."

Miranda fanned the air in front of her. Lee watched as he slid the box back into the cube and turned the lock.

He twirled the key ring around on his finger as he said, "The fee owed on this box is $500." His crooked yellow teeth showed as he grinned with pleasure.

Miranda put her hand on her hip and turned toward the man. "What? Well, you can keep it then. There isn't anything in there worth that kind of money." She poked her chin forward at him.

He raised his hand into the air, turned and walked toward the door.

"That's fine with me, miss. Have a good day." With a slight bend at the waist and a sweeping gesture with his arm, he told them it was time to leave.

Lee and Miranda walked out of the bank, driving straight to the airport where they waited for their ten o'clock flight.

They'd be back in Bridgetown in time to meet with the police chief.

Lee whispered into Miranda's ear as he looked over his shoulder. "Did you get it?"

She glanced from side to side. "Yes, it's in my purse, but I think we should wait until we get back to the mansion to look at it."

Lee grinned. "For once, I agree with you."

CHAPTER 27

Present Day

The trail was growing cold and Lee was left wondering if he was headed in the right direction. Digging and scratching beneath the surface he gathered clues that made no sense. He wanted information that would lead him forward, not stop him at a brick wall. Staying the course, he continued to press forward, pulling down the wall, brick by brick. At last, he saw in front of him clues that at first glance lied to him, but as he persisted in his search, laid out all the information like pieces to a big jigsaw puzzle. They were starting to fit together and the picture crystallized in front of his eyes. Maybe, just maybe, it wasn't the picture he expected to see.

***

They had a few minutes before their appointment with the police chief, so Lee and Miranda stopped at the Coffee Grind for a welcome short break.

At the appointed time they were sitting in the police chief's office.

Chief Williams, a thick-bodied man with thinning sandy hair, was soft spoken but authoritative. He said his pleasantries and seemed anxious to start.

With thick, stubby fingers, he reached down into a side drawer of the desk he was sitting behind, coming up with a twelve-inch-thick manila file folder brimming with papers, which he placed on top of his desk. After a short pause, he looked first at Lee then Miranda, while pointing to the folder.

"The department spent many months investigating the Grayson murder, talking to everyone who had anything to do with the case. We think this folder speaks for itself, showing the department spent a lot of time on this investigation."

"Excuse me, Chief," Lee said, "but you could have stuffed old papers in there knowing we were coming for this meeting."

The chief held his gaze as his eyes narrowed, pointing his index finger at Lee. "A murder is always open until it's solved."

He looked at Miranda then back at Lee. "Before we begin, I have a message for you from the district attorney. If you write a book about this murder, you're not to use the name of Bridgetown or the Bridgetown Police Department in a negative way. If you do, we'll sue you. You're not to contact anyone involved with this case, and that includes the detectives who worked it. They don't want to talk to you. Do you understand what I've said?"

"Now wait one minute," Lee said as he started to stand, pointing his index finger back at the chief. "Are you threatening us?"

"No," the chief said as he raised both hands in front of his chest. "Not at all, that was a message from the district attorney, not me."

Lee sat down and exchanged looks with Miranda. "So are you saying the district attorney told you to point your finger at me as you spoke?"

The chief glanced up at the ceiling behind Lee, he turned to see what the policeman was looking at and saw the camera.

The officer turned his gaze back on Lee. "If we're clear on that issue, why don't we get started?"

Lee nodded in agreement, as he opened the folder, starting with the top paper.

"I'll only use first names, that way you won't know who I'm talking about and the people involved will be protected."

One hour later, they left the office, but not before Lee was handed a copy of the autopsy report as he walked out the door. Lee's head was swimming with information. Some of it, he already knew from the newspaper accounts of the murder and Lilly's letters, and some of it was new. Walking toward the elevator, Lee glanced around the halls, noticing cameras everywhere.

"After that message from the district attorney, I believe Lilly was right," Lee said. "The police were corrupt then and are still running roughshod over the people of Bridgetown. I took what he said as a threat, didn't you?"

"Yes, I did. The whole interview was tense. Did you see his reaction when I asked if they had interviewed any of the family members and he had to tell me no? That was amazing all by itself. When I inquired about the young historian's death, he fumbled around for his words."

"Remember his comments about Lilly?" Lee said. "She was crazy, someone who would read about a high-profile murder case in the newspapers, then try to inject herself into it. Trying hard to discredit her he pushed that line of thinking a little too much. He was trying to control what we thought about Lilly and this case by meshing together what they wanted us to believe instead of what the reality was." Lee held the door for Miranda.

"Yes, Lee, they were trying to shape our line of thinking rather than look at the facts and the evidence. Speaking of evidence, there was precious little of that to look at. This is crazy. It's like we're trapped inside one of Lilly's letters."

When the elevator stopped at the bottom floor, Lee, followed by Miranda, walked to the front of the building. As they approached the glass doors, Miranda said, "Look at my car.

There's a white paper flapping in the breeze on the windshield. Did someone give me a ticket?"

They hurried toward the car. Miranda pulled the paper from under the wiper, unfolded it, read what it said, and then without a word handed it to Lee.

He took the typewritten note and read it out loud.

> *If you're still alive to read this, you're one of the lucky ones. It means they haven't found you yet, or they haven't figured out a foolproof plan to get rid of you. But you can bet they will. They always do.*

Lee was familiar with the look in Miranda's eyes.

"Don't let them scare you, Kid. We'll get through this together."

She was half listening to him as she opened her door.

Lee folded the note, put it into his coat pocket, then turned around and scanned the area. He didn't know what he was looking for, but he could sense they were looking back at him. He glanced in the direction of the police station. Everything seemed ordinary with people flowing in and out. Glancing at the windows he could see men and women working at their desks. Everything looked normal—whatever normal was any more or had grown to be in this crazy investigation Lee had allowed himself to be drawn into.

He wondered how a few pieces of black print on white paper could put such fear and suspicion into his heart and mind. After all, they were only words.

"Someone is trying to scare us off. I get that. But why? After all this time it doesn't make sense. Could the killer or killers still be alive? Can it be the second generation in a clumsy, but desperate attempt to protect the people who were involved in the murder?" Lee said.

Miranda shrugged as she slid into the seat. "I don't know, but now more than ever I'm determined to find out. They aren't going to scare me off. I faced more formidable forces than this when I worked in the field with Ridgeway. We're going to get these cowards."

The thoughts rolled around in Lee's head as he slid into the car seat and closed the door, but this time, it was different.

This time, Miranda wasn't tapping her fingers and humming to the sixties music playing on the radio. Her jaw was set and Lee could see she was deep in thought as the car headed in the direction of her house.

CHAPTER 28

Present Day

"Before we go back to the house, we should stop at Jane's farm to see if Johnny is there. I'd like to pick up the gun and send it off to the FBI to check for fingerprints."

"Good thinking, Miranda. Do you mean after all this time and the condition of the gun they can get fingerprints from it?"

"Lee, with today's technology, it's amazing what they might be able to find on that gun."

He patted Miranda on the leg. "If I were you, I wouldn't worry too much about that note."

"If I didn't have you with me at the house, I might be a bit frightened, especially since Adrian is gone. Anyway, I think they're only trying to scare us off. So, you know what that means, don't you?"

"I think it means we're starting to get close to exposing the killer or killers."

"Yes, Lee, and I also think Jane may be in some danger.

They have to know she's connected to all this in some way."

Lee's phone chirped. "Hello, this is Lee."

"Who are you and why do you want to know about Bert Grayson's murder?"

Lee hit the speakerphone button so Miranda could listen as she drove. "Who is this? Why do you want to know who I am?"

"I want to know who you are and your connection to Bert Grayson."

"As the ad in the newspaper reads, I'm doing research for a possible book about the murder. I'm willing to listen to any information you'd like to share, and as the ad reads, my name is Lee Perkins. Do you have any information you'd like to share with me?"

"My name is Roger Grayson. Together we, that is my grandfather who was Bert's older brother, and Donna, who was my cousin, have extensively investigated the murder and we know who did it."

"You do? Well, what did the police say when you told them you've solved the murder?"

"They just ignored what we had to say because the guy who killed him works for the police department. They take care of their own and protect them. It doesn't matter what crime they commit."

"Do you know the man's name who committed the murder?"

"His name is Hank Cranston. He is a black man who worked in the police department and ran a tavern up on Jew Hill by the bus station. Before Hank joined the police force he worked as a butcher at a local shop."

"How did Hank commit the murder?"

"The night of the murder, Hank was tipped off that Bert was in town and pretty liquored up. He got together about twenty guys who he knew were holding grudges against Bert. A couple of the men lured him into the alley where the rest of them were waiting. Hank slit my uncle's throat while all the others stood around and watched."

"Wait a minute, Roger, are you saying around twenty people were involved in the murder?"

"That's right. That's what we came up with," Roger said.

"How do you know the others stood around and watched while Hank slit his throat?" Lee asked.

"We know because the police said there were at least twenty sets of footprints around the body."

"Do you have a motive?" Lee asked.

"I think it had something to do with the time Bert was more involved in the union. He made some enemies then."

"Okay, Roger, thanks for calling."

Lee closed the phone and for a few silent minutes stared at Miranda as she drove rehashing in his mind everything Roger said.

Miranda turned onto a single-lane blacktop road. There was an abandoned ranch house on the right. On the left was a rundown two-story farmhouse with some acreage. The road made a sharp left, and on the right was a two-story clapboard house being remodeled. Just past the house stood an aluminum-sided three-bay garage. A man stuck his head around the opened door as the car came to a stop on the driveway. He was younger with dark hair. He waved and smiled.

"That's Johnny," Miranda said. "He's a nice young man. He has his mom's personality."

Johnny moved his tall frame toward the car, smiling the whole time.

Miranda introduced Lee when they got out of the car.

"Hey, Miranda, Mom called and said you'd be stopping by to get the gun. People act strange about stuff like that. I don't know why." He handed the can to Lee. "I put a lid on it so the kerosene won't splash out on you."

"Thanks, Johnny," Lee said. "I appreciate your thoughtfulness." Lee took the can from Johnny, securing it in the trunk.

"I'm sorry I won't have time to chat with you, Miranda, but I have an appointment in town. I was on my way out when I heard your car pull up."

"Thanks, Johnny," Lee said. "We don't want you to be late for your appointment, so we'll be leaving."

They got back into the car and drove down the road. Lee looked at Miranda. "I guess we got here at the right time."

"It sure looks that way," Miranda said.

Back at the mansion, Lee carried the can to the front porch. Miranda followed him. He looked at her and said, "Where do you want me to put this?"

"I have a trash-burning barrel out back. Take the can and dump the kerosene into the barrel. I'll have Adrian take care of it when he gets back."

"Oh, okay, whatever you say," Lee said as he saluted.

"Real funny, Lee. When you've poured out the kerosene, grab the gun with this plastic bag, seal it, then use this rag to wrap it up, and put it in this box. I'll print a label for FedEx to pick it up," Miranda said as she walked into the house.

She came back out to the porch carrying a printed label and attached it to the box. About thirty minutes later a package pickup truck pulled into the driveway. The carrier jumped out carrying a metal box. Miranda met him at the door. He opened the lined container, placed the box inside, and sealed it.

He looked at Miranda, smiled, winked, and said, "Thank you, Miranda." She nodded at him then he hurried to his truck.

"Wow, Kid, that was an unusual exchange."

"You don't need to know everything, Lee. Let's get back to the computer room."

"You go ahead. I'll be there shortly."

Miranda stepped inside and closed the door. Lee stood on the front porch, leaning on one of the pillars, drinking in the vistas and going over the busy day's events in his mind. Miranda stuck her head out the door as it started to spit snow showers.

"Miranda to Lee, where are you? It's cold. Come inside."

"Sorry, I was going over in my mind everything Roger said. I'm not sure he is credible."

"Roger is the least of my thoughts right now. We'll get to him later. Right now . . ." Miranda paused, waving the manuscript at Lee.

He followed her through the door and into the living room to read it.

He read ten pages then paused and put the papers down on the sofa. "What the heck? The information in this manuscript is the same as the letters. It would seem we had the manuscript all the time and didn't know it."

"It looks like we took a trip to Florida for nothing. Well, maybe not. At least now we know," Miranda said with a smile.

"Okay, Miranda, now we've solved the mystery of the manuscript, let's get back to our other research."

"Here's what I've pulled up on the Bliss brothers," Miranda said. "Cain did die in an accident at his workplace. He was laid off from the railroad and went to work for a construction company in Maryland. The dump truck he was driving rolled over when he tried to straddle a hill of dirt with the wheels of the truck. Cain jumped out the window on the driver's side. Unfortunately, he didn't jump far enough, and the truck rolled onto him, crushing his body. He died instantly. At least that's what the newspapers reported."

"What a terrible way to die. It gives me the shivers thinking about it," Lee said.

"His brother Clay, as we know, must still have a lot of connections with all the wrong people including local mafia types."

"Wait, Kid, did you say he still has connections with the mafia? How can that be? The papers said they rounded up the mafia, put most of them in prison, and ran the rest of them out of town."

"He spent a few years in jail for his mafia ties in the 1980s. After the new police chief arrived in town they rounded up everyone connected with the mob and put them all in prison.

Since that time there hasn't been much of a mafia in Bridgetown. Well, at least I don't think there is. After that interview with the police chief, I'm not so sure," Miranda said.

"You told me that the black man working at the puritan cleaners at the time of the murder was interviewed," Lee said.

"The police chief also told us he was questioned about the murder. However, he was in Butler, Pennsylvania, the night the murder was committed. The police said they spoke with several people who verified the information. If what the police said can be believed."

"So far," Lee said, "we're getting a lot of responses to the ad, but nothing informative except the first phone call, if that guy can be believed. Will you run Hank Cranston on the Internet to see what you come up with?"

"I'll Google him." After a few minutes of searching, she found something. "Okay, here it is. Hank ran a rough bar in a place called Jew Hill. His bar was closed down because he allowed drug pushers and numbers runners to work out of it.

He was probably pushing drugs along with the booze. He was a local hood. He's still alive and is eighty years old. I can't find anywhere that he was on the local police force."

"He does sound like a local hood," Lee said. "I'd be willing to bet that Clay Bliss hung out there a lot. Let's drive down to Jane's. Maybe she can tell us more."

CHAPTER 29

Present Day

When they got there, however, Jane's office was closed. He smiled ruefully at Miranda. "Guess we should have called first."

Miranda shrugged. "Let's head back. We'll call Jane first, next time."

On the drive back, Miranda was quiet for a change. Lee was taking in the homes and businesses as they drove. Ahead, on the right, was a little amusement park.

"Miranda, is that where Lilly said she first met Bert and he told her his dad owned the park?"

"It is. Look at that merry-go-round." Miranda pulled the car over to the side of the road so Lee could have a good view of it. "It's original from the 1800s, as many of the rides are. I keep hoping they'll sell off some of the horses. I'd like to buy one as a collector's item. The owners of the park keep updating and refurbishing all the rides instead of selling them off and buying new ones."

"So this is the park Lilly talks about in the letters?" Lee said.

"Well, yes," Miranda said. "I did some checking. It was owned by one family from the early 1800s until the 1940s when a local businessman bought it, expanded it, and put in the water park on the other side of the road."

"I think Bert was trying to impress Lilly. If Lilly lived in Benson, she probably spent a lot of summers at this park as a kid. It would've been easy for Bert to meet her here for dates," he said as he took a deep breath. "Wow, pizza, it smells wonderful. They blow that out from the concession stands to make people hungry, and it is sure working on me."

Miranda pulled the car back onto the road and pointed it toward home.

Back at the mansion Miranda started working on the computer, digging out information on the people in Lilly's letters.

Lee sat in the chair next to her. "Kid, it's odd that Lilly waited three years before writing the next letter to Elizabeth."

"I wondered about that myself. Maybe she did write others, but Elizabeth and Jane only kept these letters."

"Yes, but she also said she spent a year crying over Bert's death. We don't know how long she was in the hospital," he said.

The buzzer rang. When Miranda opened the front door a red-eyed, nervous, well dressed older gentleman stood in the threshold holding his hat in his hand.

"Hello, may I help you?"

Lee stepped to the door beside Miranda. The man didn't acknowledge him. He shifted from foot to foot, twisting his scarf in his free hand.

"Nice Bentley, beautiful emerald green," Lee said.

"Yes, well, I'm not here to discuss my car or talk with you. I'm here to see Miranda," he said, looking Lee in the eyes this time and nodding.

"Alright then," Lee said.

"I won't give my name. I'm too well known in Bridgetown."

"Really, I don't know you," Miranda said.

"That's probably because we run in different circles. But I do know who you are."

"Okay then, what is it you want?"

"I have some information to tell you and I hope it will help you solve this long forgotten murder that took place here many years ago."

"Would you like to come in? It's cold out there."

"No, thank you. I won't be here long."

"Okay, what is it you have to say? Miranda said.

"I'm sure you don't know about a group of people in this town who have tried to hide the facts of this murder and the person who did it. I'm a retired Bridgetown city policeman. I worked on the railroad until 1950 when I joined the police department. I wasn't assigned to help work Bert's murder case, but I think I know who killed him."

Miranda interrupted him. "Oh. What did the detectives assigned to the case say when you told them you knew who did it?"

"They said they would look into it, but I don't think they ever did. Now, may I continue with my story?"

"Oh, sorry. Go ahead."

"The night of the murder I was on patrol with another officer. We were called to a traffic accident at 17th Street and Margaret Avenue. Before we arrived, the man who rear-ended the car parked at the light had fled on foot, leaving his vehicle behind at the scene. When we ran the license number, we traced it to a family by the name of Backers who lived on Chestnut Avenue two doors down from where Bert's body was found."

"Sorry to interrupt you again, but did you say the police said they checked into this guy?" Miranda said.

"Yes. The next day I asked a detective about it and he told me it wasn't my concern. He said I was to forget about it. Now, back to the story," he put his hat on.

"We impounded the car and went to the Backers' house.

When we arrived at the door a woman answered our knock.

We inquired if she owned this certain Ford. She said yes, it was parked behind Jim's Hot Dog Diner. We told her no, it was impounded because it was just involved in a hit and run accident on 17th Street."

"So, you're saying she didn't know he had taken her car and used it? Sorry for the interruption again," Miranda said.

"That's right, she didn't believe us. She told her son, Billy, to go upstairs and get the keys to her car. When the boy came back he said the keys were missing. She also told us she had a boarder who lived in a room upstairs who wasn't at home at the time."

"Isn't it strange that she parked the car behind the diner?"

"Look, lady, if you keep interrupting me, I'm never going to get through this story."

Lee looked at Miranda with a smirked.

"Sorry, I'll try not to do that again. No promises, though."

"Early the next morning after the murder, the detectives working the case got a tip to check out this boarder. When they knocked on his door, a large, burly fellow who had a couple of red strawberry marks on his forehead opened the door. They were the kind of marks you'd get from bashing your head into the windshield of a car. This man also matched the description of one of the men last seen with Bert at the hot dog diner earlier that night. I theorize that this fellow, his name is Will Pink, killed Bert, then stole the Backers' car, and was involved in the accident while fLeeing from the scene of the murder. He was also linked to the murder of Mr. Merritt."

"Go on, sir. Do you have more to say?" Miranda asked.

"No, I'm done. Please don't try to contact me. I'm not interested in talking to you again. I've told you everything I know. That should be enough. But I have two words of advice for you: Be careful." With that, he turned and walked to his car and drove off.

"Isn't that interesting," Lee said. "Mr. Merritt popped up again. He certainly got around. He's like an apparition—everyone seems to know him, but no one knows anything about him. He flows in and out of people's lives."

"Are you sure you're okay? You look pale."

"I'm okay, Miranda, but thanks for your concern."

"See, I do have a heart," she said.

"He didn't give a description of this man with the head injury other than he was large and burly fitting the description of one of the men who left the hot dog diner with Bert."

"I'm typing in Will Pink right now," Miranda said.

"Hope we get lucky."

"I can't find anyone by that name in that time period. There's no accident report in the police records or in the newspaper, maybe this guy is just a nut."

"Kid, didn't we look up this Merritt guy? It's strange that so many people mentioned him."

"We did look him up and couldn't find any information about him either. And yes, it's interesting everyone mentions him."

CHAPTER 30

Present Day

His phone chirped.

"Hello, this is Lee."

"Hello, my name is Harry Winston." Lee hit the speakerphone button.

"I was a patrol officer for the Bridgetown Police Department the night of the Grayson murder."

"Yes, Harry. What do you want to tell me?"

Harry continued his story. "I wanted to know if you learned anything new about the murder."

"We haven't learned anything more than what was in the papers, Harry. So what do you want to tell me?"

"It started snowing about ten that night. At about twelve fifteen A.M. we got a call from the dispatcher. I was with another officer. We always patrolled with two men on duty for protection. The dispatcher said they were receiving calls that there were loud noises coming from the alley behind 30 Chestnut Avenue. When we arrived on the scene about 12:30 A.M., we pulled the car up at the end of the dark alley, got out and walked with flashlights toward the address. With the moonlight reflecting off the snow, we could see a man sitting in the snow leaning against the wooden fence. It looked like he was sLeeping, and getting covered with snow that was falling heavy and wet. We were afraid he was going to freeze, so we went over to the man, and when we turned our flashlights on him, we could see blood everywhere, on him and in the snow. It scared me pretty good. I dropped my flashlight, backing away from the body as fast as I could. It took a few minutes to get control of my senses then I picked my light up and brushed the bloody snow off of it. Telling you what I saw still makes my heart race."

"Excuse me, Harry, so you're saying you were pretty shook up at what you were seeing?" Lee said.

"Yes. It was the first time I'd been around a dead body."

"Okay, sorry, go on with your story."

"I stepped up to the man sitting in the snow, placing my hand on his shoulder I shook him, his head flopped over to the side landing on his left shoulder, it was attached to his body by a small amount of skin and tissue. I jumped back, sucking in air as I did. I could see his neck was cut from behind his ear to almost the other ear. We decided to go back to the squad car, call headquarters, and report the gruesome scene. It was almost more than I could handle."

"Wait, Harry, didn't you see anyone out or around the body as you walked toward it?"

"Oh, yes, by the time we got back to the scene after phoning in our report, there were people coming out of their houses. They were pressing close to the victim. We had to keep telling them to get back. Some of them were pretty aggressive, and would walk right up to the body."

"Okay, go on with your story, Harry."

"Well, there were houses on both sides of the alley, and the lights seemed to be on in all the homes."

"Didn't you think that was odd?" Lee asked.

"Well, not at first. I was so shook up from seeing the murder victim at the time, all I could think about was getting away from him. I guess our minds couldn't comprehend the gory scene we'd walked into. We were both rookies, please remember it was our first murder scene. We were trained for this but to experience it first hand was something else. After phoning it in, we were told by the dispatcher to go back to the scene and guard it until backup came."

"I guess I could understand that," Lee said.

"We stayed in the alley until the detective and his crew arrived. He wanted to know about all the footprints. I told him they were in the snow when we showed up at the scene, walked up to the body to see if the guy was sLeeping or drunk, and that's when we saw the horrible sight.

"We stayed until the detective told us to go back to our nightly rounds. I didn't hear anything more about the case." He sighed before continuing, "There were moments when my curiosity would get the best of me. I'd look up the detectives working the case, and ask about the investigation. The one in charge at the time wouldn't give me any information. He said if I wasn't working on the case, it was none of my business. The department ended the investigation three months after the murder."

"Harry, I have a couple of questions for you."

"Okay, shoot."

"Do you know a Hank Cranston, a black man who ran a bar in Bridgetown at the time Bert was murdered?"

"Yes, Hank is a good friend of mine."

Lee exchanged glances with Miranda, deciding this guy was unreliable because of his connection with Hank.

"He used to run a bar," Harry continued, "in the Jew Hill district and later moved it down to the Chestnut Avenue area. He did some numbers running once in a while. If you think Hank killed Bert, I would say you were wrong. He wouldn't commit such a crime, but he could have because he was in great physical shape."

"Harry, would you know if Hank is still alive?"

"Yes, I do know that. He lives in Bridgetown with his girlfriend. They closed his bar down a few years ago for drug peddling."

"Was Hank working for the police department when Bert was murdered?"

"No, Hank never worked for the police. There was only one black man working for the police at that time and his last name was Harter."

"Do you know of a Clay and Cain Bliss?"

"Why, yes. They're both bad news—" He stopped in mid-sentence, paused, and said, "No, I don't know either of them."

Lee glanced at Miranda, she raised an eyebrow, while Lee nodded.

"Did you know or know of a Lillian Grace?" Lee said.

"No, I never heard of her, why do you ask about her? Who was she?"

"She was just someone who knew Bert," Lee said.

"Do you know if the composite picture published in the paper of one of the men who left the bar with Bert the night he was murdered could have been Clay Bliss?"

"No, I didn't know there was a composite picture in the paper."

"So I guess you didn't read about the murder in the paper?"

"No, I was too busy working and making a living to spend time reading the newspaper."

"Do you know if there was a mafia in Bridgetown?"

"No, as far as I knew there was only a small numbers running gang, and it was rumored that Bert was an enforcer for them."

"Oh, that's an interesting bit of information," Lee said as he took a seat beside Miranda.

"Harry, do you mind me asking how old you are?"

"No, not at all. I'm eighty years old. For your information Lee, I wasn't friends with Bert. I only knew of him because of the murder. After he was killed I learned of his reputation as a drinker and bar hopper. I do know that no family claimed Bert's body."

Lee nodded to Miranda.

"His body was held in the morgue for a couple of weeks and the city buried him in a pauper's grave. That's about all I know." Harry concluded with a sigh.

"How do you know no one claimed his body?"

"A friend of mine in the department told me."

"Okay, one more question for you, Harry. Did you know of a man named Will Pink, involved in a traffic accident the night of the murder?"

"No, I never heard of him."

"If I have any more questions, can I call you?"

"Yes, my number is 987-969-7150. Call me anytime."

"Thank you, Harry, you've been helpful. Bye." Lee hung up.

CHAPTER 31

Present Day

"I'm not sure I believe what Harry said," Lee mused. "Can we check to see if he was on the police force and if he's still alive? That guy could've been anybody calling to see what information we've come up with. When he said he was good friends with this Hank, I started to question what he said about everything." He stood staring out the window, at the light snow falling, melting as fast it landed on the ground.

"What about when he said he knew the Blisses, then in the middle of the sentence said he didn't know them?"

"Kid, it's getting late and I'm tired, it's been one busy day.

With this much interest I can't wait to see who contacts us tomorrow."

He moved toward Miranda, put his arms around her and nudged her body against his. Her cheeks were glowing. Her lips were an inch away from his. He could smell her lipstick.

"I agree, Lee, and I'm going to bed as well. As soon as you let go of me." Pushing him away she turned to walk up the steps.

"Don't pull away, Miranda."

"Get that out of your head, Lee. It isn't going to happen, at least not tonight."

"Oh, so you're leaving me hope."

"No, not at all. I'm only trying to let you down in a gentle way, but I'm a woman and you never know, I might change my mind at any time. Good night, Lee."

Lee was left standing in the room with the exhilarating smell of her perfume penetrating his mind.

Alone in his room he was thinking about Miranda and how beautiful and distant she was. Or was it all an act? Maybe she'd had her heart broken and didn't want to take a chance again. He walked over to the sliding door and stood staring at the outline of the tall mountains in the distance against the clear star filled sky. He shivered at the eerie look of daylight from the moon as it lit the expansive manicured lawn back to the black forest, causing the hair on the back of his neck to stand up. A quick glance at his watch told him it was midnight. Yawning, he took one last look at the night scene.

What's that? He was trying to get a better look with his eyes riveted on what he thought was a tall figure stepping out of the tree line.

He moved to the other door that didn't have a screen. The figure looked like a man walking in the direction of the house. He rubbed his eyes. *Focus, eyes, focus.* Maybe it was a deer, but it looked like a man picking his way toward the house. With the lights off in his room the figure couldn't see him.

There, he moved again. It was a man, now he was running toward the house.

Lee stepped back into the shadows of the room, his eyes followed the interloper up the steps. The ski mask only revealed the nose, eyes, and mouth. He pulled on the door handle, but it didn't budge. When he looked down to jimmy the lock, Lee made his move to the door. The burglar must have caught the movement in his peripheral vision and glanced up.

Lee grabbed for the door, at the same time flipping the outside light on. In one powerful jerk, he opened the door with such force it almost broke the glass. Lee bounded onto the deck but the intruder was already halfway to the woods.

Running hard and fast in pursuit he was soon out of breath.

Ten feet away from the intruder his lungs were burning. Stopping he bent over, resting his hands on his knees and sucking air.

His eyes were riveted on the man who stopped suddenly at the edge of the woods. On instinct, Lee started to run for him again. The stranger smiled and disappeared into the black forest. By the time he reached the woods his chest was aching and his heart was racing. Sweat was rolling down his face. He stopped at the entrance to the woods staring, not knowing the path that the intruder seemed to know so well. Lee thought he might be standing in there looking back with a smirk on his face. As Lee turned to walk back to the house he saw a light on upstairs in the mansion. He had a quick glimpse of Miranda's black outline standing at the window, then she disappeared.

Lee walked back toward the house, he paused to look up and saw Miranda standing in his doorway, then she moved out onto the deck.

"Lee, what's going on? I heard all this noise, then I saw you running toward the woods."

"We had another visitor. It happened that I couldn't sLeep and as I stood in the dark looking out at the night I saw this figure come out of the woods. He came up to my door and tried to open it. When I jerked the door open he took off like a speed racer. I chased him to the edge of the woods, where I stopped, thinking it would be foolish to follow him into the darkness."

"Did you get a look at his face?"

"Oh, yes he had on a ski mask and was dressed like a ninja.

But I got a good look at his teeth and his eyes. A lot of help that will be. He seemed to be familiar with the woods. He didn't hesitate to run into them."

"Well," Miranda said, "you never know."

"But he made one mistake," Lee said.

"What was that?"

He held up a set of keys and smiled.

CHAPTER 32

Present Day

"This guy is persistent," Lee said, "if nothing else."

"Yes, he is, if it's the same person. Lee, what kind of vehicle do you think the keys fit?"

"I don't know, but he must have had a long walk back to where he came from."

Lee rolled the keys around in his hand thinking about who this person might be, while trying to figure out what kind of vehicle the key would fit.

"There's no symbol on the key chain."

"Hopefully when we go out there in the morning the vehicle will still be there, but if I were him, I'd get it out tonight. He must have someone working with him. The question is, who and why do they want the letters? I'm assuming the letters. What else could it be?" Miranda said.

"Come on, Kid, we should try to get some sLeep. We have another busy day ahead." Lee put his arm around Miranda's tiny waist as they walked up the steps leading into his room. He stopped, and turned toward Miranda. "Kid, will you be okay? I mean, you're not afraid to go back to bed by yourself, are you?"

Miranda backed up a couple of steps with a sLeepy smile.

"Lee, you wouldn't be trying to take advantage of a girl at a time like this, would you?"

Lee moved toward her and wrapped his arms around her warm body. She didn't resist. He stared into her eyes. His mouth was an inch from hers. He closed his eyes as the sweet smell of her perfume filled his mind. In that moment nothing else mattered. It was exhilarating. His heart started to race when her soft voice broke the silence.

"Not tonight, Lee." She pushed him away with a gentle touch, jolting him back to reality.

He smiled, and touched the tip of her nose with his finger. "Hey, you can't blame a guy for trying." He watched as she walked away toward the stairs, and listened for the faint sound of her bedroom door closing.

CHAPTER 33

Present Day

In the morning Lee and Miranda walked the winding path through the dense forest behind the mansion. After adjusting their eyes to the bright sunlight as they stepped out of the darkness onto the power line road. It wasn't hard to find the tire tracks, but no vehicle.

"Either he had a second set of keys," Lee said, "or he had someone come and tow it away."

"Four wheeler tracks, the same type of vehicle they used the last time. The local kids must have started using this as a path through the woods for riding," Miranda said.

Lee stood silent for a moment. "Come on, Kid, let's get back."

At the house, Miranda was on the computer while Lee was thinking through what they had learned.

"Dr. Seller is in a nursing home suffering from the late stages of Alzheimer's disease. Mrs. Jones, the state psychologist, died twenty years ago. From the old newspaper accounts, it looks like Lilly was in and out of the mental hospital for the first three years after Bert's murder." Miranda paused, looking Lee.

"Miranda, how did you know she was in and out of the hospital?"

"In that time period, the newspapers printed anything just to fill space. So every day they would send a cub reporter to all the hospitals to find out who was admitted and discharged that day, printing it as news."

"Do you remember when the police chief told us they had information that the person who committed the murder moved to Florida?" Lee said.

"Where did Lilly die? In Florida!" Miranda said as she turned toward Lee. "Could she be the murderer? Or was it a coincidence that she moved to Florida? Or maybe she's the one who wrote the name on the wall in the hotel, then moved to Florida out of fear for her life. Lee, I think you might be onto something with that theory."

"Don't forget, Miranda, there is one more person who moved to Florida—Robert Mason. We can't be absent minded about him. The questions are all good ones. I hope we can find the answers."

"Lee, I'm going to get some fresh air by taking a stroll down to the mailbox. Would you like to stretch your legs?"

"Sure, why not? I'll get the door, ladies first," he said, holding the front door open.

Miranda paused on the porch for a couple of seconds, looking around.

"Is something wrong? Why did you stop?"

"I always try to pause out here to remember when I didn't have this million-dollar view of the mountains."

"That it is, and you can enjoy it anytime you have the desire by stepping out on your front porch. You should turn this place into a bed and breakfast."

"Yeah, right on, Lee. I'll get to work on that."

Lee shrugged and smiled.

They strolled down the long driveway until they reached the mailbox.

"Huh, look at this, Lee. A letter postmarked from Bridgetown. No return address on it."

When Miranda removed the letter from the envelope and unfolded it, a newspaper clipping fell out and drifted to the ground before she could catch it. Lee plucked it from the ground and read it without looking in her direction.

"Huh, it's an obituary for Charles L. Darrell. Didn't Ridgeway say he stopped to visit the family on his way to Maine? You said you didn't know him."

She was so engrossed reading the letter that she didn't hear what he was saying. "Lee, listen to this. This obituary appeared in the *Bridgetown Mirror* on February 21. This same man openly and willingly stated that he killed Bert Grayson. Bert Grayson was dating his mother, who ran the local brothel in Bridgetown. He claimed Grayson abused and beat her. Several years later Darrell went to prison for manslaughter after the death of his wife, who died while being tied up during rough sex. While Darrell was in prison he told a fellow prisoner that he killed Bert Grayson for beating up his mother." Miranda pointed to the letter. "Look, no signature and no return address."

"Listen, Kid, right now I don't know what to say, other than what we're learning is amazing. I've never been involved in a research project with so many twists. But it sounds like Darrell was one mean guy."

On the walk back to the house they discussed how to proceed.

"If Darrell killed his wife, the old newspapers will have the information on the murder and the trial," Lee said.

Back at the house, Miranda searched through old newspapers online. "Let me see. Here's the newspaper account of Darrell's murder trial in August 1977. This is interesting. They have it tucked away on page three."

Miranda read the article out loud.

"Charles L. Darrell, 41, of Wilson Township. The former director of the Bridgetown Mobile Emergency Department was sentenced yesterday to seven years in prison for involuntary manslaughter in the death by strangulation of his nineteen-year-old wife, Ruth C. Darrell. Darrell was found guilty last week of strangling his wife in their mobile home while having rough sex, according to prosecutors."

"This is one maniacal dude," Lee said. "And it sounds like he was someone important in Bridgetown at the time of the murder."

"So, why did the person who mailed the letter wait until Darrell died to reveal such important information? Why didn't he go to the police?"

"Here's what I think, Kid. If he murdered Bert for roughing up his mother and got away with it, then murdered his wife and spent only seven years in prison, I'd be afraid of him. But once he's dead, the threat is gone. The newspapers wrote an article about him above his obituary. In it, they said he was the head accountant for the city, so he had power." Lee shook his head. "Look at the picture the newspapers published of him when he murdered his wife. He doesn't look anything like the composite picture of the man who left the bar with Bert the night he was murdered."

"The killers are beginning to line up," Miranda said.

"Okay, Kid, so how many people do we have now who we think might have killed Bert?"

"So far there are too many," Miranda said.

The doorbell rang, and she went to open it. "Willow, what brings you out this way? Come in. It's cold out there. Have a seat in the living room."

Lee stood and smiled at Willow as she strolled into the living room, glancing over her shoulder at Lee.

"Thank you, Miranda. Sorry to come over without calling."

"Oh, that's okay, Willow. When has that ever stopped you?"

"Now Miranda, be nice. I know you love me."

"You're right, Willow. Sit. Sorry I missed our session. I had some important things to take care of. Willow, this is my friend Lee. He's helping me with the investigation I told you girls about."

"Hello, Lee, it's nice to meet you. Miranda keeps all her men to herself."

"Nice to meet you, Willow. Miranda's a busy girl," he said as he winked at Miranda and chuckled to himself.

"Miranda, I decided to come to see you after running into Wilma Wythe yesterday at the coffee house. We were discussing the Grayson murder and you won't believe what she told me."

As Willow talked, she used a lot of hand gestures.

"Oh, I can't wait to hear this," Miranda said.

"Wilma told me, and I will try to use her exact words," she said while crossing one leg over her knee before continuing. "She said she has been haunted by your ad in the newspaper."

"Oh, haunted, that's an unusual choice of words, go on," Miranda said.

"Well, Miranda, that's exactly what I said to her and this is what she said to me. She said I wasn't to dare to tell anyone what she was going to tell me. So I promised her I wouldn't, but you're different—I can tell you."

Lee grinned at Miranda.

"What did she say?" Miranda said as she shot Lee a cool stare.

"She said her father was a fifth-grade teacher at the Bridgetown Elementary School in 1962. The day after the murder of Bert Grayson he told her that one of his students, a boy, came into class excited because he said his uncle who lived with them had come home last night covered with blood, demanding money from the boy's mom and dad and saying he had to get out of town in hurry." Willow paused, taking a deep breath.

"What was her father's name?" Miranda said.

"James Wythe."

"Did he tell the police what happened?"

"Well," she said, "that's where the problem starts. He didn't tell the police because he didn't want to get involved with the Grayson murder."

"What was the boy's name?"

"She said every time she would ask her dad the same question, he would become so upset she had to stop. Her dad passed away in 1996, never telling her the boy's name. I questioned her to see if she had the class logbook with the names of the students from that fifth grade class. She said her mom packed all his belongings into bags and boxes and stored it in the third bedroom, where it stayed for about two years until she donated everything to the Salvation Army." Willow winked at Lee, he winked back.

"Where's her mom now? I would like to talk with her, to see what she remembers about the murder, or how I could find the name of the boy." Miranda said.

"Her mom has since passed away. I asked her the same question. She didn't know how I could find the boy's name or the list of students from her dad's class. She said it was a relief to get this out in the open." Willow stood.

"So, I wonder why she didn't tell me this herself, it was my ad in the newspaper."

"She told me this when we ran into each other in the coffee shop. We decided to share a table since we were both alone.

When we sat down Wilma mentioned she had been seeing your ad in the newspaper so it was natural to start discussing the Grayson murder."

"I see, thanks, Willow."

"Miranda, will you be in class tomorrow?"

"I don't know. We're pretty busy with this investigation. I may not be back until we're finished, however long that takes," Miranda said as she walked Willow to the door.

Willow turned in Lee's direction, "Bye, Lee. It was nice to meet you. Hope to see you again soon."

"Bye, Willow, have a great day," Lee said as he winked at her.

Miranda closed the door, moving into the computer room, Lee followed close behind.

"Wow, Lee, do you believe what people are telling us?"

"Can we believe what she said?"

"If it were anyone but Willow, I wouldn't believe it. She might seem a little wacky, but she's rock solid. I've never known her to tell a lie."

"We have to investigate everything these people are telling us. We've collected a big bowl of puzzle pieces, now is the time to move each one around to see if any of them fit together," Lee said as he took a seat next to Miranda.

"It looks like her dad did work at Bridgetown elementary," Miranda said.

"Miranda, would you call the elementary school and ask them to give us the classroom log of the boys that were in Mr. Wythe's class."

She called the school offices. "Hello, I'd like to get a copy of the class roster for all the boys listed at Bridgetown Elementary fifth grade class for February 1962."

"One moment please."

There were a couple of minutes of waiting before another voice came on the line. "Hello, what do you want to do with the information?"

"We're conducting research and may use the information in a book we might write about Bridgetown's history," Miranda said.

"I'm afraid that's private information, we're not allowed to give it out to the general public."

"But I'm not the general public, I'm a researcher and writer."

"I'm sorry miss, I can't give you that information."

"Thank you anyway," Miranda said, and hung up. "They won't give out that information. They said it was part of the privacy act."

"Do they list the classroom assignments in the newspapers here? They did when I was a kid growing up," he said.

"Great idea, Lee. Let me look. They would've published the classroom listings in August of that year."

Miranda pulled up the old newspaper clippings online.

"Here it is. Bridgetown Elementary." She read for a minute. "Ha, can you believe it? A new Bridgetown Elementary School was built and put into service that year. The students were assigned to their classrooms as they came into the school the first day. Can you believe that?"

"Listen, Kid, if that boy was related to Darrell, there has to be a way to get hold of the information." Lee nodded at Miranda. She stopped working on the computer and started to tap her fingers on the desk.

CHAPTER 34

Present Day

"None of this makes any sense. It's like Lilly has sucked us into her crazy world and we're living inside the letters, while the characters are coming out of the past itching to tell what they know. I'm not complaining about the response to the ad.

I'm trying to piece together all this information coming at us." Lee looked perplexed as he stood and started to pace.

"Lee, why don't we switch channels and look at something else."

"Okay, that sounds good to me. Kid, the one big question I have stored in the back of my head nagging at me is why does Lilly keep saying she was responsible for Bert's death? It doesn't make sense unless she was somehow involved with the murder."

"Yes, I agree. It makes no sense at all. Those same thoughts keep rolling around in my head." Miranda returned to the computer.

"Here's something interesting, Lee. In her letters, Lilly said Art Cassel died out of state. She thought it had to do with Bert's murder. After reading that nugget of information

I called Jane, to question her about Cassel. I wanted to know who he was and his relationship to Bert. She said they grew up together and he was one of Bert's best friends. He came to the funeral home the night of Bert's viewing. As he stood at the casket looking down at Bert, Jane walked across the room, stopping at his side. He put his hand on hers before saying, 'Jane I'm going to be next.' Jane asked him why he would say such a thing, and he repeated it. 'I'm going to be next.' Then he walked out of the funeral home. Jane said a couple of months later they found him dead of acute alcohol poisoning in Maryland."

"You have to drink a lot of booze to die from too much," Lee said.

CHAPTER 35

Present Day

When people are forced by fate to expose their secrets and lies, how do they retrofit them into today's time continuum? How do they walk out of the past, present their side of the story and make it believable? Time doesn't stop for anyone. How would someone go back into the past to search for the truth about a secret many men and women willingly or unwillingly took to their graves? The problems start when the secret begins to leak like a broken faucet, drip by drip. The lies slowly ooze out of the control of the people who were alive some fifty years later and had been entrusted with the secret.

They could no longer keep it bottled up inside. It devoured first their hearts, then their minds, forcing their souls to seek relief.

All it took was one seeker, Lee Perkins, to doggedly pursue the truth, scratching and picking the encrustations from the memories of the people who tried to forget and protect. When the scabs were at last jerked off, reality began to bubble up to the top. Then, like a volcano, the veracity of it all exploded, covering each of them with the pus and blood of their secrets and lies. Exposing their secrets at last, they've become unable to conceal the truth of their actions any longer.

***

"We should take a break," Miranda said, "and have dinner. It's getting late and I don't like to eat after six. I don't sLeep well if I eat much later."

"That's okay with me. I like to eat anytime."

Her phone chirped. "Hello, this is Miranda." She hit the speakerphone.

"Meet me at the Coffee Grind in Bridgetown tonight at eight," a voice said. "Bring the letters and leave the tall guy at home. I'll make you an offer for the letters that you won't be able to refuse." The man hung up.

Lee looked at Miranda. "You're not going alone, Kid. Don't even consider it. It's four o'clock now. We should eat, then scout out the coffee house before tonight."

"I know the Coffee Grind," Miranda said. "We were just there yesterday morning."

"I know, but I don't remember how the inside was laid out. I need to find a place to hide so I can watch you while waiting for this guy. If I remember right, it was in a bad part of town."

"I've always felt safe going there. I know it looks pretty bad from the outside, but you have to admit how nice it was inside."

"Let's get going, we need all the time we can get. This could be dangerous for you tonight. I don't like it."

"Don't worry. I'm good at taking care of myself. Don't forget,

I was a special ops agent before going into the research end."

"Oh, I do remember, but that was a long time ago."

"What are you saying, I'm too old for this stuff now?"

"Well, you're a woman. I feel the need to protect you. Your skills might have gotten rusty."

"Oh, Lee, you always had a way with words. No one ever accused you of having a silver tongue, did they?"

He winked at Miranda as they moved to the garage.

CHAPTER 36

Present Day

Lee parked the car in the only vacant space in front of the dingy brick building. The Coffee Grind was well past its prime. There had to be a good reason the owners let the outside look so run-down. He wondered what they were hiding, perhaps certain people who didn't want to be seen from the street.

Lee held the door open for Miranda. The aroma of strong coffee and lattes filled the air. Soft music from the live band mingled with people talking and laughing. Lee scanned the numerous tables and booths spaced around the room. There was a large section separated from the main floor by a latticework wall, the tables were empty and the lights were off.

"This place has all age groups," Lee said.

"Yes, look at the tall husky guy standing beside the coffee barista. They appear to be in deep conversation with a couple of Bridgetown's finest perched on the stools at the counter,"

Miranda said.

"Did you see them turn and look at us when we opened the door?" Lee said.

"I wouldn't have noticed if they hadn't stared at us all the way to the table."

"Let's sit over here," Lee said, holding the chair at a table in the middle of the coffee shop. "I want to make sure you're in the safest place in the room."

"Good thinking, Lee."

"Here's my plan. Tonight, I'll come in early, get a coffee, and find a seat behind the latticework where I can see you, but won't be seen. You come in about 7:45, and sit at this table with your back to me so I can watch whoever you're going to meet."

"But what if this table is taken?"

"For heaven's sake, let me worry about that." He glanced at his watch.

"It's almost six o'clock, so we have an hour and a half to get ready. Let's head back to your house, and since we're in the area I would like to stop where the murder took place, or should I say Bert's body was found. I already programmed it into my GPS."

"Sure, Lee, it's just around the block. That place has changed a lot in fifty years, all the old shacks that stood on Chestnut Avenue have been replaced by a parking lot. It's still daylight so you'll get a good sense of the area."

Lee turned right off Chestnut Avenue then a quick left onto a blacktop street. He pulled the car into a parking space facing a row of ramshackle narrow houses behind a chain-link fence.

"This is it?" Lee said.

"There in front of you is the alley behind 30 Chestnut Avenue."

"I thought the newspaper said there was a wooden fence?"

"Yes, it did, and there was one there then, it has since been replaced with that chain-link fence in front of you."

"So, we're looking at the exact spot were Bert's body was found."

"Yes, right there. Lee, try to picture in your mind a mud-rutted alley, an old wooden fence and this parking lot a mirror image of the ramshackle houses you're looking at on the other side of that chain link barrier."

Lee studied the scene for a few minutes from the car. "I need to get out of the car," he said.

"I'll stay here." She watched him as he walked up and down the now blacktop-street, and what used to be a dark, mud-rutted alley. He came back to the car.

"Amazing, isn't it Kid, the contrast. It's as if on the other side of the fence time has forgotten them and they're still living in the 1960s, while just the opposite is true here on Chestnut Avenue where they've moved into today's world."

"Yes, it is. We should get going, Lee. We have plans to make before our meeting tonight."

CHAPTER 37

Present Day

They walked into the computer room, where Miranda noticed she had another e-mail waiting for her.

"Look at this, Lee. It's from a reporter at the *Bridgetown Mirror*." She read it out loud.

> *Hello, I saw your advertisement in today's newspaper and it sparked my interest. My name is Glen Roberts. I've been a reporter at the Mirror since 1979. I'd never heard of the name Big Bert Grayson, but I asked my co-worker. He remembered the newsroom talk from the past about Grayson's murder. Apparently, it occurred not too far from the Mirror's downtown location. The Mirror has since moved out of downtown.*
>
> *Our archives here at the Mirror have information published at the time of the murder, plus an advertisement that was later published, offering a $10,000 reward, but not for any police officer or public official.*

It all sounds interesting to me. I'm wondering if there might be a story there, and what you may have learned.

Glen

"Oh, sure. Does he think we're going to share what we've learned with him?" Miranda said.

"I guess a lot of people would share what they've learned, eager to tell someone all the interesting and surprising facts they've uncovered, hoping to get their name in the paper. But we aren't those people."

Lee stood in front of Miranda with his arms crossed. "Listen, Kid, I need a way to hear what this person you're going to meet is saying to you."

Miranda got up from her chair, moved to a door in the computer room, and opened it.

"Come in here, I can solve that problem real easy."

When she bent over rummaging through some boxes, he couldn't help but notice how slim and sexy she looked.

"Okay, Lee, that's enough. I can feel your eyes ogling me."

"Who, me? I don't know what you're talking about. But you are a beautiful woman."

Lee was just about to reach out and put his arms around her when she stood, turned around, and handed him an earpiece while putting one into her ear.

"Put that bud in your ear, go outside, and tell me if you can hear me talking."

"The cool air will be refreshing." He stood on the front porch.

"Hey, Lee, can you hear me?"

"Loud and clear, so these should do the trick."

On the way back into the house he spied an envelope lying on the porch beside the front door and snatched it up. He handed it to Miranda when he got back into the computer room.

"You got mail, Kid. This was lying on the front porch beside the door."

"Mmm," she said as she read the return address. "I don't know a Tommy Carson."

Miranda read the letter and handed it to Lee, who read it out loud.

> *Miranda, I have been seeing your ads in the newspaper. I wonder why you want this information from so long ago. What is your connection to this murder? I happen to know that there have been many stories and rumors told over the years. I'm sure that people meant well, but everyone remembers things differently, especially after fifty years. I would love to hear some of what you've been told. You see, Miranda, I'm the person who found Big Bert's body that night in the alley, and I have to think hard to remember what I know. If you're interested in talking to me, meet me at seven o'clock tomorrow morning at the Coffee Grind in Bridgetown. Tommy.*

Lee placed the letter on the desk and turned to Miranda.

"You'd think the Coffee Grind was the only coffee house in town."

"Well, it is."

"We're certainly giving them our share of business this week," Lee said. "That should be an interesting meeting tomorrow morning, but for now we need to concentrate on our meeting tonight."

"Let's get going," Miranda said. "We don't want to be late."

They pulled into an empty space in front of the coffee house.

"Hey, Kid, did you remember to grab the phony letters?"

"Yes, I'm ready for whatever comes my way. Try not to forget to put your earpiece in."

"I'm ready for this, Miranda. You need to concentrate on your part. Stay in the car until 7:45. I'm going in now. Don't forget to sit where we planned."

"I'll sit at the right table if it's empty when I come in."

"Oh, don't worry, I'll take care of that."

With a steaming cup of coffee in one hand, he dropped a reserved sign on Miranda's table, then walked to the back of the room. Behind the latticework wall he found a chair with a good view of the room and Miranda's table. At the right time, Miranda walked in, went to the bar and ordered a cup of coffee.

"We'll bring your coffee out to you," the barista said.

"Okay, thanks."

Lee watched Miranda as she turned around, moving her head from side to side. "What are you looking for," he whispered in her earpiece.

"I was looking at how full the room is," she whispered. "Oh, good, the table is empty."

She walked to the table, picked up the reserved sign, put it in her pocket, and smiled.

"Good work, Lee."

"I told you I'd take care of it."

He saw her glance at the latticework wall.

She sat in the chair at the table facing the door. It was 8 P.M. The husky guy behind the coffee bar walked over, set her coffee on the table and slipped a piece of folded paper under her cup. She glanced up.

"The man sitting at that table over there . . ." He pointed to the back corner where an older gray-haired man was sitting. "Told me to give you this note."

He turned, crossed the floor and returned to his place behind the bar. Miranda glanced in the direction of a well-dressed elderly man sitting alone, leaning on his cane and making eye contact with her. She couldn't help but notice how handsome he was for a gentlemen who appeared to be in his eighties or older. Nodding at him, she unfolded the note, reading it loud enough that Lee could hear.

"I'm glad to see you came alone, walk over here and take a seat at the table with me. I hope you brought the letters." She paused for a moment, "Lee, what am I going to do now?"

"I'll move to another seat back here where I can see you.

Don't forget, I can hear everything that's said, so you'll be okay. Don't worry, I have your back."

"Lee, it was hard for me to catch my breath for a few seconds.

I think I was starting to panic, but it's going away now."

Miranda looked up at the man again. This time, he tipped his hat, smiling at her. She picked up her coffee and made her way over to his table.

"Thank you for coming, Miranda, please have a seat. I see you already have coffee."

She placed her cup on the table and took a seat, holding the man's eye contact as she talked. "Coffee is one of my favorite drinks, it has lots of antioxidants that are good for you and helps fight aging."

"My dear, you are stunningly beautiful. You make me wish I were twenty years younger, but that is for another time. The only thing coffee does for me anymore is keep me up at night. Insomnia, I think, or maybe old age."

"So who are you, and why do you want these letters?"

"We will get to that in a minute, but first I want to see the letters."

"Oh, no, that isn't going to happen until you tell me why you want them."

"Good girl," Lee said.

"Okay, I'm a local historian. I tried to buy the rights to the letters from Lillian after she wrote them many years ago, but she wouldn't sell them to me. She wanted nothing to do with me back then."

"You're Robert Mason?"

"Yes. I think I had Lillian convinced to sell me half of the rights until old piano legs Sara Dowell stuck her nose in telling Lillian not to deal with me at any price. Both of them are dead now.

"To answer your question. Fifty years ago I wrote an exposé on the Conn Railroad, exposing to the world the iron fisted control they had over their employees and the people of Bridgetown. Lillian had all the information on the police department as well as the corruption of the government officials running the town. She intended to write and publish a book revealing their great cover-up of the truth. I wanted to add what I knew to what Lillian knew and clean up this town, but Lillian didn't trust me."

"Why didn't she trust you?"

"I think it all goes back to Sara. She convinced Lillian not to have an alliance with me. Sara was my cousin, and we never got along. I think she was jealous of my success."

"That sounds like a good story, Robert, but I'm not buying it."

"Good girl. Keep him talking."

"There are a lot of incriminating statements in those letters.

I know the people who want them burned so no one can read them. I want to prevent that so I can finish my book."

Miranda pointed her finger at Robert. "Finish the book or continue to keep the truth hidden? Who are these people who want the letters burned?"

"You do not understand what you are getting involved with, missy." His eyes were beginning to narrow and turn cold.

"Wow. But you just said you wanted to finish the book Lillian started."

He leaned back in his chair in a simpering manner. "I am, but it will be different to what she would have written. Mine will make sense and clear up all the crazy things Lillian said."

"So, Robert, who is backing you?"

"Good question, Kid. Keep him talking," Lee said.

"I do not know what you mean. I am independently wealthy.

I do not need a backer. I own my own satellite company worth billions." He leaned forward, raising his eyebrows while holding her eye contact.

"Kid, maybe he's the one spying on us."

"Now that we have that settled, I would like to get back to the book and the letters," Robert said.

"Who said it was settled? Have you been using your satellites to watch us and listen to everything we were talking about? We could sense we were being spied on by someone, but we didn't know who or why."

"My company builds and sells satellites to anyone who has the money. I don't know what they do with them, that is their business. I have sold them to businesses and people living in this area."

"Well that may be, but someone is watching and listening to everything we say and do. If it isn't you, then who?"

"I didn't ask you here to talk about my satellite business. Now I would like to get back to the letters and the book."

"Wow, is he avoiding the question or what?" Lee said.

"My book will be far better than the one Lillian would have written. Lillian was bitter and full of hate for her husband and men in general," Robert said.

Miranda gestured with her arms. "Oh, come on can't you do better than that? Why is it when a man is opposed by a woman he accuses her of being filled with hate for all men? That's what a man says when he's cornered, and Robert, that isn't what I got from her letters. I'm not so sure Lillian would have wanted you to have them. There has to be a reason she didn't give them to you back then. I don't know what it was, but I think for right now I'll keep them. There's no deal. Not now, maybe not ever."

"You tell that old goat, Kid," Lee said.

"But Miranda, I am willing to give you twenty thousand dollars for them."

"Wow, this guy wants them in a bad way," Lee said.

"I don't think so." Miranda's eyes narrowed into a glaring stare.

Robert slammed his fist on the tabletop. Heads turned in their direction. She watched his handsome face transform into an ugly, twisted mass of wrinkles. The cane in his hand shook under his uncontrollable anger. What Miranda saw next engulfed her entire body with fear as his eyes were flooded with a cold, distant, blinding, intensity. She had seen that look only one other time as an FBI agent, in the eyes of a cold-blooded killer just before she shot him to death. She shook her head, trying to bring her thinking back to the present.

"You will change your mind Miss Witherspoon, and when you do you will sell them to me."

"I will? Why?"

"I have my ways, young lady. You will come around to see things my way. You can't continue to suppress the truth." He paused, started to chuckle, and shake his head in uncontrollable frustration.

"Mr. Mason, that sounds like a threat. Are you the one sending people to break into my home looking for what could only be the letters? While we were in the cemetery the other day someone shot at us. Did you have anything to do with that?"

"Oh. I don't know anything about a shooting. I do know that someone other than me wants the letters. I don't know the other people but I know of them. I would suggest that you be extremely careful. Watch your back. I am not the kind of person to come at you from behind. I will face you straight on and tell you what I want, no matter how it looks, in just the same way I am doing now. I guess you could say I have no shame. Listen to me, Miss Witherspoon. I am too old to be concerned with what people think of me. Heck, I could die tonight in my sLeep and this would all be for naught. Watch your back, Miss Witherspoon, and by all means enjoy the rest of the evening."

Robert smiled, and tipped his broad-brimmed hat at Miranda as he got up, and wobbled on his cane to the door. When Miranda turned around in her chair, Lee was standing by her side.

"What do you make of that, Kid?"

"He wasn't surprised someone else was trying to get the letters, or he's a good actor. I believed him, but I don't know what to make of any of this. Did he threaten me? I'm not sure."

"It sounded like it to me. Kid, I think the bigger question is who else is trying to get the letters and why? We must be missing something in them."

CHAPTER 38

Present Day

At 7:00 A.M. the next morning Lee and Miranda sat at a corner table in the Coffee Grind watching each man who walked through the door. At five minutes past an older man with thinning gray hair opened the door and took one look around the room before walking over to Lee, sticking out his hand. Lee returned the gesture.

"I'm Tommy." He shook Miranda's hand and sat in the chair across from her.

"How could you know who we were?" Lee said.

"Oh, that's easy, you're the only strangers in here. I know all the regulars."

"I guess I should have known," Lee said.

"Tommy," Miranda said, "thank you for contacting us. We're anxious to hear what you have to say. Would you mind if I record our conversation?"

"No, I don't, but let me get a cup of coffee before we begin."

"Oh no, let me get it for you, Tommy," Lee said. "What do you want?"

"That's kind of you, Lee. I'll have a large regular black."

While Lee was getting the coffee, Miranda set up her phone to record everyone's conversation.

"Here you are, steamy hot and black."

"Thanks, Lee."

"Anytime you're ready to begin talking, go ahead," Miranda said.

"You two might be digging around in something that will get you hurt."

"Why would you say something like that?" Lee said.

"Well, for certain I wondered why your ads were running after all this time. It's been over fifty years, but there are still a lot of people in town who remember the Grayson murder and may have had some involvement with it."

"Tommy," Miranda said, "why don't you tell us what you want us to know?"

"Okay, that sounds good to me."

Miranda pushed the phone in front of Tommy.

"I was nineteen when this all took place. My girlfriend, now my wife of forty-nine years, and I were returning from the dance. After walking her home, I hurried down the street and into the alley. Mom never liked it when I was late. The alley was the sidewalk to my house at 32 Chestnut Avenue. I don't know why, but the front door to all the houses fronted onto Chestnut Avenue except ours, which fronted into the alley." He paused to sip his coffee.

"About ten o'clock that night the sky let loose with a heavy wet snow. By the time we were on our way home there was about six inches on the ground. The only light in the alley was from the moonlight reflecting off the new fallen snow."

"Excuse me, Tommy, but didn't the newspapers say a couple of kids found the body on the way home from roller skating?"

"Yes, they published that story to protect me. I'll get to that later." Tommy shifted in his chair and smiled at Miranda.

"As I was saying, halfway down the alley by Switzer's fence– it was called that because in those days there was a tall wooden fence that ran the length of the alley that Mr. Switzer erected the year before - I saw what looked like a man lying in the snow against the fence. I thought it was my friend Butch.

"He was a big man, like Bert. He would get drunk, sit down or stretch out on the ground wherever he was at the time and fall asLeep. He only lived around the block. I figured he couldn't make it home."

"That is probably what I would've been thinking," Lee said.

"I thought about going over, giving him a good shake hoping he would wake up, then I would take him home. He was covered with snow. I was afraid he was going to freeze to death lying there. Then I thought maybe I shouldn't in case someone saw me and thought I was trying to shake down a drunk. So I decided to go home, tell mom what was going on and get my younger brother, who was sixteen, to help me take Butch home.

"I walked three doors down to my house. When I opened the door my mom and sisters were sitting around the kitchen table. Mom was drinking and listening to music. I went upstairs, found my brother, told him the story, and asked him to help me. He agreed. I never knew what kind of a mood he might be in, sometimes he was disagreeable and sometimes he was easy to get along with."

"Was it unusual for your mom and sisters to be up so late?" Lee asked.

"No, not at all. Mom worked late as a waitress at one of the bars and my sisters were doing homework. They were both straight A students. My dad left mom when I was five. She kept the family together and raised us the best way she knew how. She didn't like living in the shacks on Chestnut Avenue, but it was all she could afford. With five mouths to feed she did the best she could. When I was eleven I worked different jobs after school to help out. I wanted to quit school and get a full-time job, but mom wouldn't have it. She said she wanted all her kids to graduate from high school. She scrubbed floors and waited tables in the bars to make that a reality. So where was I? Oh, I remember." Tommy took a sip of coffee.

"My brother and I went downstairs to the kitchen and started digging around in the drawers until we found a couple of flashlights. After he put his coat on we told mom what we were doing, and she said okay.

"In the alley, we approached the spot where Butch had been stretched out, I could see he was sitting up against the fence, but when I flashed the light on him, I almost dropped it, and my mind couldn't take in the horrible scene in front of us. The light revealed a man sitting against the fence, blood splattered everywhere. My brother started to run back to the house."

"Didn't you see the blood the first time?" Lee asked.

"That's a good question and one I keep asking myself to this day. No, I didn't see any blood then." Tommy took a gulp of coffee.

"I could see a big slit in his neck, and his head was resting on his right shoulder. Needless to say, it wasn't my friend Butch, but I didn't know who it was. There were two boards kicked out of the fence beside the body. I'd like to say I was brave and acted calm, but I didn't. I ran as fast as my feet could carry me back to the house, almost passing my brother. He beat me to the door and was inside, spilling out a river of words to my mother and sisters, flailing his arms around wildly, telling of this ugly scene in the alley. After we finished the story, they said they didn't believe us, so all of them put on their coats, went out, and looked at the gruesome scene in the alley. Sorry, it still shakes me up a little telling about it." He took a big swig of coffee.

"We were too poor to have a telephone, so mom told me to run next door to the Rayburn's and tell them to call the police. When I knocked on the door, Mr. Rayburn answered, and I told him the story. He didn't believe me. So Mr. and Mrs. Rayburn and the three kids all came out to see for themselves. After viewing the scene they went back into the house and called the police.

"I was scared and ran back home, up to my bedroom, and locked the door. From my bedroom window I could see the flashing lights of the police cars and people milling around.

"About an hour later a Detective Marshall knocked on my bedroom door. I opened it and he stepped in questioning me, but the way he was going about it sounded like he thought I committed the murder. I told him what I thought, and he said they weren't thinking that way at all." Tommy paused, breathing deep.

"I was scared, not knowing if whoever committed the murder saw me in the alley, and was about to slit Bert's throat when I came along. Maybe he jumped through the hole in the fence waiting for me to pass by, and when he thought I was gone, he jumped back out, sat Bert up, slit his throat, and took off down the alley or disappeared into one of the houses on the street. I didn't know."

"So Tommy, you believe he was murdered between the time you went home and came back with your brother?" Lee said.

"I know when I walked down the alley the first time his body was stretched out in the snow against the fence, and when I came back with my brother he was sitting up against the fence with his throat slit and blood was everywhere."

"So no one heard anything out of the ordinary in the alley that night?" Lee said.

"My mom said she heard a car in the alley shortly before I came home, but she didn't pay any attention to it. She thought it was our neighbor Joe who owns a bowling alley and usually came home about that time of night." Tommy stretched his legs out and folded his arms across his chest.

"Back then I worked at a gas station on Chestnut Avenue.

Part of my job was to close the station each night at ten o'clock. I didn't have a car so I walked home. It wasn't that far, only a couple of blocks, but after the murder I was scared and ran all the way every night. I was afraid whoever killed Bert knew who I was and would wait to kill me some night."

"I can understand your thinking," Lee said.

"In the 1960's the Bridgetown police would stop every night to check the local businesses for unlocked doors or broken windows. They would drive past the station where I worked several times a night. Shortly after the murder they stopped by to chat. I told them that I was afraid to walk home at night and why. Ever after that until I took another job, the police would follow me home so I wouldn't be afraid."

"Wow, that was nice of them," Lee said.

"Yes, it was. I got married a year later, bought a car and took a job selling insurance. I never heard any more from the police until ten years later when I was living up the street at a different address. I heard a knock on the door and when I opened it there was a state policeman. He said he wanted to know what I knew about the murder. I told him everything I'm telling you. When I was finished, all he said was if I were you I would write that down, and put it away in a safe place for future reference. He walked out the door and I never heard any more about the murder until I saw your ad running in the newspaper."

"How odd that the state police would do that. Now I understand why you would be wondering who we really were. You must still live in some amount of fear, not knowing if the killer or killers are still out there, and might be looking for you," Lee said.

"I didn't know who you were or why you wanted the information. You could've been anybody. I didn't know if you were a real writer or had some other motive."

"I understand why you didn't want to come forward. Thank you, you've been more help than you can imagine," Lee said.

"Tommy," Miranda said, "let me put your mind at ease. We're not after you, we didn't know about you until now. I can't imagine living for over fifty years in fear for your life over something someone thought you might have seen."

"That's exactly what I was thinking. It's a relief to know you're not out to kill me."

"Did the state policeman give his name?" Lee asked.

"No, he just showed me his badge and flashed his ID card.

I don't remember the name on it."

"Tommy," Miranda said, "did you know a Hank Cranston?"

"He was one of my insurance customers. Once a month I would go to his bar up on Jew Hill to collect his insurance payment. In those days the customers didn't mail in their premiums. Instead, the insurance agent went to the customer, either their house or place of business and collected the money.

"Hank was always a nice guy, at least to me. I think he's still alive, living in the flats. They closed his bar down a couple of years ago.

"The police department hired a new police chief to clean up the town. It had become so bad that the state police would be called in to help with the crime situation. In fact, this wouldn't have been a safe place to come a few years ago. Hank had a long history of allowing numbers runners, enforcers and drug pushers to operate out of his bar. The new police chief forced the dirty detectives to retire and fired the beat cops involved in crimes and mafia cover-ups. They've closed down most of the known drug houses and mafia links in Bridgetown, so needless to say this is a much nicer town to live in now."

"Have you ever heard of Lillian Grace?" Lee said.

"No, I've never heard of her. Why?"

"She had a connection with Bert and lived here in town, that's all. Did you know any of the people linked to the mafia here in Bridgetown at that time?" Lee said.

"You know, it's funny that you would ask that. I had been working as an insurance agent for a couple of years, and as I said, I went in and out of the businesses collecting the premiums each month, and I would always run into Francis Como. He would be carrying a briefcase and visiting the same stores I did. I didn't think anything of it. I just figured he was selling something.

"Then one day I was in downtown Pittsburgh at an insurance convention. A couple of us guys were out on the sidewalk taking a smoke break. I looked up and there was Francis Como heading to the building across from ours. He was wearing a brown suit and carrying a briefcase. I said to the guys, 'Hey, do you believe this? We come to Pittsburgh and there crossing the street in front of us is Francis Como. What in the world is he doing in this town?'"

Tommy paused and waved at a couple of guys across the room. "Sorry. They're waiting for me. I have to wrap this up." He took a sip of coffee.

"Back to what I was saying. One of the guys spoke up and said, 'Tommy, don't you know? Francis is a numbers runner and enforcer for the mafia in Bridgetown. He no doubt is carrying the receipts from last week to the bosses.' When he said that, I nearly fell over on the sidewalk. I couldn't believe it. I had talked to Francis at different times, just chitchat. I would pass him in the street, stop and talk with him about the weather or how the day was going. He was always a nice guy." He waved at the guys across the room.

"In the 1980s he was convicted of killing a couple of people for not paying off their bets. After a long court trial they put him in prison for life and he's still there.

While he was in prison they used him as a witness against the rest of the mafia, but who am I? I didn't know about the mafia back then either. Francis would be about my age now, late sixties."

"Do you know what prison they put him in?" Lee said.

"I heard they just moved him into the state prison in Pennsylvania."

"Did you know if Bert was an enforcer for the mafia?" Lee said.

"I never knew Bert, but after the murder I heard some rumors that he was an enforcer, and he wasn't liked by a lot of people in Bridgetown. He was supposed to have beaten up a couple of women at a brothel one night when he was drunk, but as I said, they were just rumors."

After talking with Tommy for quite some time, Lee got the impression he had learned all he could from him.

Tommy said, "Oh, one more thing. Since your ads have been running in the papers it gives us something to talk about in the mornings here at the coffee shop. Let me know when the book comes out. I'd like to read it."

"I will. And thanks again for all the information."

"You're welcome."

Lee watched as Tommy picked up his coffee cup and walked over to the table where three other men his age were sitting. He pulled out a chair, sat down with them, and they began to talk.

Lee and Miranda walked out, got into their car, and went back to the mansion.

CHAPTER 39

Present Day

Human dramas and love stories have entwined themselves around our hearts and imaginations since the beginning of time. The letters as Lee read them revealed the struggles of a woman trapped in an era where women knew their place and men ruled with an iron fist, unquestioned in their motives or actions.

***

Back at the mansion, Miranda was working the computer to find out if Tommy was who he said he was.

"Tell me what you think of this. I think we need to develop Bridgetown eyes."

"What kind of eyes?" Miranda asked.

"There seems to be a lot of Bridgetown eyes and tell-tale heart syndrome around here," Lee said.

"Now what does all that mean?"

"We should start looking at Bridgetown, the way the people who have lived here since the early 1960s look at the town. They all seem to have the same plague. The tell-tale heart syndrome, you know, suspicion always haunts the guilty mind. They all seem to be hiding dark secrets concerning this murder. They all seem to want to free themselves by contacting us. They all seem to think that, once they tell us their story, the haunting will go away. They think it'll free their minds to move on to other things and free their consciences so they can begin to sLeep at night," Lee said.

"I've lived here all my life, and I don't think I have either of those things, a tell-tale-heart syndrome or Bridgetown eyes. You think if we develop them, we'll see what we've been missing so far?"

"Well, maybe," Lee said. "Right now it looks like there were a lot of people associated with this event. For example, all the men and women we've met in the last three days. It's unbelievable that this level of interest is still here, and they are all so sincere. Maybe, just maybe, we're developing Bridgetown eyes and aren't aware of it yet."

"I don't know. It sounds pretty crazy to me."

"Crazy or not, the people are coming out of the woodwork to tell us their stories," Lee said.

"Tommy seems to be who he said he was," Miranda said.

"Did you pull anything out of that computer about Francis Como?" Lee said. He stood, then walked to the living room window, the snow had stopped, but not before it covered the ground with a thin coat.

"Whew, you won't believe what I found out about him. He's still alive, by the way. According to the newspapers, he struck a deal with the D.A. to testify against the other mafia leaders so they could put them away. He was the only witness to the murders they'd committed. He testified that he was ordered by Joe Russo to murder a guy who wouldn't pay up a bet he lost. Francis told in explicit detail how he shot the guy in the stomach, then while the guy was dying on his own garage floor, Francis walked over to the guy's workbench, picked up a chainsaw, and fired it up. He cut the guy's legs off while the man was still alive. He said the man begged for mercy and he, Francis, said he just laughed at him. He then expressed how much he enjoyed murdering the man and watching him die a slow, painful death. He said it just gave him a rush. He's serving in the Pennsylvania State Pen for the criminally insane."

"I was thinking maybe we could go visit this Francis but it would probably be a waste of my time," Lee said.

Her phone chimed. "Hello, this is Miranda." She hit the speakerphone button.

"Hello, my name is Randy Johnson from Bridgetown. I'm a friend of Harry Winston, the retired Bridgetown policeman you talked to a few days ago. I'm also friends with Detective Jones, who was one of the detectives who worked the Bert Grayson murder. I'd like to know what you've learned so far."

"I'd like to ask you a question," Miranda said. "What would you like to tell me?"

"Okay, here it is. Detective Jones told me that the police always hold one thing back from the public in a murder case, one piece of information that only the police have knowledge of. The piece of information they held back, in this case, is there was a one-legged man with Bert the night he left the hot dog diner. He's the man they think killed Bert. He fled the state after the murder and settled in Ohio, and that's where he died."

"Excuse me, Randy," Miranda said, "are you saying they thought this guy killed Bert and they didn't go to Ohio to question him or bring him back to New York?"

"Well, I don't know, I wasn't told that information."

"Well, didn't you wonder about it when Jones dropped this little clue in your lap?"

"No, I figured the detectives knew what they were doing."

"Okay, go on with what you were saying."

"My second wife's grandmother ran a brothel in Bridgetown and she said she knew who killed Bert. One night when Bert came to the brothel he roughed up my second wife's grandmother while he was drunk, and she said it was this one-legged man who was in love with the grandmother and killed Bert for revenge for roughing her up that night. The one-legged man lost his leg in World War II when he stepped on a land mine. He was a white man."

"That's an interesting comment. Why would you say, he was a white man?"

"No specific reason. I just said he was white for clarification."

"What was the man's name?" Miranda said.

"I don't know, but my second wife knows his name."

"What was the grandmother's name?"

"I don't know that either."

"You mean," Miranda said, "you were married to this woman and didn't know the name of her grandmother?"

"My ex-wife and I didn't communicate a lot. That is probably one of the reasons we got a divorce."

"Okay, what is your second wife's last name?"

"Davidson was her last name."

"Okay, I should be able to find her," Miranda said.

"If I come up with more information to tell you, I'll give you a call back. Bye."

Miranda and Lee looked at each other, wondering what just happened.

"Now wasn't that the strangest phone call," Lee said. "The list of murderers keeps growing. These people have to be making this stuff up."

After some time on the computer, Miranda said, "I ran a list of brothels operating in Bridgetown at the time of the murder, and from the information there was only three."

"Who were the owners?"

"Washington was one. She grew up in Bridgetown and after a bad divorce started the brothel to make a living. She kept five women working all the time. It was a twenty-four-hour operation. It was a rough place. The police were called there often because the men would get violent and beat up on the workers. It operated for ten years, then the police closed it down in 1968. The women all left town, probably going to bigger cities for work. I couldn't find the owners of the other two."

"Can you find anything on this Randy Johnson and his second wife?"

"Yes, he's a retired railroad engineer. His second wife was Janet Davidson, and I ran the background on her grandmother. Her maiden name was Wilson."

"We've had several women who were beaten up by Bert. Or was it the same person who was beaten up, but different people reporting it to us?"

His phone chirped. "Hello, this is Lee." He pressed the speakerphone button.

"Hello," a woman's voice said. "I'm not going to give you my name. I don't want it associated with this murder. We're too well known in Bridgetown. My husband didn't want me to call."

"You don't have to give me your name. Just tell me what you called to say."

"Okay, I knew Bert Grayson's son. I went to school with him."

"Wait, did you say he had a son? What was his son's name?" Lee said.

"His name was John. He lived in the Grace Hill area with his mother."

"What was his mother's name?"

"I don't know. I just knew John. Anyway, he was big like Bert and looked a lot like his father. He was a couple of years older than me. I was thirteen at the time of the murder. He would walk me home after school to make sure I got home safe, and he wouldn't let anyone bother me."

"Why would anyone bother you?"

"The area of town I lived in was a rough neighborhood."

"Was that the same area Bert was murdered in?"

"Yes, I lived down the street from where his body was found."

"Okay, go on with what you have to tell me."

"Shortly after the murder, my mother and I went to the indoor carnival in the Hill district of Bridgetown. We were about to get on the Ferris wheel. My mom stopped in her tracks, backed up, then she said, "Come on, we have to go home." She was upset.

She went right from the carnival to the police station in Bridgetown. She told them the guy running the Ferris wheel is the same guy she saw Bert leave the diner with the night he was murdered. She used to date Bert Grayson."

"What did the police do?"

"Nothing. My mom was so upset and hysterical they didn't believe her story. As I said, I'm not giving you my name. I called because this has preyed on my mind since your ad started to run in the newspaper. Bye."

Miranda turned toward Lee.

"I'd like to think these people were making this up except for one thing."

"What's that?" Miranda said.

"The police chief, if you remember, told us about every one of these people. Of course, he didn't tell us their names, or the people who contacted them after the murder. If you think back to what he told us, he said they investigated what these people said and everything they said turned out to be false or misleading information. At least that was the police version from the chief of police."

"All of these people can't be making this stuff up. That means Winslow knew what he was talking about when he said Bert had a son," Miranda said.

"So you think these people are telling the truth?" Lee asked. "They're contacting us because their parents went to the police and they dismissed the information as unimportant or untrue. So were the police protecting someone involved with this group of people? Remember the anonymous letter we got the other day? When you think about it, the police didn't seem to believe anything anyone told them."

"Our secret keepers are breaking apart at the seams. At least that's what it looks and sounds like to me," Miranda said.

"So, do we go back to Lilly? It looks like the evidence is swinging in her favor, but it still nags at me that several times in her letters she said it was her fault Bert was murdered and that she could have prevented it. Maybe that's why she spent so much time in the mental hospital. Maybe it was from guilt and not from fear of George. Maybe that was her cover up after killing Bert. Maybe George stopped beating her because he was afraid of her.

I don't know, there are a lot of nagging questions yet to be answered."

Miranda stood, stretched, and smiled at Lee. "Why don't we call it a night, Lee? Tomorrow is another day. I'm tired. It's been a long day."

"Sounds good to me. Would you like some company tonight to keep you safe and warm?"

"No, but thanks for the offer. Maybe some other night. I will say you're good at taking rejection."

"Let's just say I'm a patient person." He walked over and gave her a hug, planting a kiss on her cheek.

"Good night, Kid. SLeep tight."

There was a loud knock on the door.

"I'll get it. Stay here," Lee said.

On the way to the door he went to the living room window and peeked around the curtain. At the end of the driveway he saw dim taillights of a car or truck turning onto the main street. He couldn't see anyone on the porch.

He opened the door and there was a small package sitting on the porch. He carried it to Miranda.

"It's addressed to you from the FBI. From the weight of it, it's probably the gun."

He set the package on the kitchen counter.

As she opened it a note was on top. "Huh, listen to this. "They could only pull a couple of prints from it. One was from the guy who found it and the other was not in the database."

"Well, at least now we know," Lee said.

CHAPTER 40

Present Day

Lee walked into the computer room.

"Good morning, sLeepy head."

"It's seven o'clock already and the morning is about gone.

Why didn't you wake me up?"

"We've had a pretty busy couple of days. I figured you could use the rest."

"Have you learned any new information?"

"Yes and no," she said. "I called Jane and talked to her about Bert having a son. She said she didn't know that, but it would be nice for Bert to have a son. I told her everything the lady said, and she seemed surprised, but didn't know anything about it."

She stood and stretched.

"Then I asked her about the accident Bert was in, and from what she told me, someone may have tampered with the brakes on his truck. He was driving home from Bridgetown after midnight. His truck was slipping and sliding down Appleton Mountain when the tires hit a patch of ice. He pressed on the brake pedal and it went to the floor.

That's when he lost control of his vehicle and crashed through the guardrail, sailing over a steep embankment. If the truck hadn't wedged itself between two big trees on the bank of the river, it would have landed in the icy water. Jane said it was strange that the brakes didn't work because the week before the accident Bert had them replaced at a garage in Bridgetown. He said a friend of his did the job for him at a great price. Jane said it was two months later that Bert was murdered."

"Wow, that sounds like a scary ride. Maybe someone was trying to get rid of him then and he just wasn't aware of what was going on. That cut-rate job nearly cost him his life," Lee said.

"That's what it sounds like to me, and I think that's what Jane thinks, but she didn't say it."

His phone chirped. "Hello, this is Lee." He punched the speakerphone button.

"Hello, my name is Sam Lowman. I'm a retired New York state policeman. I saw your ad in the paper and decided to call to see what you've learned. I'm also a friend of Harry Winston, the retired Bridgetown policeman you spoke with a couple of days ago."

"Harry has a lot of connections," Lee said.

"As do all of the men connected with the safety services in Bridgetown," Sam said.

"What did you say your name was?"

"What was that beeping sound? I hope you're not recording this because it's against the law for you to record a conversation without the approval of the other person."

"I'm not recording anything. My phone battery beeps like that when it gets low."

"Well, you know it's against the law to record a conversation. People go to prison for doing that stuff."

"Hey, fella, are you threatening me? I told you, I'm not recording this. You called me, remember? So please tell me why you're calling."

"Wait a minute, I'm not threatening anyone. I'm trying to help you. If you've learned anything new, you should call the police and tell them. I know Detective Devon. You should contact him. He could help you."

"What did you call to tell me?"

"Boy oh boy, I could get in trouble for this. Did you know they had a suspect named Runner Jones? Did you know that?"

"No, I didn't know that. What did he do that made him a suspect?

"That's information I can't give out. I could get into a lot of trouble for even talking to you."

"Oh, I see, then why are you talking to me?"

"I can tell you that I was working in Bridgetown when the murder happened and I did some investigation work on the case. The Bridgetown Police sent me out to Denver to interview a man working as a dish washer in a restaurant who had information about the murder."

"What did the man tell you about the murder?"

"Nothing. When I got there he was gone and they didn't know where he went."

"Do you know his name?"

"I don't know what his name was. He was gone when I got there, and I didn't find out what his name was."

Lee shot a puzzled look at Miranda.

"What was the name of the restaurant you went to?"

"I don't remember the name of it. Anyway, that was a long time ago."

"Oh, I see. You went to interview a man and you can't remember his name at a restaurant you can't remember the name of in Denver. Is that right?"

"Hey, look, buddy, I'm just trying to help you. If you've learned anything new about the murder, you should call the Bridgetown police and contact Detective Devon. He's a good detective."

"You said that once. Are you two trying to dig up cold cases and solve them? If you are, you'll have to do all your own work. We're not doing it for you."

"Okay, Lee, calm down. But just so you know it's against the law to withhold new information on the case. Murder cases stay open until they're solved no matter how old they are."

"I know how to contact the Bridgetown police," Lee said. "When Bert was murdered, the police weren't too interested in finding out who killed him. The police department at that time was so riddled with corruption and mafia types that they didn't want to solve the murder. The police were probably linked to the murder and were covering up for each other."

"Hey, I shouldn't be talking to you about this. It could get me in a lot of trouble. I'm trying to help you. That's all, help you. Lee, if you go on the Internet and type in Sam Lowman you'll see that I worked on a lot of crimes in Bridgetown and solved them."

"Thank you for calling, Sam. Have a great day."

"You're welcome. Bye."

"Wasn't he was quite the snippy old guy?" Miranda said.

"I think his aggressive attitude is probably what Lilly kept running into with these corrupt police in Bridgetown. They all no doubt used veiled threats to intimidate the people they were trying to get information from or when they were trying to keep someone quiet."

"They seemed to have everyone in this town under their control," Miranda said.

"Poor Lilly. Now I do feel sorry for her. What a woman. She fought back the only way she knew how without getting killed for it. I think everything she said about fearing for her life was true. I think her life was threatened. I don't think she was a nut case. Why didn't they kill her instead of putting up with her all those years? From what she said in her letters, she was at certain times taunting them. She was almost daring them to try to do something to her."

"I think they didn't kill her because every time a new body turns up it becomes harder to explain the death. The FBI tracks murders in the United States, and when a town starts to turn up a lot of dead bodies, the FBI starts to look into the way the town is run or look at what's going on in the town or who's running it. They didn't want the FBI sticking their noses in."

"Okay, so what you're saying is it gets harder to explain all the deaths. It would be safer and much easier for them to paint her as a nut case. They made it look like she was someone who would see a conspiracy in every death that occurred in the town. "Sad to say, I think she was right. They painted her with this incredible and complete picture of someone with mental illness. When they convinced everyone to believe their lies they could ignore Lilly, letting her have her rants, and no one would believe what she said.

By doing all of that, they had Lilly right where they wanted her and one less body to explain away." Lee said.

"I think you're right. If all of the policemen she had to deal with were like that Sam Lowman, she had every reason to fear for her life."

CHAPTER 41

Present Day

"Everyone leaves tracks behind but Bert and Lilly left a super highway leading straight to the police department and the local government of Bridgetown," Lee said.

"You're right. You expressed my same thoughts," Miranda said.

"When I stop to think about it, that's a scary thought. For well over fifty years the people running this town have done whatever they wanted to do," he said.

"Stop reading my mind. That's exactly what I was thinking.

It makes us sound like an old married couple."

"It wouldn't bother me to be married to you."

"Well, I had no idea you would think that way about me. I mean, you're a man and I'm a woman, so I can understand You're trying to get me into bed, but marriage? Well, that's an area I wouldn't think about, ever."

"Okay, I'm going to come right out and ask you this question that has bothered me about you since the day I arrived."

"Shoot. What's the question? After all, they are only words and they can't hurt you."

"Okay, here it is. Why are you so stand-offish? It's as though you pull open a small slit of this heavy dark curtain you're safely concealed behind. Keeping some big secret under wraps. On the rare occasions when your guard is down, you allow me a quick peek inside." Lee paused, stood and started to pace.

"You're building a brick wall of protection from intruding questions that you either don't know how to answer or don't want to answer. It would seem that your years with the FBI have given you a new skill."

He could see her eyes narrow and turn icy as she watched him pace.

"I remember a Miranda who would tell you anything no matter how it made you look or how it made you feel. I always admired that quality in you when you were young. Has life been that hard on you that you protect yourself by hiding your true feelings and emotions? I guess what I'm asking is, what changed you so much?"

"You listen to me, Mister. I can't believe that you see me that way. My true friends don't see me that way. Maybe because I've rejected your physical advances toward me you perceive that as putting up a wall. Talk about somebody changing. You better take a good look at yourself."

Lee stopped pacing and turned to look at her. He could see the fire in her eyes.

"You used to encourage me in the weak and fragile places of my life, and look at you now. You do the opposite. Take a good look at your own life. I remember a guy who was fun and adventurous, a strong competitor. Not this stick in the mud man I see before me now."

She walked to where he was standing and put her face an inch from his.

"Don't get me wrong, I always had a crush on you from the first day Joan introduced you to me as the new love of her life, and at that time in my life I could see no wrong in you until you took that job with that publishing company and started to ignore Joan."

Lee backed up a couple of inches. His mouth dropped open as he listened.

"She came to visit me often because she was lonely for you. You'd be gone for weeks at a time." Miranda stuck her face against his while poking her finger into his chest. "The cancer didn't kill Joan. She died from loneliness and a broken heart because you loved your job more than you loved her."

He backed up again falling onto the sofa. She continued to read him the riot act.

"Now you want to make up for all those years of neglect by solving this murder case. I think it's too little too late. Joan is gone and this, all this you're doing now, won't bring her back or change your past life with her."

Miranda paused, backed up and put her hands on her hips.

"Lee, I may have been holding my feelings in check but it was only to avoid this conversation. But since we're having it, that's how I feel."

He got up, walked over to her, put his finger under her chin, and with a gentle nudge lifted her face toward him. He stood staring into her eyes as he started to reply.

"Miranda, you continue to grind that into my mind. I live every day with the regret of my actions. The way I treated Joan was selfish and mean. I know that. I can't change the way things were, but I can change the way I treat people in the future. You're right. I'm doing this for Joan. When it's finished I'll move on with my life hopeful that in the end I will find love and happiness again."

Lee drifted away from Miranda and back to the sofa. When he sat down, her phone rang.

"It sounds like my phone. I'll get it. Hello, this is Miranda."

Lee was close enough to Miranda that he could hear the person talking on the line.

"Hello, this is Duncan."

Lee watched her move from one foot to the other, as he listened to Miranda's phone conversation.

"Duncan, how are you? I miss you. Hope you can stop by and visit with me."

"How nice of you. You're always such a darling. I miss you as well. I'm glad you said you'd like to see me. I was planning on a quick visit. I'll only have a couple of minutes to spend with you. I should be at the mansion in, let's say, fifteen minutes."

"I'll have strong dark coffee waiting for you."

"I'm looking forward to seeing you. Love you, girlie."

"Love you. I'll see you soon."

"Duncan. What kind of name is that?" Lee said when she put away her phone. "Should I be worried? Who the heck is Duncan?"

"Now wait a minute, Lee. Don't let that trivial exchange fool you. Duncan works with me on investigations and research.

That's as far it goes."

"Oh, I thought it was something more."

"No, it's not." Miranda shot an icy look in his direction.

"Okay, okay, I get the message. Duncan is a friend who works on research with you."

"Duncan is an old friend who I became acquainted with about twenty-five years ago while working on an investigation of stolen manuscripts from a major museum in New York. He's eccentric and a furiously loyal friend. He has a broad base of information and contacts that you can't begin to fathom."

"What kind of guy is he?"

"The best way to describe Duncan is he's pretty much a loner. His parents thought they wanted a child, but in reality they weren't ready to meet the needs of one, so Duncan suffered for their selfishness. He was a rich kid raised by a nanny. His parents gave him things to make up for their neglect.

"I'm like the sister he never had. He surrounds himself with things and avoids people as much as possible." She paused, taking a seat on the sofa.

"I've often consulted him for his knowledge of ancient history, lore and the store of information he's collected on just about anything you can think of. He has one of the largest libraries of rare books concerning ancient and modern history. His artifact collection rivals any museum." By this time, she was straightening up the living room as she talked.

"Duncan lives in Williamsburg, Virginia. Many an adversary has misjudged him because of his lifestyle." She picked up a book and placed it in the center of the coffee table.

"Duncan likes to cook, but has a chef because he likes to eat fine food and drink fine wine. He doesn't have any pets, but he should. It would be good for him. I guess he's like a character out of a book, but you'll love him. He's a lot of fun, and when he gets to know you, he's a friend for life who will go to any length to help you. We can all use one of them in our lives."

Lee was standing in the living room looking out on the driveway, as she finished with the room.

"I'll be right back. I'm going up to my bedroom to change my clothes," she said.

Lee watched as a dark blue Bentley wove its way up the tree-lined drive. This guy even had a chauffeur. The car stopped in front of the house, and the chauffeur got out and opened the back door.

"Is he here yet?" Miranda asked. She finished stuffing her designer shirt into her designer blue jeans as she made her way to the front door.

"He pulled up a second ago and is getting out of the car now."

Miranda opened the door and held out her arms. "Welcome, Duncan." Wrapping her arms around his neck, she hugged him, planting a peck on his cheek.

"Miranda, darling, how good to see you again." He wrapped his long arms around her slim waist, pulling his six-foot-six frame against her slim physique, and hugged her. He planted a kiss on her cheek and flashed a grin at Lee, showing a set of perfect white teeth. His dark tan told Lee that Duncan either spent a lot of time on the beaches or he spent a lot of time in a tanning booth. Duncan pulled off his overcoat and placed it over Miranda's outstretched arm. "You're a dear, Miranda. Thank you for your hospitality."

Lee moved to the door.

"Duncan, this is Lee Perkins, a long-time friend."

"Oh, are you Joan's husband?"

Duncan reached out with a monster-size hand and grabbed Lee's normal man hand and squeezed it while giving it a good hard shake.

"Yes, I am." Lee shot a questioning look at Miranda.

"Miranda has told me so much about you and Joan. I feel like I know you so well, even though I had never met you. I was sorry to hear of her passing. You've my deepest sympathy. It must have devastated you."

"Yes, it did, and I'm doing fine now. Thank you, Duncan, for your kind expression." Lee looked at Miranda and smiled. "Hey, Kid, don't you know any short men?"

Miranda smiled and winked at Lee with a twinkle in her eyes as her face lit up like a candle. "Don't be silly. Of course I know some short men. They just don't happen to be visiting me this week."

"Lee, it's swell to meet you," Duncan said. "Any friend of Miranda's is a friend of mine."

"Oh no, Duncan, the pleasure belongs to me. Miranda has spoken of you and had wonderful things to say about you."

Miranda led them inside. "Come in, Duncan. Let's go into the kitchen. I know that's your favorite room."

"Yum, I can smell espresso. Such a wonderful aroma."

"I like the smell," Miranda said, "more than I do the taste. I was never able to develop a taste for espresso."

"I see you put out your best china," Duncan said.

Miranda shot a look at Lee, as she said, "Just for you. I know you don't like to drink coffee from a mug."

"Miranda, please put my coffee in a mug," Lee said.

"So, what brings you out to this part of the country?" Miranda asked.

"I'll get to that in a moment, dear. Hum, the aroma is to die for. Well, Miranda darling, I've only allowed myself a half hour for this visit, so I must get to the reason I'm here."

"I thought you stopped by to visit me," Miranda said. "By the way, Duncan, I've found the book you said you were looking for in a bookstore in Boston."

Duncan twisted his head and looked at Miranda with a question in his eyes, and after a couple of seconds he said, "Oh, you mean the 1784 edition of the Cook's Pacific voyages of the Sandwich Islands."

"Yes, it's the French edition, and I got it at a great price—eight hundred dollars. But I don't want any money for it. Consider it a gift from me. I owe you much more than I could ever repay."

"Thank you, Miranda, that's so sweet. But you don't owe me anything. I insist on paying for it because I may want you to find another book for me and I won't feel I could ask you if you don't take my money. Please, dear. You're like the little sister I never had."

Lee watched as Duncan pulled a long, slim wallet from his shirt pocket, counted out eight one-hundred-dollar bills, and laid them on the kitchen counter. With his big hand, he slid them in Miranda's direction.

"Thank you, Duncan. That's nice of you. And I will keep my eyes peeled for any books you ask me to look for."

Lee studied Duncan as he interacted with Miranda, sizing this guy up, trying to decide if he was a threat. He wasn't going to give up on Miranda, he didn't care what she said. After ten minutes he decided he didn't have anything to be concerned about between Duncan and Miranda. Even after Miranda's total rejection earlier, he wasn't discouraged.

"I noticed the ad you and Lee are running in the *Bridgetown Mirror* newspaper regarding the writing project you two are working on."

"Wait, stop, Duncan. You read the *Bridgetown Mirror*?"

"You bet I do. I've had a subscription to that paper for twenty years. How else could I keep up with Miranda's and Bridgetown's goings on?"

"Duncan, I'm glad you said that, because we've run into a few snags getting some information we're looking for," she said.

"What information are you trying to get?"

Lee told him the story about the teacher who said a boy came into his class telling how his uncle came home covered in blood wanting the boys' mom and dad to give him money because he had to get out of town that night. Miranda told Duncan she contacted the school but couldn't get the roster for that class to see what the boys' last names were.

"So now we're trying other avenues to get the information,"

Lee said.

"I may have the resources to help with that. I'll give you a call later or I'll have someone give you the information," Duncan said as he took a sip of coffee.

"Anyway, back to what I was saying. After talking with you on the phone about the letters, Miranda, I searched through the newspapers on the computer website. I came up with some information that seemed too buried where the police hoped it wouldn't be noticed," Duncan said, as he uncrossed his legs.

"Someone must have put pressure on the police to place another composite picture in the papers a year after the murder.

In my way of thinking, if I didn't want anyone to notice it, I would wait a year and place it in the paper, and have the paper bury it in the back pages." Duncan paused and winked at Miranda.

"I said all that to say I think I came up with something that not many people are aware of or who paid any attention to. I came up with a second composite picture of a man who they say left the hot dog dinner with Bert Grayson the night of the murder."

Duncan slipped his hand into his shirt pocket and came out with his leather wallet again. This time, instead of money, he took out a white folded paper. He handed it to Miranda. She looked at it and handed it to Lee.

"This is the first time I've seen this picture," Miranda said. "He looks familiar, but I don't know why. Does the picture ring a bell with you, Lee?"

Just as Lee was about to answer, Duncan interrupted them.

"Miranda, thank you so much for the coffee. It was incredible, just like you are, dear."

Duncan stood from his chair, smiled at Miranda, then stuck out his hand to shake Lee's. Lee looked him in the eye and shook his hand.

"Lee, it was a pleasure to meet you. You and Miranda make a perfect couple. Miranda, I see why you like this guy. Stop and see me when you're in my end of the country. You're always welcome."

Miranda brought Duncan his overcoat and watched him as he put it on. "I'll miss you, Duncan. Hurry back to see me."

"Duncan, it was great to meet you, Miranda is lucky to have a friend like you."

Duncan turned around and looked at Miranda, then reached out his big paws, scooped her up in his arms, and hugged her tight for a couple of seconds. "I'll miss you as well, sweetie."

Duncan hurried down the porch steps and into his waiting blue car.

Miranda and Lee stood at the opened door and watched as Duncan's Bentley wove its way down the tree-lined driveway, passed through the tall gates, and merged into the traffic flowing south.

After closing the door they turned around and walked back into the kitchen. Lee walked over and picked up the composite picture.

"Why does he look so familiar? And why doesn't it look anything like the other composite picture?"

Lee stood at the kitchen counter with his hands on my hips.

"What are you thinking, Lee?"

Lee was about to speak when his phone jingled. "Hello, this is Lee."

"This is Rose May from the Bridgetown School offices. I have the information you said you were wanting. It's the school log of the children who attended the fifth-grade class in February 1962.

If you could give me a fax number, I'll be glad to fax it to you." Miranda scribbled down the fax number and handed it to Lee.

Lee read her the number. "Thank you so much for that information."

"You're welcome. I'm sending it now. Lee, I hope you have a great day and I'm glad I could help. If you need anything else, please call me."

Miranda's fax machine started to spit out paper. They had the list.

"Lee, do you think they got a call from Duncan? What could he have said to make them change their minds?"

"Isn't that just like a woman? You get what you want, then you want to question it to death."

They stood together looking at the boy's names on the list.

"I'll run each one and see who they're related to," Miranda said.

Miranda was running information on the third boy on the list when she stopped and said, "Look at this name." She pointed to the name Charles Curry.

"Do you think he's still around?" Lee said.

"I don't know, but it would be worth its weight in gold to find out. I'll check the listings in the white pages."

A few moments later she found it. "Yes, here's one, Charles Curry, and he lives in Bridgetown."

"Instead of calling him, why don't we stop by and visit him. That way he won't have time to make up anything or run away," Lee said.

"Do you think we should bring the police in on this now?"

"I think we can wait a bit longer, Miranda, then bring in the FBI, not this police department."

CHAPTER 42

Present Day

Lee followed the GPS directions to the south side of town. "Why are the houses so tall and skinny? Each house can't be any wider than twenty feet. They look like houses from a cartoon book, not real homes," Lee said.

"I think most of the places we are passing were built in the 1800s. The workers tore apart the railroad box cars and used the wood to build their houses, that would be my guess," Miranda said.

"Oh, here we are. I'll park behind that old faded red pickup truck," Lee said.

They got out and looked at the two-story wood-sided house.

It needed some work and a good paint job.

"Let me do all the talking," Lee said.

"Okay, it's all yours. I won't say anything until you give me a sign."

Lee, followed by Miranda, walked up on the front porch and knocked on the door.

After a few seconds the door flew open. There, filling the doorway, loomed a good-looking, slightly balding man.

He looked from Lee to Miranda and said, “Yeah, what do you want?”

“Hello, I’m Miranda Witherspoon and this is Lee Perkins.”

Lee’s mouth dropped open as he rolled his eyes at Miranda with the look of *I thought I was going to do all the talking*. Lee stuck out his hand and received a limp handshake in return.

“Hi, are you Charles Curry?” Lee said.

“Yeah. It’s Chuck. Why do you want to know?”

“We’re doing investigative research on the murder of Bert Grayson and would like to ask you some questions,” Lee said.

Through the opened door, Lee could see a middle-aged woman standing at the kitchen sink, washing dishes. Her jeans bulged at the hips and flared out at the bottom. Her white blouse was tucked neatly into the bulging waist, with a brown leather belt holding it all together. She was tapping her foot to some music playing on the radio.

“Okay,” he said in a whisper, “but not here.” He craned his neck back over his right shoulder in the direction of the woman in the kitchen washing dishes. He was a big guy. His blue jeans were torn at the knee and faded in spots. His checked hunting shirt was hanging loose at the waist. The bottom button was open, revealing his hairy belly rolling over his belt. His glasses were taped together on the nosepiece. His voice had a soft tone. He turned his attention back to Lee, who could see he didn’t want the woman inside to hear him.

Lee whispered, “Where would you like to talk?”

"I'll meet you at the Coffee Grind in Bridgetown in fifteen minutes. I have some things to finish up here first."

"Fifteen minutes at the Coffee Grind. We'll head over there now so we won't miss you," Lee said, as he craned his neck and stuck out his chin at Miranda, while shrugging.

Chuck closed the door. Lee and Miranda walked back to the car. After they got in and closed the doors, Lee said, "Why don't we sit here a few minutes to see what this guy does?"

Miranda nodded.

Just then, Chuck came out of his house and walked to the third house from his to the north. He knocked on the door.

An older woman opened it and stepped out on the porch and they chatted for a couple of minutes. Then the woman went back inside and closed the door. But Chuck didn't leave. He stood on the porch for a couple of minutes until the woman came back out and handed him a brown paper bag. He turned, walking away from his house, and the woman went back inside, closing the door.

They watched as Chuck got into an older green pickup truck and drove off.

"We better head over to the coffee shop. I wouldn't want to be late for this meeting," Lee said. "And great job letting me do all the talking."

"I felt, this time, a woman's touch was needed. That's all there was to it."

"Okay, okay, forget about it. Let's get going to the Coffee Grind."

"But, wasn't that strange the way the whole thing went?"

"Yes," Lee said. "It was almost as though he was expecting us. He certainly didn't want the woman doing the dishes to hear. Maybe she is his wife and doesn't know anything about it."

The snow that had fallen was all but gone and the sky was clearing. A bus passed Lee's car, splashing water and ice onto his windshield. A couple of kids were laughing and playing outside on the street. As Lee drove his car over the bridge with the railroad tracks below, the acrid smell of coal dust stung his nose.

Miranda waved her hand in front of her face. "I sure am glad I don't live around that stink all the time. Do you think he'll really show up? I mean, he wasn't just trying to get rid of us?"

"We'll know the answer to that in a few minutes. Anyway, we know where he lives, so that wouldn't be too smart."

They found a table in the Coffee Grind and were drinking coffee when Chuck walked in and made his way over to their table.

"Have a seat, Chuck. What can I get you?" Lee said.

"A regular cup of coffee would be good."

Lee got up and ordered the coffee, then brought it back and placed it in front of Chuck.

"I know why you guys want to talk to me. I've been keeping this bottled up inside all these years, but I was always afraid to say anything."

"Why? What were you afraid of?" Miranda said.

"I was afraid my Uncle Leslie would come after me if I ever said anything to anyone."

Lee's head snapped back to look at Miranda. She had caught the name as well.

"Everyone in the family knew you didn't mess with him. He was a powerful man in the city, and no one ever crossed him."

"Chuck, was your Uncle Leslie named Leslie Darrell?" Lee said.

"Let me finish, then I think you will understand. It didn't matter if what Uncle Leslie did was against the law, he got away with it. When I saw your ads running in the newspaper, the thought drifted around in my head to contact you, but I was still afraid after all these years, if you can believe it."

"Are you the one who sent us the anonymous letter with the obit in it?" Lee said.

"Yes, but I was still afraid my uncle could reach out from the grave and kill me."

Lee looked at Miranda, then back to Chuck. "Chuck, we know about the incident in the fifth grade with your uncle," he said.

"But how did you find out about that?"

"Someone stopped by the house and told us about it," Lee said.

"Wow, who would that be?"

"We wouldn't give out any names to protect the people who did come forward," Lee said. "Would you like to tell us in your own words what happened? Would you mind if we record what you're going to say?"

"I don't care after all this time, record it. It has to come out sooner or later. I just wish I had told my wife about it. I hate for her to hear it this way. Well, I guess I should tell you the whole story just as it happened."

Miranda set up the recorder and Chuck started to talk.

"It's been bottled up for such a long time. Here's the story. The night of the murder, loud noises woke me up from a sound sLeep. I made my way out to the top of the stairs. I couldn't figure out what was going on, why Uncle Leslie was there. I grabbed the banister and sat down, leaning my head between two rails." Chuck paused and cleared his throat.

"I had a perfect view down into the kitchen. Uncle Leslie was having a loud, heated discussion with mom and dad. At first, I didn't know what I was seeing. Uncle Leslie had something red all over his hands and arms, and even on his head. It looked like blood, he was holding a knife that was covered with blood in his one hand. I mean, it was all over him. He had on a white shirt and black pants. The blood soaked his shirt. Uncle Leslie's voice was angry, with a maniacal tone. To this day I could never get the tone of his voice out of my head. He was demanding that mom and dad give him money because he had to get out of town in a hurry. Dad asked him about work, and he said he'd call into the office tonight and tell them he'd be gone for a couple of weeks on business. Mom kept asking him, 'Leslie, what did you do?' He stared at mom for what seemed like hours, but it was only a couple of seconds." Chuck paused and blew his nose.

"He said, 'I got revenge, sis. I got revenge on the guy who beat up our mom that night in the brothel.' My foot was getting numb, so I shifted my position. It was then that Uncle Leslie looked up.

I must have bumped the railing, and it attracted his attention. You could have heard a pin drop. They stopped talking. Mom and Dad looked up. I could see mom starting to get up from her chair, so I jumped up, went back to my room, and got into bed. I could hear dad say, 'Chuck, you stay here.'

"Mom came up. I pretended to be asLeep. She pulled my blankets up around my shoulders, kissed me on the head, closed the door and went back downstairs. In a couple of minutes they started to talk again. I fell asLeep and that was all I ever heard about it until I was a teenager." Chuck paused and took a sip of coffee.

"Uncle Leslie killed his first wife one night while having rough sex. He had most of the Bridgetown officials in his pocket and bribed the judge, so he got off with a light sentence of seven years but only spent four years in prison. After he got out of prison he finished his education and went back to work for the city as the finance director until he died a couple of months ago."

"You were what? Eleven years old? That's pretty young to remember in such detail what happened," Lee said.

"Well, I was eleven going on twelve because of the way my birthday fell. At any rate, it was such a traumatic experience that I could never forget it."

"I could only imagine. So you went to school the next day and told the class and teacher what happened?" Lee asked.

"I was still upset by what I saw and heard, but they didn't believe me. The teacher told me to sit down and stop making up stories."

Lee and Miranda were hanging on his every word.

"So your mom and dad knew about this as well and didn't say a word. Do you know what they did with the knife?" Lee asked.

"Well, in their defense, Uncle Leslie no doubt threatened them. As far as the knife, I picked that up on my way here. I have it in a paper bag in the truck. My mom gave it to her aunt to keep and she has hidden it all these years."

"Wow, and no one went to the police? Why not?" Lee asked.

"We were all afraid of my uncle, and the police were in his back pocket. We had no choice until he died." Chuck put his head in his hands and was silent for a couple of minutes. Lee looked at Miranda. She shrugged.

"Chuck, are your mom and dad still alive?" Lee said.

"No, they both died in a car accident a couple of years ago. I always thought it was a strange accident."

"What was strange about it?" Lee said.

"They had just had the brakes on their car replaced, and that night they were coming down the reservoir mountain road. It was a snowy and icy road that night. On one of the curves I guess the brakes didn't work and they went through the guardrail and over the cliff and died when the car crashed at the bottom." Lee and Miranda exchanged glances as he continued to talk.

"A friend of mine took the car to his junkyard, and a year later I ran into him here at the coffee shop and he told me had gone out to get a brake part from my mom and dad's car and noticed that it looked like someone had cut the brake lines. The first person to pop into my mind was Uncle Leslie. I never said anything to anyone. By this time, I was thinking he was a serial killer."

"Why, when you were older, didn't you tell the police what you knew?" Lee asked.

"I ran into Uncle Leslie after he got out of prison for murdering his first wife. It was then that he said he saw me at the staircase that night. He told me if I ever said anything to anyone he would take care of me the way he took care of Bert Grayson for beating up his mother. I had no reason not to believe he wouldn't do what he said he would do."

"So how did your uncle know it was Bert Grayson who beat up your grandmother?"

"I guess my grandmother must have told him it was Bert who beat her up one night when he was drunk. Bert used to date my grandmother who ran a brothel in Bridgetown. Bert went to the brothel one night when he was pretty drunk, got her alone in one of the rooms and blackened her eyes and knocked a couple of her front teeth out. She said it was her fault because Bert was jealous. He didn't want her seeing other men. Uncle Leslie was getting revenge for her. My dad told me he was the one who sent the composite picture to the newspapers a year after the murder hoping someone would recognize him, but I guess the police were in his back pocket, and maybe the police were as afraid of him as I was."

"When and why did your dad tell you that?" Lee said

"My parents were as afraid of him as I was. Dad told me that information about a year before he died."

Lee turned toward Miranda. "Now what do we do, Miranda?" Lee looked at Miranda and back at Chuck. They all knew what they had to do.

"I think we need to go to the office of the FBI and tell them the story. After all, the threat is gone now," Lee said.

Lee and Miranda looked at Chuck.

"What do you say, Chuck?"

"But Uncle Leslie's second wife doesn't know any of this, and his children will never believe it. It will break their hearts."

Lee told him, "It's up to you, Chuck. You can go on living with this. We won't expose you. Or you can go to the FBI and tell them what you told us. I'm sure Bert's family would like to have this solved. I'll write my book, but the way it ends will depend on what you do."

CHAPTER 43

Present Day

That afternoon Lee and Miranda walked with Chuck up the steps of the FBI office in Bridgetown. Lee held the door open for Chuck and Miranda, then Lee walked in behind them. The agent standing at the front desk looked at Chuck.

"Can I help you?"

"Yes, my name is Chuck Curry."

Then Chuck told his story to the FBI.

***

It took them six months, but they cleaned up the remaining mafia types in Bridgetown and put the rest of the corrupt officials and police into prison, where they still are today. Chuck turned states witness with what he knew about the murder and was only given a six month sentence for concealing evidence.

Robert Mason was found dead from a heart attack in his hotel room the morning after he met with Miranda at the coffee shop. After his estate was settled, the NSA bought his satellite company and is putting it to good use around the world. After talking with Mason's secretary they learned that he hired someone to shoot at them in the cemetery to scare them off the investigation.

Darrell's wife and family were heartbroken by the story that had to be told. Through sources, the FBI also found out that Bert's niece was in Bridgetown the night of the murder and hired Darrell to kill Bert. She knew Darrell hated Bert for beating up his mother.

Bert's family was relieved to have closure on this murder fifty years later and relieved that the town had been cleaned up of corruption.

Lee thought it was sad that Lillian didn't live to see that she was proven to be right all along. She would have liked that.

Why did Lillian say she could have prevented the murder?

Through careful reading of the letters, they pieced together she believed if she had married Bert, he would still be alive.

CHAPTER 44

Present Day

Lee drifted close to Miranda, reached out, and pulled her next to him. This time, she hugged him back. He kissed her cheek and released her.

"Goodbye, Kid. Maybe we'll get together again to work on another case."

He looked at Adrian, "It was nice to meet you. Take care of our girl."

"It was nice to meet you. Don't worry. She's my number one priority. Have a safe trip home."

Miranda looked into his eyes. "Goodbye, Lee. Maybe I don't mind being called Kid after all. You never know, we might work together again soon."

Lee drove down the winding driveway and stopped at the wrought-iron gates. He got out and looked at them one last time.

"Yep, they're classic Miranda."

Nine hours later Lee pulled into the docks. A calming peace washed over him at the sight of his houseboat. It seemed like he had been gone for a year. That night he fell into a deep sLeep in his own bed.

Early the next morning he was standing outside on the deck leaning on the railing just before dawn, sipping a cup of steaming coffee waiting for the sunrise. As the light splashed across the water his phone rang.

"Hello, this is Lee."

"Lee, this is Clint. How are you, old buddy? It's been a couple of months since we last spoke. We need to get together and catch up."

"Clint, it's good to hear from you. I would like to get together."

"Thanks, buddy. Glad to hear you say that. I'm calling because I need your help if you're available. I'm working on a hard to solve case and I was wondering if you'd have the time to work on it with me? I have bad news about an old friend of ours."

"Clint, I now have all the time in the world. What's the bad news and who is it about?"

CHAPTER 45

Present Day

Lee wrote his book. It became a number one *New York Times* best seller. He titled it *For Joan and Lillian.*

END

LETTER 1

March 1962

Dearest Elizabeth,

You may think that is an odd way for one woman to start a letter to another, especially when it is doubtful if they have ever seen each other. I wasn't going to write this, but last Saturday I went to Dr. Denny and he told me to do whatever I felt I had to do. I thought I was losing my mind, but he said I was sane enough. He said I was just grief-stricken.

You see, Elizabeth, I should have been your sister-in-law. I should have married Bert, but I didn't, and the reason was plain to me. It wasn't that I didn't love him. It was because I thought I wasn't good enough for him. I wanted him to have the best, and I knew what I had done. I thought he didn't know about it at the time, and I could never marry a man I couldn't tell what a tramp I had been. I know now that he knew all there was to know about me and it didn't matter. He felt about me the way I feel about him. If he did something bad, it wasn't wrong. Not if he did it.

I didn't know about his death until that Sunday night, the 11th. My husband came home from work and told me. I had to make him stop. I couldn't bear to hear it. I cried so hard I almost forgot to send flowers. I hope they came in time.

I think all of Appleton and parts of Bridgetown knew we were in love. I was never out with him, but it wasn't because I was afraid of him. I was afraid of myself. I couldn't even let him hold my hand. My brother had told me Bert had gotten drunk and roughed up a couple of girls on several occasions, and I had made up my mind years before I even met Bert that I would never marry a man who would do a thing like that. I had seen my father beat my mother.

I told Carl Winslow when I found out Bert was serious that I couldn't go out with him because I knew I'd let him push me around and I didn't want to do that. I didn't think it was right for a girl to mess around with a man she knew she couldn't marry.

I never knew until two weeks after Bert was dead what my brother told me. He said he had seen Bert pound his fist on the table and say he wouldn't marry the best darned woman living, and I told him that Bert must have thought I was a little better than the best because he wanted to marry me.

My brother said I was the dumbest girl he had ever seen. He said Bert was only trying to make a pass.

It's a long story, Elizabeth, far too long to put in a letter, and parts of it are sweet, but most of it is sad. I told the doctor only parts of it, and I told the police what I knew, about how Bert watched over me because he promised years ago that he would never let anyone hurt me and that I would never want for anything as long as he lived. But I never took a cent from him myself. I know that he gave Hap Mills money, and that he even gave him four hundred dollars to divorce me, and he even got someone else to help me give Hap the grounds for a divorce. When I asked why he didn't do it himself, he said because he knew he couldn't marry me until after I was divorced and he didn't trust himself.

How honorable can a man be? They don't come any better than Bert. No matter what he did?

I want to write a book. The doctor told me to go ahead. He thinks I can do it. I want to do something to make it right, and I can't even ask Bert to forgive me now, but if I had known the night of February 10 what I know now, all this would never have happened. It wouldn't have mattered that he was broke, or that he had been in a mental hospital, or that he had run around with the wrong kind of people. I could have saved his life and I didn't, and I have to live with this knowledge as long as I live, and only God knows how much it hurts.

In the book I want to tell anyone who will read it about the Bert I knew. The good clean, decent, kind, and honorable man he was. Most of the readers will think it's fiction, but it won't be.

They won't believe that a man could be as good as Bert was. But God will know and I will know, and perhaps a few of you who knew him and loved him will believe what I write.

You see, Elizabeth, a lot of years ago I told him to find someone else. Someone worthy of him, and he said he didn't want anyone else. He knew I was in love with him. I had told him I was, and when I tried to deny it later I couldn't look him in the eyes and do it. I had to look at the floor.

From all this I have learned a lot of things, but the most important one is this. When you really love someone, it's forever, and you go on loving them as long as you live no matter what they do.

There are a lot of things I don't know about Bert. I don't know when he started to wear glasses or if he got bald or not. I remember his hair was a medium shade of brown, as if he might have been blond when he was younger, and I think his eyes were blue. I hadn't seen him for a long while, until that night in the hot dog place. I remember I looked at him and he saluted me, but he didn't say anything. I was married to someone else.

He was the only man I ever knew who meant every word he ever said to me. I didn't know it then; I know it now. He said he would love me until the day he died, and he meant it. In all my life Bert Grayson was the only person who ever really loved me. My mother never forgave me for some of the things I did, but Bert forgave me. The doctor said when you love someone you don't need to ask them to forgive you. If you do something you shouldn't, it isn't wrong in their eyes. I know he's right, but I know, too, that no one ever hurt Bert the way I did. Not even at the very last.

I hadn't even heard his name until last summer when he was in the mental hospital. Herman Heritage told me he was in bad shape, and I thought it was best to let sLeeping dogs lie.

I'm not referring to Bert as a dog—I mean I thought he had forgotten me, and I didn't want to open an old wound. It only hurts worse than it did the first time, and I didn't want to hurt him ever.

When I found out he was sick I shook until I couldn't hold a cigarette. It fell right out of my fingers. We were going to Harrisburg and I never had such a miserable time in my life. I spent most of the trip in the ladies' lounge crying. I told George I was carsick. I get that way sometimes, you know.

I hope this letter hasn't hurt you. I wouldn't want to hurt anyone who was dear to Bert.

If there is ever anything I can do for you or the other members of your family, I'll try my best to do it, if you let me know. Bert would want it that way.

George, my husband, knows all about this. He knows the only reason I came back was because I thought it was the right thing to do at the time. He knows I'm not in love with him. I've slept alone for fourteen years.

I don't even sLeep in the same room with him. He doesn't mind. When I'm at myself I'm a fair housekeeper and a good cook.

I made him a home and that's all he asked of me. He has known since long before we were married that I was in love with Bert. I told him.

I hope whoever has Bert's flag will take good care of it. I think it's sacred.

Please forgive me, Elizabeth, and if you can find it in your heart to do so, come and see me. I love you because you were Bert's sister and you must be a little like him. I have cried for more than four weeks now. I don't know where all the tears come from. The doctor said not to try to suppress them, but that Bert wouldn't want me to grieve this way. He would want me to be happy the way he knew me. I ran out of writing paper. That's why this page is written on both sides. I look like an old hag, and I'm ashamed to go to the store to get more.

Thank you for reading this, Elizabeth, and please try to forgive.

Bert's Lilly P.S. I still think Grayson is the prettiest name I ever heard.

And something else you should know. I didn't know Bert was shy until Herman told me. I knew he blushed easily, and I thought he was a little shy, but not the way he was. Herman said he never saw such a shy man in his life, and I knew then that when I told Bert I didn't like men who drank I tied his tongue, and I thought it was too late. I didn't see how Bert could even like me after all the things I had done, and since. I'm a little shy, too. I didn't try to find out if he liked me or not. I didn't think I had the right.

LETTER 2

April 1963

Dear Elizabeth,

I hope you will forgive me for opening an old wound, but it is as painful for me as it will be for you. I have hesitated about writing because what I will put in this letter may cause you to be in danger, and I don't want to do that. There are a lot of things you or some member of your family should know, and since you are the only woman in the family I thought it best to write to you and let you do whatever you wanted to do with the information I will give you.

To begin with, I do know you, or at least I met you once. It was in the park during the summer when I was a young teen. You were thin and blonde and you wore your hair long, with a bun at the nape of your neck. I had come to the park at Bert's request. He was going to ask me to marry him. He didn't, but it was neither my fault nor his, and it is a detailed story so I won't go into it now. When I wrote you before I didn't remember about knowing Bert when I was a child until Dr. Denny pulled it from my memory. Bert kissed me on the cheek when I was eight years old, and that was the only time he ever kissed me. Your father owned the park, and you and Bert worked there in the summer.

I have been told that Bert lost a lot of his amazing strength after he was in that terrible accident. I have also been told that he was a diabetic. I have no way of knowing if he was a diabetic or not, but I feel sure that part of the statement is true.

Cheney said it, and he would have no reason to lie.

When I knew Bert, he lied about his age one year. I don't blame him, and I know now exactly why he did it. It was because of something I told him when I was a child. I was lying about my age, too, only it was a lot more than one year. I wasn't kidding Bert a bit.

He knew exactly how old I was, and it puzzled me because I couldn't remember how he knew me. He even remembered when my birthday was from when I told him when I was a child. Bert wanted me to write a book about a grown man who fell in love with a baby, but I didn't know what he was talking about at the time. I do now.

To say the least, it is frustrating to know something you can't prove, and I may have to tell something I don't want to tell later on. It is something I think Bert knew, but he wouldn't tell it either because he wouldn't have done anything to hurt me. I used to look at him and know he knew what I was thinking. I told him I knew something horrible about a member of my family and if he knew it, he wouldn't want to marry me. He said he thought he knew what I was referring to, but he would never tell because it would hurt me, and if anything hurt me it would hurt him, too.

No one knows about this letter but my husband, and he did not kill Bert. I'm sure of that. If I thought he had even a slight part in it I would kill him myself and not wait for the law to take its course. I'm convinced that I know who did do it, though, and that's the reason for this letter. Cain and Clay Bliss did it, probably with help from someone who is now working, or has worked at the puritan cleaners, which is right next door to me. I can tell you how I know, but it, too, is involved and would take up a lot of space.

I had a nervous breakdown after the murder and had to be hospitalized, but I was not insane even though I was in a mental institution. I couldn't stop crying, and after what the doctor thought was a reasonable length of time he suggested that it was the only thing left for me to do. He had done everything he could to help me. I was sick for more than a year, but I wasn't hospitalized but a couple of months at the time. I went in twice because when I came home the first time things did not go well for me. George objected to the book because it will put him in a bad light and he didn't want the world to know him for what he is. When he learned that I was to be allowed to write the book and he was going to have to support me, he changed his attitude about a lot of things. One thing he didn't want to do was support me, and Dr. James said she would see to it that he'd do it whether he wanted it that way or not.

I live here because I feel that George owes it to me to look after me until the book is written. If it sells, I can look after myself. Otherwise, I'll have to go back to scrubbing floors and I may as well stay here if I am going to do that. I am only an unpaid housekeeper anyhow and that's all I've been for more years than I care to remember.

The picture in the paper looked more like Clay than it did Cain, but the written description fitted Cain perfectly, except for the age, but then Cain always looked a lot younger than he was. They did it for money and revenge, and I can tell you how I know.

I talked to the police, but all the pieces weren't in the puzzle at that time. There were a lot of things I didn't remember that came to me afterward. I was hysterical when I talked to the police, and I don't think they paid much attention to what I said. I also think Clay may have killed Mr. Merritt. He was connected to the local mafia, and I keep wondering who will be next and how he will do it. As you know, Cain was killed in the fall of 1962, so he couldn't possibly have had anything to do with the second murder, but no one will make me believe he wasn't in on the first one.

I would suggest that you talk to your brothers about this letter and let them decide what would be best to do. I am willing to tell you everything I know, or I will tell the police if you'd rather I did it that way. If I don't hear from you, I will know that you would rather I kept still. I don't want to hurt you or your family in any way; however, I feel that something should be done to stop these horrible atrocities. I also feel that what I have to say would have more of an impact if you or some other member of your family were interested enough to back me.

The way I know who did it was a simple process of elimination. It had to be someone who knew me and also knew Bert, and knew that Bert was in love with me. Not many people knew me or about me. Bert would get drunk and tell people then, but I was only a name to most of them. They would have no way of knowing where I lived or even what I looked like. There was also a psychic element, but you can't prove things by feelings.

When I was in the hospital, Mrs. James, the state psychologist, said she bet I could remember every word Bert ever said to me. I can. I can also remember every conversation I ever had with anyone about him.

In any event, Elizabeth, I am not letting anyone know what is in this letter. I do not want to put you in any danger and I might if anyone found out what I wrote. Eventually, Clay will get even with me for telling it. He has ways of finding out everything. I don't know how he does it, but he does. He'll try to get me another way and make it look like an accident. That's why I'm being careful where I go and what I do. If anything happens to me, you will know what I have said here is true. I don't want it to happen until after I have finished my book.

My best to you,

Lilly

P.S. I have taken every cautionary measure I can think of.

We even have aluminum siding on our house now because aluminum won't burn. In any event, if something should happen to me, I told Bert once I'd die for him, but I couldn't marry him. I meant it.

LETTER 3

March 1965

Dear Elizabeth,

My book is nearly completed, and you will be glad to know that I have corrected all the lies and insinuations that were in the newspapers.

There is something you can tell me, if you will be so kind. I have all the answers, except for one thing; I was told that one of your brothers had gone to Baltimore and became a policeman. After Bert's death, he tried to put pressure on our local police and had died of a heart attack. Is this true?

People can tell anyone anything, so it may have been idle chatter.

I have a specific reason for wanting to know this. Bert was of the opinion that his brothers didn't like him. I'd like to think that Bert was mistaken and that someone besides me cared enough to try to do something about his death.

Don't trust the Bridgetown Police Department. Everything you tell them goes right back to Clay, and you will only put your own life in danger. I don't know if it's even safe to trust the state police because one of them lied to me when he was here. However, this may not have been intentional.

I know that the police department is going to protect its members no matter how rotten they are.

My phone number is unlisted because Clay had been calling me late at night, and when I answered he wouldn't talk. He did the same thing right after Cain told me the whole story, and I was so frightened I left town. My phone number is 944-9208, in case you want to call me. If I don't hear from you, I will know that Bert was mistaken about something he told me once, and I'm hoping he wasn't.

What the world thinks of me as a person doesn't matter. Bert knew everything I ever did and my reasons for doing what I did. He loved me in spite of my own dumb stupidity.

I know that I will be crucified over the book, but I have to have it published, even at the cost of my own life.

Sincerely,

Lilly

P.S. What was this brother's first name and did he have a history of heart trouble?

LETTER 4

April 1965

Dear Miss Grayson,

I have a guest today. It is a girl I met while I was in the state hospital, and she is reading what I have finished of my book. She likes it and said that there was no doubt in her mind that Bert was a man of high principles and good moral character.

She never even saw Bert, and I am happy that this is what a total stranger got from the material I have written about him. It is the precise message I meant to convey, and every word of it is true. I would swear to it, and I am a woman who wouldn't swear to a lie, not even to protect my own reputation.

I have to correct a couple of things I told you in my last letter. I think I told you I hadn't seen Bert for years.

Actually, I was in the same room with him one night since that. He was in the Hot Dog Lunch, and I only saw him from a distance. I was in the back booth by the window. I was raised to believe that it wasn't proper for married women to talk to other men, and I have never done it when I lived in the same house with a husband. It wasn't that I didn't want to see Bert. Once, after we moved into this house, I walked clear to Green. I live quite close to Lake Park. I think Green is nearly seven miles from where I live. Anyway, I lost my nerve and came back. George and I had had a battle and I wanted to leave here. George had taken my bus pass and all my money so I couldn't leave. That's why I walked.

Bert had told me that love lasted forever, but so many men had told me the same thing that I had a lot of doubts. I had no way of knowing that Bert might not be married. I hadn't even the nerve to call him on the phone or ask someone who would know if he were married or not.

I said that Bert only mentioned you once. I meant directly to me. I heard him mention your name to his drinking buddy Carl on occasion. I remember thinking you must have a sense of humor because Bert repeated something you'd said. I was busy and didn't hear it, and they were both laughing when I got back to the bar.

I have had a lot of unnecessary work to do after George, too, as a result of his drinking. Doing his work has never been a pleasure. It never will be. Work really isn't work when you love someone, though. I remember I told Dr. Denny I'd be willing to die if I could just see Bert long enough to ask him to forgive me.

My last letter was a pretty blunt statement of facts. Believe me, it wasn't told to me that way or I'd have wiped up the street with Cheney. At the time I didn't believe most of it since the papers had been printing cover-up stories. I had no proof for most of it, and I didn't get most of the proof until last summer.

I advertised in *Labor* newspaper for names and dates, and the proof originally came to me from Florida. From it I learned how to get most of the rest of it. The elderly couple he shot in their living room while they were watching TV. The paper said the police theorized that a child had gotten a loaded gun and that both deaths were accidental. Both people were shot to death with different bullets.

At the time Bert was killed I imagine you were too upset to even suspect why it had happened. I know that, for me, all I could think of was the horrible way in which he died. I know it was my fault, but I couldn't even remember why it was my fault.

It came back a little at a time, just the way Dr. Denny said it would. He, Dr. Denny, was the first person to encourage me about the book. He was a wonderful person. My attorney said Dr. Denny admired me.

I fault myself that Bert drank. I thought I had nothing to do with it when he started, but he told me that he knew I didn't love him enough to marry him, but he wanted me to tell him I cared enough to ask him to stop drinking. He said he believed he could quit if I asked him to. I didn't tell him, and I was pretty brutal about it.

I said I didn't want the responsibility of him on my shoulders, and I didn't care what he did. Hate me for saying it if you like, but I had my reasons. You'd have to talk to me or read the book to understand.

Forgive me for writing that last letter. I wish now I hadn't, but I may have told you this before. I'm more afraid of the local police than I ever was of Clay, and I'm plenty scared of him. He can't get into our house. The police can. I can't keep them out.

Miss Grayson, I can't believe that Bert would tell a deliberate lie, except for me. Carl was Bert's best friend at the time. Carl was trying to talk me into marrying Bert. He said he wished he was my daddy so he could make me marry Bert even if he had to take me over his knee to do it. Carl said that Bert wouldn't know how to pretend. When you told me that Bert was due to be sent overseas, I knew Bert hadn't lied to Carl. They don't take men into Foreign Service over 6'6'. They make too prominent a target. They may have some in the States who are that tall, but not in Foreign Service. Bert hated to talk about his height.

The reason he told Carl was because he knew Carl would tell me. I was so hurt for Bert that I cried. I have no doubt that his age may have had a lot to do with it, too.

If he had been younger, they could have trained him for another job and kept him in the service in the States. George got out of the service on age (he's a year younger than Bert) and on the back of his discharge it says by reason of being transferred to the reserve corps, and because he was over thirty-eight.

When Bert went to Missouri, he was evidently in a separation center. He wasn't trained there. Bert wouldn't lie to me—for me, but not to me.

Did I tell you that Bert asked my dad to marry me when I was sixteen? Bert didn't drink then. He started the summer I got married. Cain told me that Bert was blue about it, and he, Cain, suggested Bert have a few drinks to cheer him up.

Forgive the pencil! My pen went dry. I have about a dozen, but it's the only narrow one I have. I've written so much that I have a lump on the big finger of my right hand. It gets sore if I put too much pressure on it. Then I can't write for a while at all. I have to keep it bandaged.

There is only one thing wrong with Bert's grave that I can see. It's too close to Hap. Hap's body defiles the soil. I even hate his memory for what he did to Bert.

I don't drive, either. We've never even had a car. I objected because I was afraid George would have an accident and kill someone. He's a big pig head. You can't tell him anything. I quit trying long ago. He spent his money on booze and women, and I wouldn't give him what I'd earned for a car. There were too many more important things that were needed.

Miss Grayson, an accurate description of my life with George would have to read like this; I worked for my room and board. Clothing and personal necessities I had to earn outside of the house. I only lived because I didn't die. Bert knew it. He wanted me to be happy and he knew I never was.

Maybe you'd better see a doctor about your nerves. They can help you. They helped me and I was in worse condition than you are. At least you didn't have to feel that you were responsible for his death. I did. Bert mentioned to me that a brother or cousin of someone kept hounding him to sell them some land that Bert owned, and it was next to where you lived. Whatever came of that situation?

I wish I had known he was sick. If I had, I don't think principles or anything else could have kept me away from him. After we moved out here I didn't even know anyone who knew him. He tried to give me hints, but I never took a hint in my life.

I didn't know that he was the one who had put the rose bush down by my garage. When it bloomed, the roses were white. He told me once that I reminded him of white roses, little, pure, and sweet. He took all the blame for the awful life I'd brought on myself because of the incident at the park. He told me once that I'd had everything I ever wanted right in the palm of my hand all of my life and I didn't know it.

Maybe I'd better not write to you anymore, if it upsets you. I don't want to hurt anyone. I guess I'm a lot like Bert said he was. I can't seem to help myself.

My friend only got to read fourteen chapters of the book before she had to leave. She liked what she read. I would have let her take the rest of it with her, only I was afraid something might happen to it. George destroyed five chapters of it. I was furious. I told him if he ever touched anything of mine again, I'd kill him. I didn't mean it, but I had to make the threat strong enough to scare him. He said I'd go to the chair if I did anything like that. I told him I would not. I've been a mental patient and they might put me back in an institution, but they wouldn't electrocute me, and that being in an institution would be preferable to living in the same house with him. I have to live here now, but I envy you and your freedom. It must be wonderful to be able to do whatever you like, whenever you want to do it.

Fondly,
Lilly

LETTER 5

February 1967

Dear Lizzie,

Thank you for answering my letter. I didn't call you back because I got a lump in my throat and I was afraid I would start crying again. I cried for two years, and I know what it can do to me. I'm not good at talking on the phone anyway. I like to see people when I talk to them. Also, forgive me for taking liberties with your first name. Bert always called you Lizzie and he had the faculty of making me feel I knew people I really didn't know. I didn't know Bert had two sisters. I thought you were his only sister, but that he had two brothers. I never asked him about his family at all. Carl told me he thought Bert had two brothers.

I know Clay murdered Bert, and that the police covered up for him and why. I know it was Cain's picture in the paper the first time. They must have gotten too many correct identifications and changed it. I don't know where Clay is now, but I know that he murdered Brian Merritt in 1965. He was in Bridgetown then.

It was Councilman Jones's sister who told me about your nephew, only she said it was your brother. I don't know if she was trying to warn or threaten, or if it was just casual conversation. I do know that it's not safe to put pressure on the police here. It's a good way to get yourself killed. I'm a lot more afraid of the police than I am of Clay. Not all of them, however.

I can understand how you would miss Bert. He was a wonderful person. Maybe you will see him a little differently when you read my book. Everything that happened was my fault. Sometimes I think my remorse is more than I can bear. Nothing I can do now will ever make it right, but I'm hoping God will forgive me for being so stupid, once my book is published.

I still have some loose ends to wind up. So many people are afraid of me because I admitted from the first that I knew who killed Bert. I know that Clay killed at least eight more people, too. I haven't been able to learn the name of the man whose body was found in the Cricket Field and a girl who turned Clay in for exactly what I knew about him. Clay did them and I know why.

I'll appreciate your utmost secrecy in this matter. It can cost me my life and put your own in danger. There's nothing we can do anyway. Cain told me I couldn't fight city hall. I'm going to try with my book.

Actually, I don't feel the book is even mine. It's Bert's. I'd never have written it but for him. I was offered a new car not to write it.

I was sorry to hear about your accident. I hope you're in good health now, also your sister.

I hope you weren't angry because I put flowers on Bert's grave on Decoration Day and his birthday. Actually, I had

Anne do it. I was afraid of getting bawled out if I got caught doing it myself.

You see, Miss Grayson, the thing that nobody seemed to know was that I was almost as shy as Bert was. The difference was that Bert was shy in a crowd. I was shy out of one. It's a hangover from my childhood. The book will explain a lot of things no one knew. Writing it is the hardest work I have ever done. It will probably be the saddest book you ever read. I'm hoping to have it finished by late this summer. I'm copying the most important chapters to give to various people in case something should happen to me before it's finished.

Write to me or call me. You can even come to see me if you wish and aren't afraid.

Best wishes,

Lilly

I don't use Mrs. in front of my name.

P.S. My life is sad and dreary, for in my heart I find that love can never end with death for the one who is left behind.

LETTER 6

June 1968

Dear Miss Grayson,

I've been trying to answer your letter for some time, but I couldn't seem to get around to it. Something always seems to crop up. Right now my sister is in the hospital. She has had three operations in the past week. One was a minor one to remove an obstruction from the tube between the kidney and the bladder. Right now she is in great pain, but I think she will be all right. I was afraid she had cancer, but the doctor says she has no signs of it.

My red Persian cat got killed by a car last Tuesday, and I was terribly upset about it. He was such a beautiful cat and never ran away. He did get out of the yard, and that was the end of him. I don't need more cats, though. Heavens! I have five now. About four weeks ago two little neighbor boys brought me a pair of kittens whose eyes were barely open. Their mother had been killed by a car, and I had to find a formula that would agree with them and raised them with a medicine dropper. They can eat alone now. I didn't intend to keep them, but I don't see how I can bear to give them up now. They look a lot alike, only Shadow looks as if he's wearing glasses. Pixie has a black nose. Butterball had pneumonia, and I had to take him to the doctor twice. He's getting better now, but the vet charges as much as a regular doctor.

I clipped Bowtie yesterday, and it was an awful job. She didn't want to be still. I used to have a man come to the house to do it for me and he does a neater job, but now I'm afraid to have any man come into the house. Too many people are willing to do anything for a lousy dollar. I painted the porch floor this week. It needed it badly. I hate to paint, but there are lots of things I hate to do that I have to whether I want to or not.

About this Art Cassel, is he the illegitimate son of Ellen Jacobsen who was Ellen Cassel? The reason I ask is because she says he's her brother, and all the neighbors say he is her son. They say he got drunk and told it right in front of her. She still denies it, and she told me she had a brother whose wife swore he was murdered. If this is the same man, do you know where his wife lives now? Ellen didn't seem to know much about what had happened, but she did say that his wife was up in arms over the whole thing. She said the police did a good cover-up job on the murder. Do you know where he was murdered? Everyone here seems to think it happened in another town, but no one seems to know just where.

Some of my cherries froze this year. I had a lovely peach tree, but George let it die when I was sick. He's too stupid to know enough to take care of anything.

I hope you weren't foolish enough to sign off your rights to the land Bert owned. I still think you should put in a claim for what is rightfully yours. Your nephew probably wants to wait until the seven years are up and sell it until everyone is satisfied. All claims have to be satisfied before a piece of property can be sold. I know. I've been buying and selling property for more than twenty years now. Take a mortgage on it and file it at the courthouse.

Call me anytime you're in the mood. It's easier for me to talk to someone when they start the conversation. I want to set a nice artificial arrangement for on Bert's grave. Fresh flowers are nicer, but they don't last long. I'm afraid to make a practice of going anywhere on a regular basis at the present time.

I sent my book, *Only Sissies Cry,* to Carper and Stow. I haven't gotten it back yet, but there's always the possibility that I will. I wish I had known about the contest sooner. The book wasn't my best work, due to lack of time. I've been working on Bert's book for more than six years now and isn't the way I want it yet. It won't take long to finish it up now, though.

I think I know why Bert wouldn't buy a bed. Once when we were talking about getting married he asked if I like twin beds. I told him these were the only kind I did like. I told him he'd have to get an extra-long one for himself and a standard one for me and we could push them together. We could get a little bed for in a corner and be like the three bears in the nursery rhyme. He said whatever I wanted would be all right with him. God bless him. How could I be so stupid as to think he was only kidding?

I don't drive either, and right now I'm glad I don't. It's too easy to kill someone and make it look like an accident.

That's what Clay wanted Detective Elway to say had happened to his wife. Elway was afraid to take a chance.

He'd already killed one girl that way, and the insurance company would have been mighty suspicious of a second death in the same manner. The first one may have really been an accident. I have no way of knowing about that. I know there was only a small paragraph about it in the paper.

I have an appointment to have my hair done today. I hate to take the time, but I like to keep my hair short. It's so much easier to take care of.

What do you think of the Supreme Court's last ruling? The men on that court ought to have their heads examined. I think they're all senile and sick in their heads. They are terribly concerned over the rights of criminals, but they seem to forget that murder victims have rights, too. I wonder if some of those men are being blackmailed. I can't understand some of the decisions, unless someone in high places is putting pressure on them. Laws that have been enforced for years are no longer any good it seems. Bridgetown has never had many laws enforced. The whole of the city hall is corrupt.

I sold my air conditioner and now I wish I hadn't. I like to work in my room, and the fans blow the paper all over the place.

Maybe I'll buy another air conditioner. This place gets pretty hot during the day. It's nice at night, though.

So now its evening and I'd better get this finished. I worked in my yard this evening until it was too dark to see, and I managed to get several nice big mosquito bites. I'll have to scald and scrape to get clean. I can get more dirt on myself than anyone I know.

My sister is worse today. She is bLeeding from the bowels and I can't understand it. The doctor said he never had such a thing happen before. I don't know what to think about her.

She was too ill to talk, and for any Sanders that's something. We're all talkers once we get to know someone.

Let me hear from you real soon. I'm sorry to be so late about answering, but I've been up to my neck in work. My best to you.

Lilly

P.S. I was offered half of the rights to the book *Where Your Treasure Is* for half of the rights to my book, *Something for Bert*. I'm not taking it. I feel as if I'm being offered a dime for ten dollars, if you know what I mean. Robert Mason would like to get his hands on some of the proceeds. He read a portion of the book. The old goat would also like to marry me. Thank God he's in Florida and I'm here. I don't even write to him anymore. I only ever saw him once, and that was enough. He's nice enough, I guess, but I'm not interested in marriage. I only want to be able to earn a decent living. Husbands are the easiest things in the world to get and the hardest to get rid of.

LETTER 7

June 1969

Dear Miss Grayson,

Ellen Jacobsen lives across the street from me and two doors up. There's a divider strip out this way, you know. If you talk to her, please don't mention that I told you about the circumstances of his birth. After all, he didn't tell me. I never talked to the man. He was drunk, and he was hunting Ellen.

Toots Johnson's daddy was dead and he went in there to see if Ellen was there. That was when he was supposed to have told it.

I didn't even know Toots at the time. We didn't live out there when her parents were alive. I wouldn't want her, Ellen, to be embarrassed by what I said, though I suppose everyone down there would know it anyway. If she wants him to be her brother, as far as I'm concerned, he can be her brother.

Toots told me that Ellen went away at the time Art was killed. It was all kept quiet out here. Until you told me what you did, no one even suspected he had been murdered. Ellen did, but I hadn't mentioned what she told me to anyone.

My phone number is 944-9208, and I would prefer that you call me. It's always easier for me to talk if someone else starts the conversation. I can write scads and scads, but I'm not good at talking on the telephone. I would have little difficulty talking to you in person. I like to see people when I talk to them. Not only that, but I'm always free to talk. I have an extension in my room and I can always talk from there in case there's something I want to say that I don't want overheard.

I'm glad you liked the flowers. That florist always sends such nice arrangements, I think. I used to buy from the other one, but when my father died, I sent flowers and they weren't nearly as nice as some that came from the other one and cost a lot less.

Flowers are never cheap, but I believe in getting the most I can get for my money.

There was nothing wrong with the flowers from the other florist, but it was a dull arrangement. It was something you could see anywhere. They are very nice at delivering them for me, too. All I do is call and ask them and send them a check. I wanted so badly to get down and do it myself, but the weather was so miserable and I was working so hard on my book that I just couldn't. I was glad to know that the grass had been cut, and one of these days I'll go down and dig out some of the stones and plant some new grass seed. It's the least I can do for Bert. I don't care if you tell anyone that I put flowers on the grave. That is entirely up to you, but I don't blame you for letting them wonder. Maybe it's just as well that people don't know.

Clay said he had this town sewed up and no one was going to make him leave. I have to be awfully careful what I do, so I don't end up the way so many others did.

I was in to the hospital on Saturday night. My sister is in semi-private and visiting hours are from seven 'til eight. I went in a little early and came home on the seven-thirty bus. It was still daylight and some man tried to pick me up. I was scared stiff. When I was younger, I used to be terrified to walk on the streets alone. Men were always trying to pick me up, even in the daytime. I'm nearly fifty-six years old now and it doesn't make sense to me that anyone would try to do it now. I'm not even pretty anymore.

I used to be, but after Bert got killed I cried so hard it ruined my eyes. I have puffs under them all the time. Nothing makes them go away. My hair is gray, and I don't look quite my age at times, but I'm still past the age limit that men would want to pick me up. I'm not going in anymore in the evenings alone. I had been going in the evenings because my oldest sister wanted to go in the afternoon. She drives, but she doesn't like to drive at night. I'm not allowed to have anything to do with my oldest sister. That was one restriction the hospital put on me and it was the only one. The doctor said that no real sister would try to do to me what she had. She didn't only try. Some of the things she accomplished. She slept with my husband when I was sick. She thought she was going to get my house, but I fooled her. I'm in a perfect spot for a party house, and she runs one. Her neighbors all hate her because she started a party house in a residential area and now there's no place for them to park their cars when she is having a party. I didn't give a hoot that she slept with George. He has been sLeeping with other women for years now. I even gave him my own money so he could take them out. If he ever kissed me, I think I'd vomit all over him.

Miss Grayson, I wouldn't worry about the buildings other than the house. Your house roof isn't leaking, is it? Why should you spend money for someone else to get advantage of, after you're gone? Why don't your brothers fix up the buildings? Isn't as if you needed them, or do you?

I got a card of acknowledgment about my book from Carper and Stow. They said it would be several weeks before there would be anything definite on it. I hope they accept it for publication. I'll have it made if they do. If they don't, I'll give it to an agent to sell for me. I have a list of names of agents, and they are begging for books to sell. They get ten percent of the gross when they sell one.

Sara Dowell said I should just ignore Robert Mason's last letter. She said he was only trying to horn in on my work and take credit for something he didn't do, also money. The world is full of people like that. George and Kate (my oldest sister) said that if I made any money on my books they would put me back in the hospital and take it from me. I told them about it out at the hospital and it's written in my dossier that I can do whatever I like with the proceeds of the book. The work is mine. The proceeds should be mine, too. It's strange, but it's always the people with the most to hide who didn't want me to write the book, but who wanted to grab all the money they could get. I wouldn't give them a nickel if they were starving to death. I can hate as intensely as I love. I really don't hate anyone, though, except Clay and Lieutenant. Zale. The rest of them aren't important enough to hate. The hospital gave Kate specific instructions to stay away from me.

She used to park her car in my driveway when she went to get her hair done. She can't even do that anymore.

Call me anytime at your convenience. I'm here practically all the time. My sister is going to be discharged from the hospital and I will go down with her in the ambulance and my brother-in-law will bring me home, but other than that I have no plans to be away from the house. Take good care of yourself and write.

Best wishes,

Lilly

LETTER 8

July 1970

Dear Miss Grayson,

If it were safe for me to come down, I would help you fix up your house. I'm good at it. I've been doing it for years. Not because I particularly enjoyed the work, but for lack of funds. I never outgrew the depression. I know how you feel about the way Bert died. Try not to dwell on it. Bert wouldn't want you to.

The worst part of it all is that I could have prevented it if I had done the right thing at the right time. I think now that Cain wanted me to tell him what was going on. He liked Cain, but Bert didn't know that I didn't like Cain. After he tried to get my fingerprints on a gun that time I didn't trust him. I was afraid to see Bert after that for fear Cain would find out about it and tell Clay. Clay would have murdered us both. He had already threatened to murder Bert, and he would have killed me because I knew too much. I tried to warn Bert. Next to the last time I talked to him, he had Cain call me on the phone. I wouldn't meet him because he had Cain place the call, and I told him not to trust Cain. I would have told him why, except that my conversation would have been overheard.

Didn't Bert tell you that Clay had murdered Mr. McCune?

Cain told him that their mother had lied to get Clay out of it. Clay was bragging that he had murdered a man and gotten away with it. Bert had Clay tell me that he (Bert) was in love with me.

I have always been afraid of Clay. The only other man I've been afraid of was Hap, after I married him, and George, and I'm not afraid of George anymore. When he's drinking, he's a beast, but he isn't drinking now. I use George's last name for my name because that's my legal name. George and I lived under the same roof, but that's as far as it goes.

The only good thing I can say for George is that he was good to my animals. He was never good to me. It was the law that straightened him out. His mother had taught him that wives were nothing but unpaid housekeepers. I've been afraid of older people all my life. My parents started that when I was a child. She made it worse.

Miss Grayson, Bert never talked much about his family at all. I was trying to give Bert an argument about marrying him. I always felt that he was too good for me. This was right before he went into the army. I never had a conversation with him except in the bar room. I thought it was you who I met at the park that day, but it may have been your sister. Mrs. Work had told me Bert wanted to see me so he could ask me to marry him.

Right before I married George the first time (I married him twice), Bert came to my sister's and asked her to have me call him. I'd forgotten that he'd wanted to marry me so I didn't do it. By that time, I knew that most men only wanted to take me out to put me in a bad spot. I didn't like wrestling matches. I didn't trust anyone. The reason I liked George was because he hadn't acted like that. I found out why, later on. He was visiting a brothel all the time he dated me. The first time I was married. He made me come back by threatening to have people arrested. I had nowhere to go but to my sisters, and I was afraid he could get her in trouble. I left him three times before I finally got away, then I went to Sis's and told her to hide me. I didn't know anything about the law, and I thought he really could make her trouble. She knew better. I had been married only three months and I was covered with bruises. The next week I discovered I was pregnant, and the doctor who examined me asked what had caused the big bruise on my hip and if I'd been in an accident. I was almost ashamed to tell him. The baby was abdominal and I lost it two months later, so I didn't have to go back to live with George.

My sister died the following February, and I stayed on and looked after her children until her husband decided he wanted to remarry. During that time I met Detective Elway. He was a friend of Bud Kay's, my brother-in-law, and he took me and the Kelly kids swimming in the mornings. He worked at night. I rather liked him, but I wasn't considering marrying anyone. Elway didn't ask me, and I'd had enough men to last me a lifetime.

It was during the depression, and Bert got me a job in Ebensburg. I'd already forgotten him. I'd made up my mind to forget what had happened when I was married to George. And I did, but the forgetting took a lot of my former life with it. Anyway, Bert had me go to the house of one of your relatives to talk to my future employer. She lived up in Fairview somewhere, and I think she said she was your aunt, but she looked terribly young to be anyone's aunt. While we were waiting for the man from Ebensburg she told me that Bert was in love with me and what a wonderful man he was. I didn't know who she meant. I went to Ebensburg and Bert came to see me, and I'd gone to Bridgetown to see friends.

Three weeks later back in Ebensburg I married the town druggist. He was the only man I ever married who was kind to me. He died of a strep throat five months later. I came back to Bridgetown practically broke and got a job in a Jewish restaurant. Bert tried to see me then, but I didn't remember him.

My sister had married and was living in Syracuse. She was homesick and coaxed me to come up there. I went, and while I was there, Bert had a detective find out where I was. My brother wouldn't tell him.

Bert said he came up to see me twice and after he got there he hadn't nerve enough to knock on my door. He said he didn't want to be drinking because he wanted me to like him the way he was. The second time he came up I went to the movies with Culp. He said he went, too, but there were so many people he didn't get to sit near us. He came out when we did and stopped the car right beside us. We were walking.

He said he slept in his car that night because he wanted to be as near to me as he could get. The next morning Culp came in his cab, he was a cab driver, and took me to work. When I got out of the cab I leaned over and kissed Culp. Bert said he didn't come up after that because he knew I was safe with Culp. I adored Culp, but he was nothing in comparison to Bert. Culp and I had a misunderstanding and I came back to Bridgetown to work for a former boss while her regular help was on vacation. When I went back, I met a man who turned out to be a bigamist. He hadn't even used his proper name when we were married. He was a blond Italian. He was killed at the beginning of the war.

I had seen Bert from time to time before I went to work in the bar room. I was with my brother one night and he came and sat at our table. It was obvious that Harry didn't like Bert and, when we got outside, he told me that Bert had roughed up a girl and nearly put her in the hospital. I didn't believe it, but I promised Harry I wouldn't go out with Bert as long as he was in the service. Harry went the next week.

After I met Bert in the hotel I wrote and asked Harry to release me from my promise and he wouldn't do it. Harry had indirectly asked me to marry his sergeant. I'd partly promised, even though I never seen the man. I met him when I went to California to see Harry and he was a big puke. After the war, I found out that Tack was a miserable person, and Harry had used me to protect himself.

I started the flower shop because I was sick, but I still had to earn a living. I had some teeth drawn and nearly died, and Bert sent Hap Mills up to see if I needed anything. I thought he sent Hap because he didn't want to come himself. Bert got Dr. Busser to check me over, and Dr. Busser gave me three months to live.

Sis had started divorce proceedings, and Hap started putting pressure on me to marry him. Hap was a pathological liar, but I was stupid enough to believe the lies he told me. The day after we were married he burned all of my mail and sent an insurance man to sell me some insurance. I was well by that time, but I was thin. Hap wanted me to take out a policy for ten thousand dollars, but the insurance man said he couldn't issue me one without a thorough physical. Hap knew I couldn't pass it. We settled for one thousand. Hap had been with me when I went to Dr. Busser's, and he made me do everything the doctor said I shouldn't. He wouldn't even let me sit on the porch.

I got sick again, and Hap told me that if I were going to die he wished I'd do it and get it over with.

The last time I saw Bert he was in the Hot Dog Hut with Cain. Bert saluted me and I cried because you're only supposed to salute a superior officer, and he was so far above me that I wasn't even fit to touch him.

I told Dr. Denny that Bert was the most God-like man I'd ever known and I meant it. Dr. Denny knew Bert and said he had just gotten into bad company. What Bert didn't know was that he had been in bad company for years. I should have told him what I knew. Bert told me that he was afraid he was going to get murdered. He said he knew it sounded crazy and he didn't know how or where or when. It was just a feeling he had and that I could prevent it if I married him. It had to do with his drinking. I thought such a thing was impossible.

After we moved out here, Bert didn't have anyone to tell me he loved me anymore and that's why he became friends with the colored man who works at the cleaners next door. The man's name is Smith.

Bert said he was always afraid some man was going to hurt me and that he intended to see that it didn't happen as long as he lived. The black man was carrying messages about me. I wish you could come up and I could show you a lot of things, and you could understand better how I know a lot of this information. Bert had known all along that George had beaten me when we were married the first time. I told him, and he didn't trust George. Bear in mind that anything I told Bert was told while I was working in the hotel. I never talked to him after that. I didn't know that Bert was a diabetic until after he was dead. Someone told me, but I had no way of making sure. I do know that he was in a terrible accident, and it hurt too much to read about it. I looked at the picture and started to cry. Most of my life I've been an Agnostic, but I prayed then. I didn't want Bert to suffer. I guess God didn't hear my prayers. After Bert was killed, a minister told me not worry about Bert's soul. Bert was in heaven and his death had helped me find God. Isn't it too bad that it couldn't have happened sooner?

Bert didn't only recite poetry. He wrote it. I'm sorry I don't have it all, but some of it must have been among my letters that Hap burned. I only have the one I sent you and two more, but I liked the one I sent you the best. They all said practically the same things, but the words were different.

When Bert said his brothers didn't like him, he said his mother and sister were all right. I may have misunderstood; he may have said sisters.

He mentioned you by name when he wanted to buy me nylons down in Harrisburg. He said he'd bought you some and mentioned your name. To the best of my knowledge it's the only time I ever heard it until I read it in the paper.

There's something else that you probably don't know. Hap Mills told me that if I had anything to do with Bert that he would shoot Bert and make it look like a hunting accident. I was afraid he would. I'd tried all my life not to do anything to hurt Bert. Everything I did was wrong.

Bert thought Cain was an all right guy because he was a friend of Zale's, Lieutenant. Bernie Zale. Bert didn't know that Zale was a homosexual and that Cain had tried to set him up for Zale. Bert said all people like that should be put on a ship and the ship blown up.

Clay has an obscene picture of Elway and Zale that he got for murdering Mrs. Elway. Zale knows that if Clay's caught, he is caught, too. That's why nothing has been done and nothing will be done.

When I heard that Bert was in the state hospital I walked almost the whole way out to see him. When I got to the top of the hill and the hospital was in view, I lost my nerve and came home. I didn't know that love lasted forever. I only knew that I was hurt for Bert and I wanted to help him if I could. I was afraid he didn't like me anymore or that I'd run into some of his family and they wouldn't like it that I was there.

I think you're mistaken about the height business. I know that during the Korean War they passed a rule that they wouldn't accept people over 6'6', and I know there was a lot of talk about it during World War I. I know that Harry's sergeant said he wished he was two inches taller so he could get out of the army. He had been a career soldier, but he had enough money to go into business.

Bert wouldn't even have had to go to the Army in the first place. He told me he couldn't have anyone saying a big thing like him was too yellow to go to war.

Bert was evidently a lot more secretive than you thought. My maiden name was Sanders. Didn't you know anything about me? Bert was the first person to ever call me Lilly, and I used it exclusively, Lilly, until I married George the second time. I got conned into that and I have never been happy.

Now, you can see why I felt Bert was too good for me. I had been married three times. Right before I had an operation, Bert sent Cain out to see me. He said Bert was worried sick about me and he didn't want me to have the operation if it wasn't necessary. I thought it was because I had to go to work and I was in no fit condition to be around people. I had fibroid tumors and I hemorrhaged a lot. Cain told me that Bert said I didn't have to work, that he would look after me as long as I lived. I couldn't let him do that, and by that time I was deathly afraid of Hap.

I think I told you about the time I took the overdose of sLeeping pills intentionally. I think Hap wanted me dead. I know that he bled Bert for money, and that's why I worked when I wasn't even able. Hap borrowed so much money from me that my boss wouldn't advance me anymore for him. She said he should be looking after me, not the other way around.

I tried to find Culp after Bert was killed. I'd heard about some cute things that Bert had done in the service and I wanted to verify them. I'm positive they were together because Bert told me that if I wanted to marry Culp it was all right with him. He said Culp was better looking than he was. I didn't think so.

No man was ever more handsome than Bert, before that accident, to me. Bert said that he only wanted me to be happy, and I wouldn't be happy if I didn't love him. He said he knew I loved him, but I couldn't help it if I loved someone else more. I didn't. I was fond of Culp, but I didn't love him, or at least not the way I loved Bert.

I hope you will forgive me if I repeat myself. I've written you several letters and destroyed them, so I'm not certain what I may or may not have told you.

When I came to Bridgetown, it was not with the intention of staying. George had promised me that he would get a job in Benson and we could live there. I've been afraid all these last twenty years. I watch a lot of TV, too. I think I'd have lost my mind without it years ago. I'm married to a stupid man. Most of the time I don't even speak to him, and when I do, it generally concerns finances.

I told you I was shy. Bert said no two people were ever more alike than we were. I have only seen Bert's grave once because I cry so hard I get sick. I'm crying now, just thinking about it.

When I came back to George, it was supposed to be on a temporary basis. I wanted to make it work, but it never did. He has always had his girlfriends and at one time even expected me to entertain one. She made me sick. I guess I haven't enough jealousy in me.

I was only ever jealous once in my life and that was over Bert.

I guess you have to care a lot about someone before you can be jealous of them. With Bert, it was a fLeeting thing and nothing he had anything to do with. A woman told me she'd divorce her husband any day in the week for Bert Grayson. I don't know why God lets such people as Clay and Zale live either. Maybe the devil has more to do with it than we realize.

I see by the paper that a new unit was formed to fight crime.

I was wondering if it might not be a good idea to send them a couple chapters of my book. It tells how I happened to be sure of what I know. I had no positive proof of some of it until last summer. My informants are scared to death of me now.

I hope you've some protection. Do you have a good watchdog? I have six. Someone might kill one or two, but they couldn't kill them all without getting bitten. I'd buy a gun, only I'm afraid I might be tempted to use it on someone.

I don't mean that really. I put myself in the state hospital to keep from it at one time, though. I'd have really lost my mind if I hadn't. When I was out there I saw people who were withdrawn and envied them. I thought it would be wonderful not to know where I was or why I was there.

Anything I may have told you in this won't get you in danger unless you repeat it. It won't hurt you as long as no one knows you know it. Don't trust anyone I sent a partial chapter to, the P.D., the Mayor, and D.A. I may have told you, I only mentioned Clay's name and nothing about the police department.

Cain told me that Zale was the rottenest man he ever knew. He said that most of the men were decent honorable men, but they couldn't do a good job as long as Zale was on the force.

He blackmailed them, and if they wouldn't be blackmailed he had them killed.

Among the proof of the material I got was a listing of two policemen who had died. Cain told me the paper called them heart attacks. Officer Crooks was supposed to have been poisoned, but no one had proof. Officer Irvin died a week later. He was found on the street with a lump on his head. No one could find out the names of the men who found him, and the coroner said he died of a heart attack. There wasn't even a doctor's signature on his death certificate.

After Bert's death, several more died of heart attacks, and one of them had been out here when I found footprints in the snow. I was frightened. I thought the black man at the cleaners had made them. I wanted it stopped.

Miss Grayson, I honestly don't think you knew your brother any better than my family knew me. We're the kind of people who keep the things that hurt us deep inside. I don't mean that unkindly. You couldn't understand anything you didn't know about.

It's a long story and a sad one. It's hard to explain in a letter. You'll have to read the book to know what went on. I can make myself clearer that way.

In any event, be careful. I don't want anything more on my conscience. I could have prevented a lot of deaths if I had told Bert what I knew. He would have known what to do about it. When Bert was killed, Cain's picture was in the paper. That's why Cain's dead now. The world is better off without yellow curs like he was. He won't lure anyone else to their deaths.

Thank you for writing to me. The reason I don't call you is because I never know what to say on the phone. All I'm any good for is to answer questions. I don't want to get killed until my book is finished. After that it doesn't matter.

If you didn't know about me, I'll bet you thought I was some kind of nut when I wrote you those first letters. I thought everyone knew. Was the nephew who was on the

Baltimore police force Hap's nephew? If he was, he knew about me. I met him at Hap's mothers when I was married to Hap.

Would you believe that the P.D. put the pressure on George after Bert was killed? They did, and Zale was one of the men who questioned him. George was working at the time and had to prove it. If I thought George had anything to do with such a thing, the police wouldn't have gotten a chance to question him. I'd have killed him myself. A lot of the men who worked with Bert thought George might have had something to do with it. I knew better. George is a heel, but he's no murderer. He didn't even know Cain or Clay, and he's as afraid as I am. That's why he quit drinking.

Sincerely,

Lillian

P.S. I know it's none of my business, but are you living in the house Bert started to build? Or didn't he ever finish it? I'm inclined to think he did. I saw it and it was similar to a house that I had once described to him.

LETTER 9

Florida 1980

Dear Elizabeth,

I'm sorry to be so late in thanking you for the lovely Easter card. I've been busy. You probably know how it is. It's not much fun to have to do practically everything alone.

My graduation class is having its fifty-year anniversary Sept. 6 at the Elks in Benson. I don't know if I can get up or not. It depends on if I can get someone reliable to look after my pets.

My Siamese cat is totally blind now, and I have a deaf cat, too.

I don't let these animals outside at all, and many people wouldn't want to bother with litter boxes. I'd try to get up harder if the reunion was a month later. I'd love to see the leaves turn.

The last time I saw Bert I had been to the doctor with my back. We went into a restaurant while we were waiting for the bus. It was the Coney Hot Dog Diner and he was in there. I didn't go back to talk to him because I was wearing black and white oxfords and a fur coat. I was embarrassed by my appearance, and I could only wear those shoes because they had flat heels and didn't hurt my back too much. I've wished a thousand times that I'd gone back and talked to him, but wishing doesn't help a bit.

Well, take good care of yourself and write when you can. I hope you soon get to feeling better.

P.S. My book was never published, but I put the manuscript in a safe deposit box at my bank, along with what was left of my dad's estate that I inherited when he died. I also put the jewelry that George's mother left him when she passed. The diamond ring and ruby necklace are valuable. His dad was a coin collector, and there are about one hundred gold and silver coins.

I didn't keep them for sentimental reasons. I kept them in case I needed money I could sell them.

Everything should be safe there. I put the key to the safe deposit box in an envelope and put it in a safe place.

Love never dies; it just mellows with age. Friends and lovers help hide what we hold dear. Bert has always held the secrets to my heart. As he protected them in life, he will protect them in death. Oh, well, at least the manuscript is in a safe place now. In a place where I know that old coot Robert Mason won't be able to get his fingers on it.

Love, Lilly

If you enjoyed this novel would you post a review on Amazon book page,
"Secret Keepers and Skinny Shadows."
Your review would be appreciated.

Books by this author:
Trimble's Christmas
The Escape
Lilly: The Letters
Secret Keepers and Skinny Shadows